'Fast-moving, very funny and deserves the label "black comedy" ... it is a stinging send-up of the sad nonsense the great powers make of manipulating weaker countries for their own ends ... well-informed, crisp and ironic fiction can underline events, gauge the shift in the balance of power, and, above all, expose the essential immorality of humourless power-seekers' – Elizabeth Berridge, *Daily Telegraph*

'Superbly funny and tragically true ... Few areas of the world are as absurdly but richly extraordinary as Indo-China has been for the last ten years. Mr Bloodworth understands better than most the unfathomable darkness of the American "serving his country" abroad, he understands even more clearly (and ironically) the tragedy of Indo-China as big powers, utterly ignorant of the area, have thrust themselves upon it. His book is as macabre and as exciting, as sad and as complex and as alluring as Indo-China itself. More instructive than most textbooks, infinitely more enjoyable than most novels; anyone who thinks he's interested in the area should read it' – William Shawcross, *Sunday Times*

'A lusciously written novel ... Bloodworth has had the brilliant idea of applying the religious ideas of illusion and reality to the spy novel. The result is a book crammed tight with revelations, cross-purposes, disguises and black comedy ... and for good measure there is the most hilarious sex marathon one could hope to read. Altogether a complexly plotted book, continuously interesting. And on top of that, Bloodworth is a real writer' – *Scotsman*

ANY NUMBER CAN PLAY

DENNIS BLOODWORTH

QUARTET BOOKS LONDON

Published by Quartet Books Limited 1973
27 Goodge Street, London W1P 1FD

First published in Great Britain by Martin Secker and
Warburg Ltd 1972

Copyright © 1972 by Dennis Bloodworth

ISBN 0 704 31074 0

Printed in Great Britain by
Hunt Barnard Printing Ltd, Aylesbury, Bucks

Chuang Tzu once dreamed he was a butterfly that fluttered about happily, quite unaware that it was Chuang Tzu. But then he woke up, and after that he never knew whether he was Chuang Tzu who once dreamed he was a butterfly, or a butterfly now dreaming it was Chuang Tzu.

The Book of Chuang Tzu

DRAMATIS PERSONAE

Paul-David Hippolyte Font-le-Baume	The renowned French naturalist
Larry Ivansong	Foreign correspondent of the Worldover Syndication Service
Thinking Lotus	His Chinese wife
Hsiao Mang-ti ('Mango')	Their adopted six-year-old Chinese daughter
Ah King	Their Chinese amah
Prince Saravane Sissomak	The Ruler of Mekong
Prince Norivong Kitay	His cousin, the ex-Crown Prince
Yaksha	An anti-colonial rebel warlord
Charles O. Strawbury	American presidential adviser to Prince Sissomak
Calvert Kirkwall Eldritch	American Ambassador to Mekong
Dave Inqvist	Head of the CIA in Mekong
The Paramahamsa Bonze	A Hindu-Buddhist seer
Short March	Senior responsible cadre for the Chinese Intelligence Service in Mekong

Max Alias	Eurasian press adviser to Prince Sissomak
Charles M. Polak	Correspondent of the North American Broadcasting System
Catullus Yip	His cameraman
Sir Nigel Pawkinson-Convoy	British Ambassador to Mekong
Dorothy Pawkinson-Convoy	His wife
Oliver Clarence	First Secretary of the British Embassy
Greeen	An officer of the British Secret Intelligence Service
Flodden	His shadow
Jacqueline Cannabière	A French *poule*
Suzy Lee Flowerclass	A correspondent of the Worldover Syndication Service
Felicity Clipstream	Zoologist and spinster

Scene: The Kingdom of Mekong
Time: The present

I

Paul - David Hippolyte Font - le - Baume
stumbled on it a little after dawn on a Thursday during that
glorious June of 1872. The renowned French naturalist was
cutting a path through thick jungle thorn at the time, but every
now and then he would peer upwards from the floor of the
Indochinese rain-forest to where wan shafts of sunlight pierced
the curtains of liana above him. Since, therefore, like most men,
he was not always looking where he was going, he inevitably
fell over something. It was a slab of sandstone as big as a door,
and on it was carved in bas-relief a topless *apsara*, a voluptuous
heavenly dancing-girl with a smile hardly more veiled than her
enticing spherical geometry and a crack in one eye that gave
her a knowing wink. Paul-David Hippolyte Font-le-Baume
had rediscovered Nakhara.

Font-le-Baume knew the legend of the lost cities of Nakhara,
swallowed by the concupiscent Mekong jungle as the ocean had
swallowed Atlantis, and he was now to open a new era in Asian
archaeology. By the turn of the century all scholarly works –
the massive if somewhat tedious study of Burghausen*

---

* Nakhara: Versuch in 3 Bänden einer Fundamental-Analyse der
historischen Einflusssphären innerhalb einer originären Zivilisation

I

prominent among them – were confidently describing that marvellous realm as the centre of a unique Hindu-Buddhist civilization whose golden age opened expectantly in A.D. 954 and closed resignedly in 1425. At the height of its power, the God-king of Nakhara was 'master of one hundred states', and it was during this period that all available men and elephants were drafted for the sacred task of constructing the complex of sandstone temples and tombs that made Nakhara the most awesome monument in the world.

'For you must know,' recounts Marco Polo, who passed that way on the business of Kublai Khan, 'that these people are most devout, and among them it is believed not only that men live many lives, but may be born again as birds or bees, as it were. It is therefore accounted sinful to kill whatsoever living thing, and I assure you that these idolaters will deliver turtles and deer and sundry other brutes up to the priests in the temples so that they may be given sanctuary. I must tell you that at the season of the *Feast of the Beasts*, one day is set aside for this meritorious act, and on another all congregate wearing masks fashioned to resemble this or that animal, thus reminding themselves of their solemn destiny . . .'

Piety can be a costly investment. Top-heavy with temples and tombs, riches and ritual, the kingdom was sacked by the Thais in 1425, and the luckless monarch fled across the river with the remnants of his court. Nakhara was deserted. The first tendril of the first creeper reached out gently towards the first apsara frozen in stone in the forecourt of the nearest shrine, and for the next 400 years Nakhara sank slowly into the jungle's embrace.

But from the moment that a shocked Font-le-Baume caught them *in flagrante*, time began to move forwards instead of backwards, impelled by that noble sense of cultural mission inherent in all good Frenchmen. Once it was discovered that the site lay within the territory of a somewhat incoherent

unter besonderer Würdigung der kulturellen Bezüge. Von Professor Dr. Phil h.c. Gottfried Burghausen, Ordentlicher Professor für Alte Orientalische Geschichte an der Karl-August-Universität. Biographisches Institut Leipzig.

state currently known as 'Mekong', a small armed party was despatched by boat to its capital, which was now on the opposite bank of the wide river and was called Nava. A treaty was signed with the grateful king, who ceded Nakhara to France in exchange for protection. This was the beginning of a natural process whereby France ultimately acquired the whole of Mekong as payment for guaranteeing its sovereignty and territorial integrity, given the rising cost of defence.

Stone by stone, Nakhara was put together again. Frenchmen came to plant a little rubber and pepper and cut timber, to open small but excellent restaurants and subtly discolour the dusky population. For the most part, however, the indolent Mekinese continued to live as before, and every morning the saffron-robed Buddhist bonzes shuffled past the doorways of the devout, their begging bowls held out so that kneeling housewives could 'gain merit' by silently filling them and thus move nearer to the ultimate, unknowable bliss – Nirvana.

However, after World War Two the natives, fired by the novel notions of liberty and fraternity unwisely propounded to them by their white masters, started their own anti-colonial struggle under a feudal lord from the provinces named Yaksha. The French were considerably inconvenienced, and when the old king was found dead in bed one morning they passed over the fiercely nationalistic crown prince and put on the throne his pliable playboy cousin, the 25-year-old Saravane Sissomak. They were then able to take the heart out of the rebellion by slowly paying out independence to Mekong through this amiable francophile ruler fresh from the tables at Monte Carlo. Yaksha went into hiding in the hills, and by 1954 Mekong was a sovereign state.

Inheriting a country of few natural assets, Sissomak adroitly restored political stability by giving his police chief profitable concessions in gambling and prostitution, and sharing out among his regional military commanders the nation's principal sources of revenue – the customs service, the gold-smuggling, and the traditional traffic in home-grown opium. This equitable distribution of favours kept all armed factions reasonably docile. For himself, the young heir of the god-kings reserved certain beneficial agencies (including both of the Colas) and personal control of the Department of Tourism, whose possibilities he exploited with uncharacteristic energy. The tourists flocked in to see 'Fabulous Nakhara', the Royal Palace and the Royal Ballet (where the take went straight into the king's private purse), and 'Instant Mekong', the park in which all aspects of the Mekinese scene could be comfortably toured in two hours, making it quite unnecessary for foreigners to undertake tiresome journeys upcountry.

Quaint old ceremonies were revived. A 'Feast of the Beasts Week' was firmly inserted into the calendar, and thousands of cameras blinked their reptilian eyes at the colourful processions of devout Mekinese taking live turtles and pigeons to the Buddhist sanctuaries, or dancing at the open-air carnivals in their animal-masks. Cunningly crossing these local rites with the Christmas customs of their American guests, hotel managements put gifts of toy animals outside rooms occupied by children, who would find them on awakening on the last day of the Week. The practice quickly spread, and the Mekinese themselves were soon creeping up to each other's houses after dark on the tenth day of the seventh month, to leave some zoomorphic lump of wood or rubber or clay on the doorstep.

Then, gauging that their country had fallen into a suitable state of confusion and neglect under its debonair young ruler, political cadres of the communist guerrilla movement in the hills seeped southwards to mobilise and arm their paid-up supporters in the provinces around the capital itself, and filtered insidiously into the outer courts and crannies of Nakhara.

Mekong was neutral, but instead of summoning either his American adviser or his unofficial confidant in the pay of Peking, a worried Sissomak for the first time consulted his official oracle, the wizened, dying Bonze-Superior who was the head of the Buddhist hierarchy. No one knows what passed between them, but the King came away a changed man, stripped of the puppy-fat of his profligate past, suddenly mature, enlightened, cleansed, and contrite. And that was when the real trouble began.

2

I

The old Thai Embassy was still burning well, for it was built mainly of teak – Ivansong could see the flickering reflection of the blaze in the night sky – but the streets were now empty except for knots of soldiers and police at the temporary checkpoints of untidy concertina wire. The mob had dispersed, and students who had not been shot or dragged off to Nava's one unattractive jail had gone home. Mekinese retired early, and it was customary to bring all riots, demonstrations, public lynchings and similar expressions of the popular will to a close before the evening meal, which was eaten at seven.

Ivansong turned from the balcony and was pouring himself the first regulation scotch-and-soda of the evening when Thinking Lotus came out of the study in stiff black Chinese day-pyjamas, carrying two sheets of freshly-typed copy and a glass of dill-pickle juice diluted with water and ice (she did not drink or smoke).

'The new lead,' she announced, with the gentle catch of breath that prefaced everything she said, 'distilled from the exquisitely indecipherable calligraphy in your filthy old notebook.''

'That was quick work.'

'Time,' she replied in a voice of faded elegance, 'was pinching my bottom. The main cable office closes in one hour and twenty minutes.'

Ivansong took the copy from her, sank into a rattan chair

5

and read: WORLDOVER LONDON PS4   COLLECT

PRESS NAVA IVANSONGS NEW LEAD MEKINESE
TROOPS AND POLICE TODAY SHOT SIX TEENAGERS AND ARRESTED
FORTY MORE WHEN RIOTING STUDENTS SET FIRE TO THE THAI
EMBASSY HERE IN PROTEST AGAINST BANGKOKS SCATHING
CONDEMNATION OF THE NEUTRALIST POLICIES OF PRINCE
SARAVANE SISSOMAK PARA ANGRY THAI DIPLOMATS THIS
EVENING BRANDED THE STUDENTS AS COMMUNISTS WHO WERE
ENCOURAGED TO LASH OUT AT THE THAIS BY THE DISCLOSURE
THAT SISSOMAK HAS BEEN INVITED TO VISIT PEKING AND
MAY LEAVE FOR CHINA LATER THIS WEEK PARA POLITICAL
OBSERVERS DISMISS OUT OF HAND SUGGESTIONS THAT THE
THAIS MAY HAVE ENGINEERED TODAYS FRACAS IN ORDER TO
PROVIDE THEMSELVES WITH AN EXCUSE TO INTERVENE DIRECTLY
IN MEKINESE INTERNAL AFFAIRS STOP BUT IT IS WIDELY
SUSPECTED THAT THE RIOTS MAY HAVE BEEN MANIPULATED TO
THIS END BY SISSOMAKS ROYAL RIVAL AND COUSIN PRINCE
NORIVONG KITAY PARA THE TRADITIONAL VENDETTA BETWEEN
THE NORIVONG AND SARAVANE BRANCHES OF THE ROYAL FAMILY
INTENSIFIED IN 1954 RPT 1954 WHEN THE OUTGOING FRENCH
COLONIAL POWER PUT SARAVANE SISSOMAK ON THE THRONE
INSTEAD OF THE CROWN PRINCE NORIVONG KITAY STOP
RELATIONS WERE FURTHER EMBITTERED TWO YEARS AGO WHEN
SISSOMAK ABDICATED IN ORDER TO TAKE AYE MORE ACTIVE
PART IN THE POLITICAL AND ECONOMIC DEVELOPMENT OF
MEKONG FOR INSTEAD OF CEDING THE THRONE TO KITAY HE
HAD HIS MOTHER CROWNED AS CONSTITUTIONAL QUEEN PARA
THE MOVE COINCIDED WITH AN ASTONISHING CHANGE IN THE
ONETIME ROYAL WASTREL SISSOMAK WHO NOW DEVOTED HIMSELF
TO TRANSFORMING THIS BACKWARD COUNTRY INTO AYE MODEL
STATE BUT IN MAKING MANY CHANGES FOR THE GOOD HE HAS
ALSO MADE MANY ENEMIES PARA UPPICK ON PARA TWO OF MY
MAILER TO END ENDIT.

Larry Ivansong made two small changes and heaved
himself out of the chair in order to kiss Thinking Lotus
thankfully. 'Great,' he said, 'and now I suppose I had
better start The Bitch and take this rubbish down to the
cable office.'

6

'No,' she objected, 'you have been out all day incinerating embassies with indignant students, you have all the fragrance of a shaggy dog, and I do not know what you tackled in that poor, old maltreated shirt of yours but it has two broken collar-bones. You need a bath and a change and a number two regulation scotch-and-soda. I will go.'

But Ivansong went. The empty street outside looked too silent, and he did not trust The Bitch out of his sight. She was a dove-grey two-litre Salmson tourer from the heyday of the Fourth Republic, and he had picked her up for two hundred American dollars from a second-hand car dealer next to the Thieves' Market on Boulevard Siho a few days after he had arrived in Nava from Singapore. Like Ivansong, she had a long, rakish, piratical look and a narrow, suspicious stare, for the windscreen was about six feet wide but only five inches high. She was a lush for petrol and the battery ran flat if she were not given a good romp daily, since at anything less than forty miles an hour it continued to discharge.

On this occasion, The Bitch started without trouble, however, and he drove slowly down rue du Bassac, a narrow, poorly-paved street which ran past the back of the oddly-matched string of artefacts facing onto the river itself – the Hotel de l'Asie and the Hamsa Hilton, the Great Pagoda and the Royal Palace, their pointed golden roofs and graceful upswept eaves like the elaborate headdress and fastidious fingers of Thai dancers. Next came the paddock of Sissomak's white elephants, and finally a line of unpretentious riverine bordellos built over the water on stout wooden piles.

Prince Kitay's mansion was on Bassac, and so was the British Embassy compound, and Ivansong had been lucky to find nearby a big, two-storeyed wooden house built on a rise in the ornate Nava style by a former comptroller of income tax now in exile on the Côte d'Azur. He had rented it for six months after the London editors of the Worldover Syndication Service, for whose four hundred client-newspapers he struggled to write at least two background articles a week, had politely ordered him to move his base temporarily from Singapore to Mekong, and since the house on Bassac had a big swimming-pool in the back garden with concealed subaqueous lighting he could not conscientiously object.

And his editors had been right, he reflected, as a sleepy soldier in jungle green and sandals waved him down with a sten-gun, and police picked their way with dignified incomprehension through his passport and international driving licence, his car registration book and his press accreditation card. Mekong was a good running story. No wonder saints so easily became martyrs, for, if Sissomak was anything to go by, their first qualification must be an outstanding flair for arousing fury and suspicion. The reformed western-educated Prince had first taken the unheard-of step of making all smuggling – even the time-hallowed traffic in gold and opium – illegal. He had purged the Customs Department and outlawed official corruption. He had introduced free medical service to a people who doted on solid silver false teeth, and he had built secular schools at which the country's future peasants could be taught to want something better than the parcel of soggy riceland to which they would inevitably have to devote the rest of their lives.

He had shamefully embarrassed the more expansive Mekinese polygamists by moving into a modest little complex of three bungalows, in which he lived with only one wife. He had attacked the abuse of power, even executing one hapless provincial commander for doing no more than chop the knee caps out of a mother of nine who refused him a discount when he bought her eleven-year-old daughter. By these acts he had earned the hostility of all Right-thinking men. He had also destroyed the main sources of national revenue while overspending on his welfare state, economic experts protested. And what was there to set against all this? Nothing – unless you counted the fact that ninety per cent of the population adored him.

The police waved Ivansong on, and he turned left into Siho, switched on a fixed searchlight on his front bumper to pick up the great stone, bell-like *stupa* in the middle of the traffic circus ahead, and accidentally blinded the unwary driver of a trishaw pedalling a solitary tart slowly down the boulevard.

No, Sissomak had not done anything about sex. That one, after all, had survived all censure since the days of Eden, when life had presumably been less complicated.

But his performance in foreign affairs had been an un-mitigated disaster. In order to befriend the Laotians he had ceded to them an entire border province on the specious, even frivolous excuse that Mekong had annexed it by force in the first place. He had refused free rice from the Americans and continued to buy from Bangkok instead in order not to deprive the Thais of their traditional Mekinese market. He had offered to fix frontiers and sign non-aggression pacts with all neighbouring states, and had suggested that he send one of his children to school in each of them as a hostage for his own good intentions and in order to establish better international understanding in the future.

What could have been better calculated to sow distrust at home and abroad? He was sacrificing the interests of his own country for the sake of others. He was building up merit for himself at the expense of the Buddhist nations on his borders. The proposal that he send his children to infiltrate the capitals and cultures of friendly neighbours was blatant treachery, and his protestations of good faith part of a plot which was self-evidently dark and devious since no one could divine it. And when he invited the Mekinese People's Conservative Congress to inspect his personal accounts it was obvious that he was seeking to undermine the authority and probity of certain other heads of state around him. He infuriated the communists because he ran too just and egalitarian a kingdom to suit the sacred cause of red revolution, and he infuriated the anti-communists because he had decreed that the state which they had so vividly described as 'the keystone of South-east Asia'* should remain strictly neutral.

Ivansong passed the Thieves' Market, and the glowing remains of the Thai Embassy swung into view on his left over its shacks and stalls. The street was still a sloppy spaghetti of water and hoses and the firemen were squatting under the

* Final Communiqué of the Ministerial Meeting of the South-east Asia Treaty Organisation (SEATO), Manila, April 1964.

roadside tamarinds, dozing or drinking tea. But a tall, familiar all-American figure with a light bouncing stride was coming away from the guttering building, and he leaned out of the car window to shout 'Chuck' as the man drew level.

'Oh hello, Ivansong,' Strawbury replied in a light bouncing New England voice that went with the stride. 'Will you just take a look at these guys? I tell you, the fatigueability of the Mekinese fireman is positively prophylactic. He's so pathologically predisposed to self-induced hypnoidal conditioning that it kinda constitutes an inbuilt defence mechanism. He'll just never get near enough to a conflagration to risk his life before he falls fast asleep.'

'My guess is simply that the Thais refused to pay them double overtime after six. Are you assessing the damage?'

A corner of the slowly collapsing pile of embers burst feebly into flames, and Strawbury looked Ivansong over carefully, his pale watery eyes shifting behind spectacles with colourless plastic rims like some early and vulnerable form of marine life.

'Just checking,' he answered briefly, his finger to his tie. His trousers stopped well above his ankles, but otherwise he was always impeccably dressed in lightweight suits cut from one of those shiny Japanese synthetics that look like anodised tinfoil, Ivansong noted disapprovingly. He glanced down at his own sweat-stained pink cotton shirt. 'Well, what does Sissomak think of this one?' he asked before raising his head.

The prince's American adviser leaned his elbows on the car door and shook his head slowly. 'I wouldn't know,' he replied. 'I haven't seen him yet.' He stopped and blinked once.

'Oh, just back from Bangkok, then, are you?' Ivansong's resonant voice sharpened with suspicion. 'You know, some people are saying that Kitay organised the riot to give the Thais a pretext for coming in against Sissomak.'

'Yup,' said Strawbury, 'and with us Yanks right behind them with the navy and the napalm. Have a heart, Larry. You think we want to start another war? Haven't you heard about the President's doctrine – his withdrawal symptoms, total recall, all that? Military detumescence is his thing. He's positively cycloid about it. Phooey to you and your Thais.'

'All right,' conceded Ivansong, brushing back the hank of burnished, curiously silky brown hair that fell to his wiry right eyebrow, 'no Thais. But is Sissomak still going to Peking?'

Strawbury stood up and pulled out both of his trouser-pocket linings. A nail-clipper fell to the dirt. 'Search me,' he said, as he picked it up and examined his thumb. 'I wouldn't know.'

'What, a right-hand man like you?'

'Always the last to know what the left hand is doing,' Strawbury pointed out. 'Be seeing you.' And he walked off abruptly with a wiggle of well-manicured fingers. He always did.

2

Ivansong handed in his copy at the post office, learned without surprise that there was a fourteen-hour delay on cables to the outside world, and drove home slowly, thinking about the singular Chuck. The Pentagon had pulled him out of an associate professorship somewhere in Vermont, turned him into Colonel Charles Orpington Strawbury, US Army, and given him a laboratory outside Bangkok. It was there that Ivansong had first found him, dreaming at a tin desk behind a door neatly labelled 'Ecological Warfare'.

Strawbury had been mildly suspicious when Ivansong had asked him what he was working on, but only for a moment. 'Well, let's see,' he began. 'The whole thing's quite elementary, really. You know about defoliants? Maybe you remember that in 1970 Professor Matthew S. Meselson, the top biology man at Harvard, reported that pesticide-spraying missions in Vietnam had stripped the country of twenty per cent of all forest lands, and destroyed enough crops to feed more than half a million people?

'Quite an achievement, you see,' he raced on, without waiting for a signal from Ivansong. 'So the United States, over-compensating as ever for its usual state of pseudodementia, went through a period of maximalized obsessional repentance. Consequently, what I am working on now is a refoliant so's everyone will feel good again. You with me?'

'A *refoliant*?'

'Uh-huh.'

'But why not just plant the devastated areas with ordinary crops and trees? Or is that too easy?'

'Negative. Just too slow. The problem is to work up really fast-growing strains and then spray the seeds over the waste land, maybe with a variant of the aerosol bomb we used in Vietnam.' His voice bounced like sorbo from the white walls of his office. In spite of a receding line of what appeared to be short hay above a long, naked face the colour of cottage cheese, Strawbury looked like a big American basketball player.

'So we started to go into requirements, and, of course, as you will have already divined, we were soon concentrating on the problem of hybridization, mutations of genes within the seed accelerated by irradiation and bombardment with X-rays, cobalt rays or beta rays so that it germinates faster. Rudimentary stuff, really. Got it?'

Ivansong shied away from the question and attacked from the flank. 'What plants are you working on, then?' he asked. 'Something simple to begin with, like grass?'

Strawbury snapped his fingers. 'Nope, it's a question of fast things first. The quicker the natural speed of growth, the quicker could be the synthetic acceleration and the easier it would be to measure. So at the kindergarten stage we play with things like calamus rattan and lianas, negatively photo-trophic climbers insensitive to gravity that will shoot out two hundred yards of stem even in dark forests. And banyan. That works the opposite way, of course. If the seed is hung up on something high and sprouts, the aerial roots shoot downwards until they find solid ground. But it's when we get the basic dynamics we want out of that kind of junk that we'll revolu-tionize agriculture and forestry. Well, it's five. Sorry. Got to go.'

But that was not all that Ivansong was to see of him. For when the Thais became openly rude about Sissomak, the sensitive prince decided that Mekong must stop buying their agricultural surplus and become self-sufficient in food. He had heard about the IR-24 miracle rice developed in the Philippines, and with his characteristic weakness for the overcure, therefore, he drew up an elaborate if strictly hypothetical programme for developing not only a Mekinese strain of miracle rice, but miracle sugar, miracle bananas, miracle chillis, miracle coconuts, miracle frogs and miracle fish. When this priceless piece of information came to the ears of the senior presidential aide on Far Eastern affairs who sits three floors underground in the White House, it immediately suggested to his conniving mind a scheme for 'getting close to that Mekinese monkey Sissomak'. So the American military adviser to the prince was recalled, and Colonel Charles O. Strawbury posted to Nava in his place.

A sort of sword-and-ploughshare appointment, mused Ivansong, leaving The Bitch under the porch and taking the red wooden stairs to the first-floor lounge two at a time. 'Home and dry,' he shouted, and poured himself a drink. 'In the shower,' came a muffled cry from the direction of his wife's bedroom-study. 'Soup and sandwiches on the trolley.' He nodded and walked over to the balcony that ran around the four sides of the house.

It was very quiet now. The moon was rising, and gazing diagonally down the street he could see against the furtive flow of the river behind it the priapic silhouette of the bridal suite in the gardens of the Hotel de l'Asie, a domed love-nest built to resemble a temple to Vishnu. Usually a flashing sign on the Hamsa Hilton next door blocked out the background, but it was switched off tonight, and he could make out other, fainter spires like phallic reflections along the far bank of the Mekong.

These were the five tall towers of Nakhara Wat, the vast riverside sanctuary that Font-le-Baume had rediscovered. Half a mile beyond that rose Mount Kham, its base ringed by a complex of more antique ruins like a necklace of carved stone and its summit crowned by the moonlit Mayon.

The Mayon was a disquieting precinct of forty-nine square,

tapering piles, each one carved on all four sides into a huge mask, so that when Ivansong first climbed up to it, he found himself in a forest of faces and followed wherever he went by their blind gaze. No one knew its significance.

He shivered, and pitched the remains of his drink into the front garden. Even the communist guerrillas, the Mekinese Reds, had not tried to live on the sacred mountain itself, but they seemed to proliferate in the string of temples and shrines around it like polyps in coral. He turned back into the room to sample the soup, and at once froze where he stood, his hands raised to the level of his shoulders.

She was wearing an obvious wig wrapped in cellophane and an absurdly large pair of dark glasses that almost obliterated her face, but the hand that held the gun was steady. It was an old-fashioned six-shooter and her finger was crooked tight against the trigger.

'Kneel and say your prayers,' she ordered peremptorily, adding after a moment's thought: 'like a good boy.'

Ivansong obediently knelt down in front of her, but his eyes narrowed. 'You don't scare me,' he said crushingly. 'You don't look mean enough.'

'Mean?' echoed Mango, taken aback. 'Mean,' repeated Ivansong, gently taking the toy pistol out of her hand as Thinking Lotus came through the bedroom door in a silk kimono.

'Kindly do not liquidate number one and only daughter tonight,' she admonished, 'it is the amah's evening off. *And Mango, where did you get the key to my wig?*'

Hsiao Mang-ti removed her mother's dark glasses with a shake of her head, and lifted off the wig as if it were a bishop's mitre, revealing the smooth, square-cut cap of hair of a six-year-old Chinese doll underneath. 'I haven't dirtied it,' she said, with a child's usual genius for pre-empting the arguments of the enemy. 'It's all wrapped up in the wrapping paper the Christmas wrapping paper came in. See, it's quite clean.'

Thinking Lotus stripped off the cellophane, put her head on one side and nodded doubtfully. 'And what happened to bedtime? The cat get it?'

14

'Wait a minute,' said Ivansong, 'why did you buy a wig?'

'Because it was only twenty-five dollars, of course,' replied Thinking Lotus. 'I saw it in a shop in Singapore, and could not dream of resisting it. I was going to surprise you at the Beast Feast by wearing my secret mask and *her* hair.'

'Whose hair?'

'Well, I do not know, of course, but it is not mine, so it must be hers, unless it was cheap because it was cut off a horse or a carpet or something.'

'It looks like real human hair, all right.'

'How would you know? You can hardly see. That was why you were refused a ticket for the Navy and married me, or so you told me.'

'Hardly see? Dammit, I'm only colour blind, you know,' replied Ivansong, putting an arm around her waist, 'and, as I've told you before, colour-blinds often have sharper eyesight than other people. Here, let's put it to the test. Can you see the towers of Nakhara Wat across the river?'

'Yes, but they are almost illegible.'

'How many lights are there on them?'

'How can I know? They are all out.'

But Ivansong could see a faint illumination in the central tower. That would be the lamp of the Paramahamsa Bonze, the venerable anchorite whom even the guerrillas left alone, and to whom Sissomak often went for advice without fear of ambush, for it was said that he could read the future clearly in the polished mirror of his own beatitude.

A tug at his crumpled, unbuttoned shirt-sleeve wrenched Ivansong from his thoughts. Mango was looking up at him through sloe-black eyes bright with new urgency. 'Daddy, tell me something, how do I look mean?' She tugged again. 'Listen, Daddy, how do I? You're old, so you know. You can teach me.'

3

The palace launch bumped softly into the motor-tyre fenders of the jetty on the palm-fringed east bank of the Mekong, and Sissomak sprang lightly ashore on those small, agile feet that went so oddly with his royal corpulence. Before him lay the moon-soaked magnificence of Nakhara Wat, its colonnade of polished sandstone framing a huge hollow square within which rose a symmetrical system of five great towers, built upon steep pyramids of crumbling stairway. The inner wall of the colonnade was half a mile in length, and every inch of it was carved into a tremendous frieze of kings and warriors and caparisoned elephants, of war-vessels locked in battle and many-armed gods poised to strike from their intricately-worked chariots.

On dull days in duller times this marvel had been discreetly illuminated by concealed fluorescent lighting as a concession to foreign visitors, but the natives had subsequently inflicted a decisive defeat on the tourists, for the *Mékinois Rouges,* the Mekinese Reds who now dominated Nakhara, only allowed guided parties into the riverside Wat on Wednesdays and Saturdays (from eight to six) and kept them out of the ruins beyond altogether.

Although pierced by archways at the four points of the compass, the frieze was like a magic amulet that preserved inviolate the temple that it framed. For neither government troops nor guerrillas dared risk damaging it, and within the temple lived the holy Paramahamsa Bonze who had appeared quite suddenly on one blessed day in the year *Kot* of the previous decade.

Barefoot, dressed in a worn sarong and a high-necked silk

blouse, Sissomak set off along the short causeway flanked by stone lions that led to the entrance of the Wat. He passed through the west gateway of the colonnade and the courts carved with demons and apsaras that lay behind, until he was at the foot of the narrowing cliff of stone stairs that mounted to the highest tower, and the archway giving on to the chamber of the Bonze within it.

Three young monks in yellow togas appeared silently from the shadows and, seeing it was the prince, squatted in obeisance before him. He took three packs of filter-tipped king-size Chesterfield cigarettes from somewhere under his sarong, placed one before each of their bent, bald heads, and began to pull his plump but energetic figure up the foot-high steps. The monks turned to look up briefly at his ample, rotating buttocks. Then one of them shrugged, pulled a silver gas-lighter from his sleeve, and lit a reefer.

The Bonze sat meditating in the lotus position on the stone platform at the top of the pyramid. A small, hidden fluorescent light inside the entrance to the tower behind him threw his soft, still body into shadow and, as Sissomak's head came gasping over the last tread like some disembodied phantom, the prince remarked once again that in sharp silhouette the guru strikingly resembled the Maitreya who would one day come to herald an age of happiness. He had the same polished dome of a head, the same free-flowing waves of fat, and above all the awesome Buddha-ears with their huge, pendulous lobes.

Sissomak put his hands together in respectful greeting, kissed the upturned toes, and then settled cross-legged before the Master. For a short time they sat in silence, and the prince gazed respectfully at the hairless moon-faced monk with the heavy-lidded eyes and the small, bud-like mouth from which fell those uncanny, unerring prophecies. Sissomak thought with dutiful remorse of his old mentor, the Bonze-Superior in Nava, now dead and sealed up in a funerary urn filled with formaldehyde to await an auspicious day for his public cremation. It was sad that he had neglected that good and holy man during his last days and had turned instead to the Paramahamsa Bonze for counsel, but this alien seer without a sect knew as no other man knew.

At last the Bonze smacked his lips tenderly. 'My son?' he asked, in a deep, faintly fruity voice.

Sissomak knew better than to plunge words straight into the heart of his particular problem of the moment.

'Master, I have a premonition of death,' he replied.

'Then you are blessed,' commented the Bonze, holding up a chubby, short-fingered hand briefly. 'It is the secret of living correctly. It should always be with us. Too many mortals in your position of power behave as if they had a premonition of immortality. If all had to count down from three score years and ten to an inexorable zero, instead of being born at zero and climbing towards a nemesis that is unknown and can therefore be comfortably ignored, how much nearer to Nirvana would mankind be. But you are not going to die yet, Saravane Sissomak. You are merely going to travel.'

For a moment the prince felt dizzy with shock, as he always did when the Bonze peered into his mind before he was asked.

'I am not sure that I should,' he confided after a pause. 'That is why I want to consult you. I have been invited to China, but I hesitate to go, for some say that Prince Kitay is plotting against me, even that he engineered the burning of the Thai Embassy in order to push the Thais into helping him to overthrow me.'

'No, Prince,' said the Bonze gently. 'Had he conspired to seize power at this moment, he would never have provoked a crisis which might well persuade you to stay in the country, when he could have had you safely out of the way. The incident, therefore, was a genuine demonstration by your people that they want you to go to China.' The Bonze kept his blank gaze on an empty space a million miles away and for ten minutes neither man moved or spoke. Then, with terrifying suddenness, he broke the silence as if it had never existed.

'But I perceive more than this, for my business is not with the snares of reason. It is with knowing without knowing how. And I now know that you must go to Peking, Prince. Have no fear. Your enemies do not seek to strike today, and once you return with new pledges of protection from your powerful neighbours to the north, they will never dare to strike. On the other hand, if you hesitate, you will be destroyed. For your friends in Peking are meanwhile losing their control over affairs, and their earlier promises that they would safeguard your neutral state against your enemies are becoming drained of meaning.

'If you are anxious that neither left nor right shall overthrow you, you must build your defences immediately – not here, but in the Chinese capital, and with Chinese leaders who are in the ascendant. You must see Mao Tsetung himself before this moon has gone if Mekong is not to mourn. For I tell you that if you do not, Kitay will bring you down before the rice is harvested.'

Sissomak sighed with relief. His decision had been made for him. Once again the guru had proved his infallibility, for he had confirmed from his infinite wisdom what others had deduced from equivocal evidence that never reached the precincts of Nakhara. The extremists were on the make again in China.

That very morning Max Alias had laid before him a New China News Agency report from Peking about some communist party meeting which was so insufferably boring that he had glanced up at the métis in bewilderment.

'So?'

'So, Highness,' Max had replied in his how-many-times-do-I-have-to-tell-you voice, 'so it could be a disaster. The despatch includes the official list of those present, given in order of their importance in the hierarchy, as you see. And what do we have?' Max had read out of a list of incomprehensible and unmemorable Chinese monosyllables, struck the paper as if it had hit him first, and gone on: 'Instead of being placed second after Chairman Mao in the normal way, Uncle Chou – *pardon*, your esteemed patron and protector the Prime Minister Monsieur Chou En-lai – is in the fourth position. And who has superseded him, Highness? Two ultra-leftists of the Shanghai clique whom you have never even met.'

'Should I go to Peking, I wonder, then?' the prince had

mused doubtfully. 'After all, my invitation was from Chou En-lai.'

'But it is essential,' Max had urged. 'This is the time to find out the truth at first hand and perhaps to mend fences with the out-and-out Maoists up there, if they are gaining strength again. For what will happen if you do not? You may suddenly be without a protector at all, and meanwhile those turncoats in Thailand who prefer your cousin to yourself are capable of jumping ahead of you to smile winningly at whoever comes out on top in China.' He had shrugged until his shoulders almost touched his ears, and suddenly stopped talking.

And the voluble métis had been right, reflected Sissomak, as he worked his way cautiously down the stairway into the well of moonlight below. For the Paramahamsa Bonze had now told him he must go to Peking. And the Paramahamsa Bonze was never wrong.

Sipping lotus soup in the Teahouse of the Tranquil Fish on the Peninsula of Ten Thousand Years just to the north of Nakhara Wat, Short March heard a faint but purposeful bubbling as the palace launch started up and headed slowly back across the river to Nava with Sissomak aboard. The teahouse was the centre of social life in a tiny village of stone-cutters that had sprung up on this barren tongue of land, after an indulgent god-king had granted it to loyal Chinese immigrants as a burial ground. Could he be described as a loyal Chinese immigrant? Well, he reflected, as he stroked the seal-point Siamese queen on the chair beside him, he was certainly Chinese and he was certainly an immigrant. The comrades might call him 'Short March', but he had come a long way.

Short March Lee was from Swatow, where the best lace and the most beautiful girls of South-east China are painstakingly fashioned by the diligent poor, but as soon as he was old enough his impecunious father had sold him for a pig-soldier to a local warlord. Not long afterwards, the warlord was chopped into small pieces by the troops of a Chinese Nationalist butcher who thus acquired the unfortunate fellow's army at a knock-down price and joined it on to his own.

This general was then ordered to the north-west to help wipe out a pocket Soviet set up by the Chinese Reds in Shensi province, but his underpaid forces were infiltrated by an ingenious communist commander who lured away all the available turncoats among his Nationalist following. By now pig-soldier Lee, who was one of these, was on his third side and none too sure where the fourth one might be. However, Mao Tsetung and the main communist army in the south were coming to the end of their epic 6,000-mile 'Long March' in search of a new and safe base of operations. By the time the slow-moving column reached Shensi, it was no more than 10,000 strong, but just five miles from the point at which Mao made contact with the leaders of the local Soviet and called a halt, it was joined by Comrade Lee.

Lee was a small, round, smiling man with a large square head and short bandy legs, built on the principle of the round-bottomed Japanese Daruma doll that always springs upright however much it is pushed around, a vulgar peasant with quick wits, a slow, dry humour, and a bass voice full of sharp cinders. It was K'ang Sheng, Mao Tsetung's intelligence chief, who picked him out for training and dubbed him 'Short March' ('Even a journey of a thousand miles ends with one short step,' he had misquoted).

Lee was eventually transferred to the Te Wu, the Chinese 'Special Service', and in 1956 carefully established under sound commercial cover as its chief unofficial representative in Mekong, where most of the 300,000-strong Chinese minority were Teochew like himself. He had since become the most prosperous of stone-merchants with an export business in marble and the top cut of the local tomb trade. Stonecutter Village was his sanctuary.

The sound of Sissomak's launch had faded, but Short March showed his pleasure by shouting peremptorily for milk for the cat. So far, so good. The prince had been worried by the rumours about the Thai Embassy and the news from Peking, and he had duly consulted his fortune-teller. 'Come on, you mangy petit-bourgeois anarchist,' he said to the disdainful cat harshly but happily, 'drink up and none of your modern ultra-democratic factionalism or I'll denounce you as a class enemy and a danger to the proletarian revolutionary line. Which, of course, you are.'

High above the river at the threshold of his tower, the Paramahamsa Bonze gazed down at the silver-white wake of the royal launch as it shrank towards vanishing-point, took in the faint lights of the village on the Peninsula of Ten Thousand Years, and then turned to pass through the archway behind him and stride on to the big inner chamber beyond.

4

When Prince Norivong Kitay came back to Nava the next morning after he also had consulted the Paramahamsa Bonze in his turn, the raucous loudspeakers outside the Ministry of Information were already announcing that Sissomak would leave for Peking within a few days, just as the holy man had foreseen. But that was not all the Bonze had told Kitay. 'Your star rises in the heavens, Prince,' he had murmured softly, after ten minutes of utter immobility. Kitay had waited a moment, and then asked tranquilly: 'And Yaksha?' 'Stars rise,' had replied the Bonze, 'even as comets burn out and fall into darkness.' Then the heavy lids had fallen over the unseeing eyes in gentle dismissal.

So the moment had come. It only remained to deal with the Americans, Kitay thought distastefully. He stepped from his Mercedes, crossed the bridge over his lotus pond, and clapped twice as he entered the first cool, dark hall of his rambling wooden mansion on rue du Bassac. A manservant in a short embroidered jacket and sarong appeared and wormed his way towards the prince on his elbows and knees.

'Is he here?'

'In the inner room, Your Royal Highness.'

Kitay strode into the wide reception gallery, one wall of which was simply a long, fretted screen that gave on to an enclosed garden. The sunlight filtered through the carved teak on to the carpets, the low lacquered tables, the black and gold model of the Royal Barge with the Hamsa, the sacred goose, as its figurehead, the incised chests of camphorwood, and the two throne-chairs.

A white man was quite unwarrantably seated on one of these, but rose as he entered, and joined his two palms in a Mekinese greeting. He did not lift his hands high enough to show respect, and he failed to give a half-bow, Kitay noted coldly. But at least he did not try to shake hands in that insanitary way they had. President Johnson had even shaken hands with the Prime Minister of Thailand with his hat on, he had heard. Hardly credible.

'Thank you for waiting for me,' he said stiffly, 'and please be seated. It is a great pleasure to see you.'

He looked at the American attentively. A flat field of short grey stubble sprouted above a face as square, as evenly tanned and as expressionless as a cigar box into which had been set eyes as blind as Wedgwood blue. How like monkeys they are, he thought. All that hair on their hands, and those thin lips. This specimen was at least clean and even scented, yet obsession with cleanliness was itself suspect. It could be the greatest enemy of godliness, of the simple, ascetic life.

Dave Inqvist waited until Kitay had seated himself gracefully on a red cushion and lowered himself carefully on to another opposite him. Christ, they really are like monkeys, he was thinking, gingerly crossing his right leg over his left, only to find that this stranded one of his feet high in the air between them. Take this specimen squatting on the floor, with his broad, flat nose, and his protruding ears and thick lips. But we need his support, and you have to mind your manners with these people, especially royalty. They're so damned touchy.

Accordingly, Inqvist did not open the conversation but,

picking up the glass of iced tea that had been placed on a table beside him and taking a genteel sip, deferentially waited for Kitay to speak.

Kitay looked at Inqvist expressionlessly. What will he do next? First he has the ill-manners to display the sole of his shoe almost in my face, then he starts drinking his tea without waiting to be asked. These so-called *Caucasians*. They live in a contradiction in terms called the Instant Age and they strut about, grimacing and gesturing wildly, as if they were not under the eyes of God but of fifty million television viewers. They are men who seem to spend a lifetime desperately trying to make sure that they are taken for men, but with their public display of emotion and their hysterical search for luxury they are more like so many badly brought up children. We need their support, however, and you have to be careful what you say to them, especially the Americans. They are so sensitive about their own absurd beliefs.

Kitay therefore suppressed vivid memories of his single visit to the United States, and obliquely began one of those dialogues in treachery at which he was so practised. The premises were simple enough. The CIA, with the connivance of the Pentagon, had side-stepped the State Department and obtained presidential approval for some minor political brain-surgery in Mekong. Inqvist, their man in Nava, had smuggled the old, disgruntled anti-colonial warlord Yaksha back into the country from exile in Bangkok, and he was now hiding in the limestone hills that stuck abruptly out of the rice-plains to the west of the capital. He had quickly surrounded himself with several resentful Mekinese generals whom Sissomak had deprived of their promising military careers in opium and the black market and, once the prince left for Peking, he was to seize Nava. The Americans would 'negativize' any immediate threat of a move by the communist guerrillas in the Nakhara complex, and Mekong would join the other nations of South-east Asia that were strengthening regional resistance to communist subversion so that the GIs could all go home.

Yaksha's record was impressive. He was anti-French as well as anti-communist. He had spent the year 1928 in Chicago, spoke the archaic American of Scarface, and even had a taste for sour mash and cole slaw. 'He's our boy, Mr. President,' one of the thinkmen who live under the White House had stressed, urging that since the best defence was to get someone else to attack for you, the best way to withdraw from South-east Asia was to help your friends to practise a little good old-fashioned aggression.

The President of the United States of America is like a novice in a Zen monastery faced with a series of mind-expanding questions: What is the sound of one hand clapping? (Is China going to war with Russia – or us?) A girl is crossing the street – is she the younger or the older sister? (Should we give India arms? or Pakistan? Or both?) The novice exhausts the powers of his intellect in futile attempts to find logical answers until his mind rejects all further reasoning and opens itself to a flash of intuitive understanding. That is *satori*, the experience of spiritual awakening. Similarly the President of the United States, having listened patiently to the conflicting views of rival advisers and agencies, finds his mind screaming with contradictions and may finally be impelled by the frustration of it all into making an instinctive, snap decision. But in his case that is not always accompanied by a spiritual awakening. So on this occasion, the President gave the green light for Operation Homework.

There was one snag, however. If certain discontented generals rallied to Yaksha, the rank and file did not, for Sissomak was beloved of the peasantry and in Mekong all soldiers are peasants. Yaksha was therefore too weak to strike, and it was decided that Inqvist must try to draw Prince Kitay into the plot, for not only could he call on all those loyal to the family of Norivong, but he could bring in the Police Chief and Commander of the well-armed gendarmerie, General Keo, whom Sissomak still found too powerful to replace and whose broad buttocks had so far remained pre-cariously perched on the fence.

As soon as Inqvist had dropped a note at his house, asking to see him privately, Kitay had realised what was afoot, and the encouraging words of the Paramahamsa Bonze had now told him what he must do. The conversation therefore proceeded smoothly, like the conversations of all men with a common aim who do not understand one another. Kitay lied throughout with dignified circumspection, for it is not meet to force-feed simple men with distasteful truths they cannot digest. The Hindus even have a word for this error — *adhikarabheda*. So the prince spoke in passing of his admiration for the West, his staunch anti-communism and his respect for the ideals expressed in the American Constitution and the *American Dream*. He described himself as deeply religious, without explaining that for a Hindu-Buddhist this could involve the principle that each man must play his appointed role in life, whether saint or assassin, and that there were no good actions or bad actions.

Inqvist unhappily crossed his legs the other way, the prince clapped for Johnnie Walker Black Label, and a grovelling servant gave the tormented American a stiff kick on the rocks. When the man had gone, Kitay asked him what in general was Washington's reaction when governments changed abruptly. 'Well,' replied Inqvist in the slurred, metallic voice which always emerged from his scarcely moving slot of a mouth, as if it belonged either to a ventriloquist or his dummy, 'when one ruler falls, we just have to get along with the next guy.' Kitay permitted himself a very slight smile. That was what he wanted to know. For while Inqvist might have been talking about Yaksha, Kitay was not.

'Naturally,' went on Inqvist, wagging the index finger of his left hand at the prince, who winced invisibly at the appalling insult, 'naturally, we shall adopt a low posture throughout, but what we're ready for is a real package deal. You're not drinking, Your Highness,' he added, and painfully crossed his legs again with a small, involuntary groan.

Savages! they both thought simultaneously. 'I do not drink spirits,' replied Kitay, trying to unravel some of this unfamiliar English. Low posture? Europeans did not make obeisance, and promises to squat could only mean one thing. What was this new impudence? And package deal? In America they wrapped up everything elaborately from

26

cheap food to cheap women. What was he offering now?

'I can assure you, Your Highness, that we're ready to pour in the aid – economic, military, educational – until you have a way of life here comparable with our own. Sky's the limit, and we've got it to give.' They are always the same, thought Kitay, always trying to shower things on others and so put the rest of us under an obligation, to gain merit in Heaven at the expense of everyone else. All this *giving*! Heaven, indeed. At this rate Heaven would end up looking like the Empire State Building.

None of this showed on the placid face of the prince, as he sat effortlessly holding his thin, brittle body bolt upright on a cushion, his legs turned to the left as etiquette prescribed, and Inqvist's hand-sewn Hong-Kong shoe two feet from his face. No, he mused, with such a person there must be no brutal disclosures. One must teach him gently, compassionately, by what Buddhism has laid down as the use of 'skilful means'. He remembered the classic example of the father who had tempted his small, uncomprehending children to come out of their burning house, not by frightening them with shouts of 'fire', but by promising them toys. Once out, they were sadly disappointed to find that there were none, but this was the lesser of two shocks.

'I would like you to know,' he said at length, 'that I think we can reach an understanding, and that I give you my royal promise, you understand, my royal promise to put Yaksha in the place of my cousin Saravane Sissomak.'

Two hours later a jubilant Inqvist rose too quickly to take his leave, staggered drunkenly as the blood flowed back into his numb legs, grabbed Kitay by the shoulder in order to keep his balance and limped towards the door. As soon as he had gone, the outraged prince clapped his hands for the midday meal, and was soon sitting alone at a dining table, attended by his youngest son, aged six.

'And what did they teach you today?' he asked, as he helped himself from a large fish laced with a sauce of lemon-grass and red chilli.

The child hesitated. 'Sir, did you . . . ? I mean, a monk

taught us why we must kill no living thing, not even a tiny little mosquito.'

Kitay looked at him perplexed for a moment, then laughed gently. 'Did I catch this fish, you mean?' The boy nodded dumbly. 'Yes, I caught it in the royal lake. I often catch big fish. You know that. But notice this: I never kill them. I simply take them out of the water and bring them home.'

Calvert Kirkwall Eldritch was the other keen amateur fisherman of standing in Mekong, but no one had suggested that he 'get close to Kitay' until now. He had heard some fatuous schemes in his time for promoting United States influence, from suggestions that Washington finance the computerisation of the Iranian carpet industry to plans for popularising baseball in North Vietnam, but in his 25 years as a Foreign Service officer he had most adroitly avoided being implicated in a single coup d'état, despite earlier postings to Laos, Thailand and Indonesia.

He sat facing Inqvist and Strawbury across his large Empire desk, a lightly-powdered example of middle-aged Harvard with the rough-hewn head of a stage-senator and a big slab of body draped in flawless white. His sleek accent was patrician Massachusetts, and he talked bearable French, Spanish and Thai. His only sin was to have passed over the possibility of a merger with a Baltimore heiress in favour of a marriage with his Texan wife, and he was more joyful over this one opportunity that was lost than the ninety-nine that he had otherwise seized in his professional and social career. She had her faults, of course, but, Heaven knew, there were worse things in this world than a harmless addiction to square-dancing.

'Kitay's not exactly a ball of fire,' said Inqvist, 'but he came through all right with a solemn promise to put Yaksha in the saddle. He finalises with General Keo tomorrow, and he's sending his brother out to Yaksha's headquarters for minute-to-minute liaison. We'll be ready to go in three days, Mr. Ambassador.'

The ambassador hesitated for a moment, gazing at Inqvist

with pursed lips. 'I'm not trying to stand in the way of any home-brewed do-it-yourself revolution,' he began uneasily, 'but are we quite sure what we're getting into here, and what the results will really be? I doubt very much whether we are acquainted with the true inwardness of the affair. For a start, we have a dangerous tendency to judge these people by our own mental processes, to read their signals as our own. That could be like saying old man Death is a friendly soul because he never stops grinning.'

'But a Mekinese is still *homo sapiens*, Mr. Ambassador,' objected Strawbury, polishing his glasses and bouncing his voice gently off the ceiling that he could just discern as a vague white blur. 'His reflexes in relation to any decisional interaction context are practically game-analysable. *You* know. Just a matter of Pavlov's little old dog.'

'Do you agree, Dave?' queried the ambassador wickedly.

But Inqvist was not a senior officer of the CIA for nothing. 'Yep, that just about sums it up,' he replied through stiff, paper-thin lips, his eyes fixed blindly on Eldritch. 'And anyway, as François-Marie Arouet said, "God is on the side of the big battalions".'

There was a startled silence, and the ambassador realized that he was holding his breath. 'Since when have you been reading Voltaire, Dave?' he asked Inqvist at last. 'Oh,' said Inqvist, and threw his left hand nonchalantly into mid-air, 'just since.' It was a sweet moment, and he was not going to give that son-of-a-bitch Eldritch any points.

The truth was that he had been seduced from his blissful state of ignorance by a mail-order advertisement in a New York glossy that had taken him by brutal syntactical force. '*You risk nothing!*' it had shrieked at him. 'First superb 240-page volume in full color worth $2.50 – *free*! Send *no* money. Just fill in the form and post it to us, and every month we shall send you yet another gorgeous addition to our collection of twenty full-illustrated matching volumes handsomely bound in red and gold, and comprising *your key* to the poise and assurance that come only with *knowledge*. Here it is, for the first time: the entire history of "Our Cultural Heritage" from

Homer to Hemingway, from Socrates to Scott Fitzgerald, in one million words of text!' The astute secret agent had weighed the odds, taken his decision, and boldly posted his form. In consequence he was now wading his way through the one million words.

But Eldritch had not risen to Class One Officer rank in the Foreign Service for nothing, either.

'I think you'll find,' he said quietly, resting his elbows on his desk and putting the palms of his hands together, 'that the same author also said we "use thought only to justify our wrong-doings, and words only to conceal our thought". Don't let's be too quick to take things at face value, because the easiest way in the world to make a moronic mistake is to talk yourself into it with cast-iron, irrefutable arguments.

'First of all, if we back Yaksha, what's Yaksha going to do for us? Oh, I know we've been all over the ground, and so has Washington, but these people don't have a western sense of obligation. They believe that whoever does them a service is rewarded by Heaven anyway, and in fact may simply be currying favour with the gods.

'The second thing is that you cannot go by their faces, because they think that they can learn to glimpse the Infinite if they firmly discipline their animal gestures and feelings, and so we are surrounded by gentle smiles and grave politeness that do not necessarily bear any relationship to their true opinion of us.

'And finally, there is the little matter of their superstition. Just look around you. Every single dwelling has an eye-level spirit-house in the front garden dedicated to the *phi* that guards the home. Do you know you are supposed to ask its permission before you go in, and that the family have to propitiate it by heaping the altar with food and flowers, and bribe it with paper images of poultry or domestic help on high days and holidays, or else? Are you aware that people around here consult a geomancer before they site their house, and an astrologer before they choose its number? That's why, as you'll have noticed, they often don't run consecutively, and you may even get two houses with the same number in the same street.

'You're both relatively new around here, but I've held four posts in this goddamned subcontinent, and I've seen us make all our mistakes – and, boy, have we made some – for one reason and one only: our blithe assumption that they think as we do. Kitay could go to some fancy fortune-teller to-morrow, some pessimistic astromancer or clairvoyant or what-have-you,' the ambassador went on, not realising how near the mark he was, 'and the whole operation could go down the nearest monsoon drain.'

He scratched the left side of his corrugated nose, and glanced sharply from one to the other. 'And furthermore,' he broke in as Strawbury seemed about to speak, 'what really sticks in my craw is our own so-called negativization plan to stop the Mekinese Reds from taking advantage of the situation. That's direct military involvement, and it completely destroys our plausibility of denial if the coup fails.' He tapped the Empire desk gently with the flat of one large hand, paused, and continued: 'No, I'm sorry, gentlemen, but as our accredited ambassador to Mekong I reserve the right to question this entire operation once again with the Secretary of State.'

'But the whole proposition has been cleared through channels already,' protested Inqvist, 'and the deadline –'

'Dave,' interrupted the ambassador, holding up his hand. 'I don't wish to seem overbearing, but I must point out that I am in authority over all American agencies in Mekong, whatsoever their nature, and the CIA does not direct the policy of the United States – yet.'

Strawbury loosened his shoulders like a boxer, leaned forward, and extended a long index finger towards Eldritch. 'But the President does, Mr. Ambassador,' he said blandly, the words bobbing lightly from his mobile lips. 'And while of course the last thing I want is to provoke any subliminal animadversion, the fact is that as presidential adviser to the Mekinese administration I hold my mandate from the White House. And the White House has given the okay for Operation Homework.'

The ambassador raised his eyes to the ceiling. 'You mean you don't want to quarrel, but you're going to have it your way?'

Strawbury nodded and smiled pleasantly.

'Well, wait until you've got that fault-finding mission of twelve Congressmen on your hands once the whole business has backfired in your face.'

'There won't be any congressional mission, because history has taught that the guys who win are automatically innocent, and the guys who lose are automatically guilty, and we have the Pentagon right behind us and we are going to succeed.'

'That sounds to me like a possible contradiction in terms you have there,' commented Eldritch.

'And anyway it's only a small military operation,' concluded Strawbury.

'Yes,' conceded the ambassador sardonically, measuring it between two powerful index fingers, 'just about the size of the last straw.'

5

Thinking Lotus caught Ivansong as he was shrugging his way into a striped orlon jacket. 'Let's see,' he murmured, 'notebook, pen, car keys, handkerchiefs, wallet, diary, airport pass, cable card, small change, dark glasses, bow tie (I'll put it on at the last minute), camera, radio. Something I've forgotten. What?'

'Stock book,' replied Lotus promptly, slapping a sheet of paper into his hand in a businesslike manner.

'Stock book, what stock book?'

'All tradesmen have stock books and you are carrying a whole shop about with you in and around that distressingly vulgar jacket. Moreover, you are sweating all over your exposure meter.'

'Oh, damn it all,' cursed Ivansong. 'I'm soaked through before I even start out, and I've forgotten to bring down the portable – I'll type a short story at the airport and cable it from there. And what do you mean, stock book? This looks like a list of chores. Three tins of powdered milk, one bottle Moskovskaya vodka, collect broken tape-recorder from bicycle shop, something cold for lunch, one pot Dolly Varden's Special Skin-care Nourishing Overnight Cream (Regular Formula), one pkt quarto typing paper, three bags of general fertiliser . . . look, Lotus, I have to go and see Sissomak off. How can I deal with all this junk?'

'But we need some of that by lunchtime and I am only going into town late this afternoon to have my hair cooked. They could not fit me in earlier, and,' went on Lotus, 'I have to see the new morning gardener and tell him to bury the holes left by the roots of the old thorn tree we dug up so that Mango cannot fall into them. And you will have the car with you. So be an angel.'

'I'm always being an angel.'

'Never mind, sometime I will give you a day off and you can be a devil for once. But I have so much to do today. Why do you complain? You know I am part of the garden.'

'Is that so,' retorted Ivansong, 'then just what am I?'

'You?' replied Lotus blinking up at him in astonishment. 'But of course you are just part of me.'

Five minutes later The Bitch was nosing gingerly down the potholed street to Prince Kitay's mansion. Ivansong pulled up by the gate and hooted twice. After he had waited two minutes, a yawning doorkeeper appeared from around the side of the house, took the two letters that were given to him, and withdrew again. This was now an established ritual, for the semi-literate postman often confused their mail.

There was still a military check-point at the bottom of rue du Bassac, and once Ivansong was well down Boulevard Siho he found the road unevenly laced with troops and police, for Sissomak would pass this way. The sun rode high and un-repentant in a bold blue sky, and the air seemed sticky with sweat. Few people were about at the airport. A guard of

33

honour drooped listlessly at ease on the white-hot apron, which was otherwise empty except for a portly Ilyushin of the Civil Aviation Administration of China at the far end. Through the glass doors of the VIP room Ivansong caught sight of a small huddle of glum ambassadors who had come to see the prince off, while around the bar in the main hall stood a group of sartorial extroverts, each clad in his own idea of the correct dress for the occasion, ranging from striped T-shirt and sandals to charcoal-grey dacron and deerskin suede. These were his colleagues, and they greeted him absently, for they were listening with care and attention to something of evident importance.

'So I've just got this gladiolus down on the rack,' explained a raw, smooth voice like undyed velvet from somewhere in the middle of the cluster, 'and I'm all set to fill this long-felt want of hers – and she's something, I can tell you, classy-looking but kinda serious, you know the type, reminds me a bit of Svetlana Whatsaname – when suddenly the door flies open and Cat here shouts "Cable, Polak, New York wants a rundown on the old priest they've pickled in mercurochrome."'

'Formaldehyde,' corrected Bernard Kalb, who was the CBS correspondent.

'Mercurochrome,' countered Charlie Polak of the rival North American Broadcasting System defiantly, 'or there-abouts. So,' he continued, his voice softening confidentially again, 'you know how it is. With sensitive people like me fire in the belly turns to ashes in the ass if you have a god-damned audience. So I give up and turn to Cat and say "Well, let's see it anyway", and start to read it in comfort from where I am, when this very sizeable bitch hauls herself off the cot, and in words of the most refined vulgarity calls me a m*th*r-fucking *bookworm*, didn't she, Cat?'

Catullus Yip nodded his head with a small Chinese smile. He was a fourth-generation immigrant from Fukien province, American-educated, sketchily bearded, hooked on grass, and the best television cameraman Polak had ever directed.

'And after that monstrous performance I trust you turned your thoughts to the holy man with a suitable sense of humility,

34

Your Grace?' said Richard Hughes of the *Sunday Times*, as the laughter subsided.

'Oh, I sent New York something to keep them quiet,' said Polak, with a shrug, 'but the one I'd like to pin down is that *Sadhu* up in Nakhara Wat.'

'The Paramahamsa Bonze?'

'Yeah, but you can't get near him. I hear he refuses to talk to anyone directly nowadays except big boys like Sissomak, even assuming you could get through to him. We've taken a few shots of him with a telephoto lens, but nothing to go and get drunk on. He gives me a pain in the sacroiliac.'

Ivansong eased his way into the group and punched Polak gently but firmly on the left bicep. The brooding eyes, set between long black sideburns in a fastidious semitic face that always seemed to be sniffing deeply on an inseparable mixture of sweat and ambrosia, sparkled suddenly. 'Where have you been all my life, Larry, which is already one whole month in this land of the Lingam?'

'It just happened like that somehow,' said Ivansong, refusing a Lucky Strike. 'Did I by any chance hear you talking chuff, as usual?'

'Chuff?' echoed Polak, taken aback. 'Who am I to talk chuff with experts around? Look who's here.'

He nodded towards a plump Eurasian with a solemn, flabby face the colour of weak tea who stood gravely in mid-concourse, wearing a Hawaii shirt cut from a handsome silver and green sarong, and a young ash-grey gibbon perched on its ischial callosities on his left shoulder. Max Alias had screwed his half-open fists into his eyes as if he were conning the mill of journalists through binoculars, and was softly crooning a verse from a fine French dramatic ballad:

> *Ce fut un combat gigantesque!*
> *Trois-cents mille périrent ou presque!*
> *Le général des morpions*
> *Examinait la position!*
> *De Profondis . . .*

'Bonjour, les gars,' murmured the métis, as he joined the enemy (for officially he was Sissomak's press adviser). 'Qu'est-

35

ce qui se passe? Where is the war?' His dog-like eyes moved from one to the other, and he shook his head sadly. 'Why the concentration of troops? The prince is not saying anything today. Ne t'en fais pas, Mini,' he added gently to the gibbon, which had flinched from the gross faces around it and buried its head in his armpit. 'They are big but they are only journalists. And among the many things they have in common with baboons is that their bark is more frequent than their bite.'

Before anyone could think of a suitable rejoinder, there was a flurry behind the glass door of the VIP room. The prince had arrived, and the correspondents abandoned the concourse bar for the scorching apron, where television cameras had already been set up by lieutenants of Polak and Kalb. 'No conference,' shouted Max at their receding backs, and morosely signed all the bills that remained unpaid.

The prince, dressed like a French banker in a pin-striped black suit and a pearl-grey silk tie, stepped smiling on to the apron from the VIP room, followed immediately by the Chinese ambassador in a smart buttoned-up tunic with matching gor-blimey, and the French and British envoys. He paused as the cameras clicked. The incongruous Max appeared suddenly at his side, whispering urgently, 'I have told them you have nothing to say, Sire,' and glared balefully at a young, ostensibly harmless Australian from Reuters. Thus discouraged, the Australian at once went off like a cuckoo clock. 'Sir, can you give us any indication why you finally decided to go to Peking and what you hope to achieve there?' he asked swiftly, 'and secondly, would you care to comment on . . .'

The prince raised his hand. 'Max says no press conference,' he said in his high-pitched harsh English. 'But I have no secrets, and I will tell you this. I hope to consolidate further the friendship between my country and the great People's Republic of China, and between myself and the present and future leaders in Peking. No more than that. Why did I decide to go at this time? Let us say it was written in the stars.'

'Nonetheless, in view of the burning of the Thai Embassy –'

persisted the agency man. But the prince walked forward, nodding and smiling affably to each side as if no one had spoken, and ten minutes later the CAAC Ilyushin spluttered into monotonous song and taxied to the runway, its ill-balanced tail-section bobbing gently.

After the aircraft had failed to crash on take-off, the correspondents dispersed philosophically. The Australian from Reuters sat down on a bench in the concourse, banged out two hundred words on a chipped and rusted portable typewriter, and was soon gone.

Ivansong put his machine on the bar and thoughtfully composed a new lead to an airmail backgrounder that he had registered to London the day before. After all, the prince had confirmed one thing, at least by implication. His journey to Peking had been 'written in the stars'. He was going on the advice of the Paramahamsa Bonze. It was good colour and would give his story a relaxed opening. He handed in his cable at the telecommunications desk and strode out towards the car park just as a long and motley string of empty buses arrived, from the first of which fluttered a gay banner reading 'Mekong Welcomes Kutprice Kamping Inc.'.

At that moment Ivansong heard the harmonious drone of several large aircraft and, being of an inquisitive turn of mind, decided to buy himself a beer. Dolly Varden's Special Skincare Nourishing Overnight Cream (Regular Formula) would have to wait.

6

The Boeing 707s followed each other down like migrating geese, and were soon lined up neatly on the apron with the same expectant, self-righteous look to be remarked among most birds after they have alighted. Only then did the doors of all five open, spilling their contents casually on to the tarmac.

The passengers were mainly men, with a few large and athletic girls in blouses and slacks scattered among them, and they were dressed in a polychromatic selection of bush-shirts, denim trousers tucked into canvas-sided boots and caps with sun-vizors, as if they were going on a hunting trip. Mekong offered tiger and bear, pig and lethal wild ox of South-east Asia to the one unnatural enemy of all jungle life, but if this group were let loose on the available four-legged fauna there would be a slaughter, thought Ivansong, for it was far too large.

'Who on earth are they?' he asked the chief ground hostess of Royal Air Mekong. She turned a bright Mekinese eye upon him, smoothed down her cherry-coloured sarong, and replied: 'It's one of these big package tours that American corporations go in for. You know. They give the staff – or the prize workers on the staff – a group holiday. I once had to help with three thousand of them over a two-month period in Hong Kong. *Three thousand*, can you imagine? There was not a transistor or a colour film left in the Crown Colony. But these are something else. I think there are about four or five hundred of them, and they work for a firm called Kutprice Kamping Inc. in Detroit or Pittsburgh or one of those.'

She left Ivansong for a moment, only to bring over to him a rather preoccupied middle-aged American in a lounge-suit with a big button in his left lapel that read 'R. & R. Tours'.

'This is Monsieur Ivansong, of the newspapers,' said the little Mekinese. 'He wants you to tell him something about your holiday group.'

The American gazed at Ivansong in silence for a moment. 'Well, there's not much I can say at this point,' he began abruptly. 'This operation is a cheap package deal for Kutprice Kamping. The men in the outfit bring all their camp gear with them, do their own cooking, and see something of the countries we're going through that way. We've just come from Thailand, and although we'll be putting up one night at the hotels in town here, tomorrow at 0600 we'll be moving off to the site. Yes?' This to one of the holidaymakers who had broken away from a long, orderly line heading towards the baggage collection centre. 'Excuse me, Major, but –' 'I'm not Major,' cut in the R. & R. Tours official quickly. 'I'm Karstang – that's Mister Major over there,' and he pointed to a saturnine Caucasian with a scar down one cheek.

'They don't go through Immigration, then?' asked Ivansong with interest.

'No, sir, nor Customs,' replied Karstang. 'We clear everything in bulk in advance – passports, their gear, the lot. And I'll say they're a pretty self-sufficient bunch. They certainly don't give much trouble.' He walked towards the mounds of baggage now accumulating, and Ivansong saw what he meant. They were manhandling what he took to be bedrolls, duffle bags, stout camping kitchen-boxes, personal haversacks, sixty-pound tents, and other bulky canvas-covered bundles – some of them obviously very heavy – out of the building and into the buses in a competent, businesslike way.

Ivansong quietly left the side of Karstang and moved across to the man with the scar who had been identified as Mr. Major. 'Is this kit all manufactured by Kutprice Kamping Inc.?' he asked. 'Sure,' answered Scarface readily, with a smile, 'and the best on the market for the price. But I don't think I remember meeting . . .' 'Oh, I'm sorry,' said Ivansong, his flecked eyes dancing dangerously, 'My name's Larry Ivansong, and I believe you're Mr. Maj –'

'Say, Cap,' interrupted a big, square-cut, straight-backed American with a badly-weathered face, 'how about a detail for –' 'I'm not Capp,' interrupted the man with the scar, 'I'm Straker, remember? That's Capp over there.' Ivansong discreetly withdrew as Straker pointed towards Karstang, and drove to the Hotel de l'Asie.

'Are you putting up the people from this American group tour?' he asked the head receptionist, a thin, elderly Mekinese in pince-nez.

'Some. In fact about one hundred and eighty of them,' replied the old man resignedly. 'We are packing them in as

4   39

best we can – often three and even more to a room. Where necessary they will use their own camp-beds, you see. Very cheap,' he added, with a sniff. ' "Monsieur," I said to the manager, "why not let them camp in the grounds?" But they don't want to unpack their tents, it seems.'

There would have been room for them in the garden, for as *Fodor's Guide to Japan and East Asia* notes under 'Mekong' (page 1178 et seq.) 'Hotel de l'Asie is set in twelve acres of tropical gardens shaded by palms and studded with ornamental ponds. By far the older of the two best hotels in Nava, it has something of the cool, spacious colonial architecture of Raffles in Singapore and it faces on to the River Mekong. Most rooms are airconditioned, there is an excellent lounge-bar of Somerset Maugham vintage, and an open-air restaurant (French cuisine). Another feature of the grounds is the bridal suite, a separate structure built to resemble one of the old temples of Nakhara itself. Single occupancy in a double room is charged at single rate. Most rooms have telephone, bathrooms and modern amenities. . .'

The heavily-laden Kutprice Kampers started to filter in, to be met by another self-confident American wearing an R. & R. Tours badge who allocated them briskly to their rooms, apparently irrespective of sex.

'Chow – dinner – at one, and a hot evening meal at seven,' he was saying, 'in the café in the garden. Breakfast at five tomorrow morning.'

'You can see now what travelling is coming to,' remarked the receptionist. 'None of the grace of the old days.' Nevertheless, that was how the Chomsky mob came to spend a night in a bridal suite together, a possibility to which hitherto they had given very little thought indeed.

'Just get a load of this,' said Chomsky as he led the other four through the door of the imitation temple to Vishnu. The walls were covered with a grey and white paper designed to resemble rubbings from the more erotic carvings of Nakhara, and depicting a riot of apsaras and potent princes. Above the huge circular treble-bed was set a large, highly-polished oval mirror, and the floor around was covered with soft off-white nylon sheepskin backed with spring rubber.

The table lights were ornate black and gold Chinese household altars and their shades were of heavy silk the colour of a light blush. The small lobby and lounge, and the opulently-fitted bathroom with its sunken Japanese sitting-bath for two and its own ceiling mirror, were decorated in the same style, and the suite was air-conditioned as one unit.

'Wow,' said Smearer, dropping his huge canvas bedroll to the floor, 'this is what I call camping out.' The other three gazed around them in silent wonderment, while Chomsky carried out a systematic inspection. It was when he came back that he noticed the row of buttons by the bed. 'Well, how do you like that?' he murmured in awe.

'Whatsamatter now, Chomsky?'

'These frigging bells – listen, this is real service. The top one says "Boy", the next one says – what's this? Gazetti, give us the old Italian.'

Gazetti came over. 'French,' he said, 'it says "femme de shombre", means something like "room woman".'

'There, you see,' said Chomsky triumphantly, 'Girl. And look what the bottom one says – *LOVE*. L-O-V-E. Well, if one's boy, and the other's girl, what the hell do you get for "Love"? That ought to sort out the hombres from the shombres. I just can't wait to see.' And he pressed it.

Even in the slanting sunshine, they were able to discern the soft pink glow that gradually suffused the room from concealed lighting all around the walls and the mirror in the ceiling. Chomsky pressed the button again, but the lights would not go out.

He shook his head in surprise, but then turned to the others. 'Okay,' he said, 'I've checked out the joint. The lounge-bar has got some kind of a davenport thing, and the other guy sleeps in his bag, whichever. So that's Helmsmann and Gazetti taken care of. That leaves Smearer and me and Miss Craddock with the fun-bed and the sofa between us, and it don't matter how we share that out because,' went on Chomsky flatly, 'I'm gonna have the boobs off Miss Craddock right here and now.'

'What the hell's that,' shouted the outraged Craddock,

41

clutching at his very noticeable bosom. 'You goddam well leave me alone, Chomsky, or I'll belt your teeth in.'

'Yeah?' replied Chomsky. 'Well, you already learned one lesson today, Miss Craddock, ain't you, insisting you got the constitutional right to grow your hair long in the outfit like some goddamned guitarist? So now they really got you fixed, girlie. I don't know why they didn't put you guys in skirts and have done, if they wanted it to look like we had some dames with us.'

'Be reasonable,' said Smearer. 'How could they? Look at the legs on them.'

'Yeh, but they still went to the trouble of giving boobs to all these long-haired buck privates, didn't they, just the same? Well, now they're coming off,' announced Chomsky inexorably. 'No boobs in my squad. Come on, Smearer, give us a hand in a little sex-change operation.'

'Get back, you bastards,' yelled Craddock, as the pair seized him, pushed him over backwards on the bed, and tore open his blouse. 'Get back, and leave me alone. These tits are official issue. I had to sign for them, for Chrissake. Give them back!'

But he was too late, a buckle snapped, and a pair of khaki falsies came away with Chomsky's victorious arm. The mood changed suddenly. Helmsmann and Gazetti moved closer, and they all peered at the offending objects. 'Wonderful what they keep in combat stores these days,' commented Helmsmann, 'but what are they for?' Chomsky shrugged. 'Could be kinda flak protection, could be for swimming if you're sunk, could be –'

'Could be falsies,' said Smearer, 'you know, for real women, you know, like WACs, that kind of thing.'

'Boy, falsies for WACs,' echoed Gazetti with a grin. 'How to scare the enemy out of his cotton-picking wits. Go on, Chomsky, let the bastard put 'em back on again. We may need them out in the field. Only trouble is, he oughta have two pairs really – one for his non-existent stack and the other for his non-existent ass.'

'Well why don't we go out and find the real thing?' suggested

Helmsmann reasonably. 'Plenty of room for a few birds here, too, without any immediate danger of overpopulation.'

'Out,' said Chomsky, 'you know it's out. We gotta stay put so's not to run the risk of giving ourselves away. We're tourists, remember? No tail, no going out on the town, and no drinks from the bar. Colonel's orders. So there's only one thing left,' and unstrapping his bedroll he pulled out a bottle of Old Grandad that lay, carefully wrapped in a pair of undershorts, next to his M-16 rifle. 'All right, men,' he shouted suddenly, 'Red Alert!'

And as they hurried to unpack the vodka, the gin and the scotch, and Gazetti swung open the door of the countersunk refrigerator in his search for ice and soda and tonic, the hidden cameras above the one-way mirror in the ceiling were able to record the evolving scene even when the sky darkened with thunderclouds, since the lights operated by the 'Love' button could only be switched off from outside.

7

On the next day history made one of those short sprints that always save it at the last moment just as it appears to be falling behind the time. The Kutprice Kampers moved off promptly at 0600 hours, crossed the leaden-faced Mekong in a string of barges requisitioned by General Keo, and landed on the far bank at a point one mile down-river and south of Nakhara. From there they humped their gear up Hill 520, which the civilised world knew as Mount Kham, and occupied their scheduled camp-site among the brooding stone faces of the Mayon at its summit. No one stopped them.

So they opened the bundles and boxes that ostensibly

contained Kutprice tents and bedrolls and portable kitchens and collapsible latrines, and they took out their M-16 automatic rifles, their 81-mm mortars, their 106-mm recoilless rifles, their M-60 light machine-guns, their 3.5-inch rocket launchers and two thousand non-returnable plastic sandbags which they proceeded to fill with earth for defence works. Snatching sustenance from their C-rations and water-bottles as and when they could, they mounted some of their weapons among the enigmatic four-faced towers around them, but established their outer perimeter just below the Mayon by linking up the tumbled stones of the enclosing wall around its base with sandbags, and digging shallow gun-positions on the slope behind them. They set up their command post in the main pinnacle of the monument, and by five o'clock in the afternoon they were no longer Kutprice Kamping Inc. but half a battalion of United States Marines.

Their imperturbable commander ('I've seen some pretty funny landing zones in my time, but this looks like one of the original Halls of Montezuma') announced this metamorphosis over his radio, and was assured by his superiors at sea in the Gulf of Khammax that the first helicopters carrying more sandbags, wire, rations, ammunition, claymore mines and – above all – water would be above him before dusk.

The Mekinese Reds had shown no sign of life, and the Marines now held the one feature that dominated the surrounding terrain, the river, and the capital itself. Operation Homework had been executed with the same clockwork precision that had characterised its mindless conception.

Assured that the Marines had already reached the top of Mount Kham, Yaksha gave the signal for his coup d'état when the traditional three-hour siesta started at midday. This devious ruse took the loyalists by surprise, and by three in the afternoon Yaksha's rebel forces held the airport, the main post office, and all the principal ministries, and were laying seige to the barracks of the Nava garrison. The heavily-armed gendarmerie of General Keo had surrounded the Royal Palace where the Queen Mother was in residence and seized control of the radio station, and its armoured cars had isolated the main arsenal.

There was sporadic shooting and looting throughout the city, and the Mekinese took advantage of the turmoil to indulge in their favourite pastime of setting fire to the shop-houses of Chinese moneylenders in the hope of incinerating not only the inmates but their own IOUs. In general, however, it was the most orderly and dignified life-or-death struggle Ivansong had covered in his career.

At three-thirty in the afternoon the streets were still filled with smoke and soldiers, and light tanks or scout cars of the defected Fourth Armoured Regiment from Yaksha's own province commanded all main crossroads. But apart from a few abrupt outbursts – sudden, confused shouting, the brief ebb and flow of running feet, the neurotic babble of a lonely tommy-gun – Nava seemed to be falling quiet, as if waiting.

For a few minutes, Ivansong was puzzled. He stood in the middle of Quatre-Faces, the big intersection of Siho and Chulalok with its four-faced Gate of Vishnu in the middle, and tried to think what was missing. He thumbed through his half-torn notebook with grimy fingers, but his jottings, a scrawled battle-scene in themselves, gave him no clue. Then the corner of his eye registered movement and he swung around, ready for trouble, to see an incongruous figure teeter-ing delicately towards him across the flat, empty square as if it were walking a very narrow plank over a raging torrent – the half-bent arms were stretched out on either side for better balance, the slender hands drooping from the wrist, and every now and again it would suddenly drop to its haunches and crouch motionless, glancing nervously this way and that. As it drew near, Ivansong realised that it was Max's grey gibbon, and that she was obviously distressed not only by the frighten-ing noises of the past few hours, but by the terrible horizontal expanse before her which compelled her to run on her short legs, and gave no proper play to the long furry arms with which a gibbon swings along the branches of trees or the wire of a cage.

At that moment Ivansong heard a far-off yell, and made out the wildly gesticulating figure of Max himself, well behind the animal. 'Mini,' Ivansong shouted urgently. 'Mini, *here*, you damn silly monkey, you.' But as she came closer and saw him, she veered off towards the gate itself, and with one smooth, simian leap hooked her long fingers into the beringed stone toe of a carved warrior and swung to and fro nine feet up, gazing nervously this way and that. Ivansong moved below her, held out his arms, and shouted 'Jump, you cretin, jump,' and, miraculously, she landed on his shoulder without even making him stagger.

'*Mince, alors,*' panted Max as he came up with the pair, his chest heaving with pulmonary exertion and distress. 'Toi, petit salaud, toi,' he breathed at the gibbon, enfolding her in his arms, from which she peeked out accusingly at Ivansong. 'The stupid animal got scared by some imbecile of a *vache* who started firing the fifty-calibre on his armoured car at nothing, and I have been trying to catch up with her ever since. Larry, a thousand thanks. But the trouble is I don't know what to do now. Yaksha's gangs of pigs are everywhere, including in the prince's quarters. I am out on my ear.' Max paused to catch his breath. 'Look, Larry,' he went on, 'please, please do something for me. You have a house, you can help.'

'Of course,' said Ivansong slowly, 'come and move in right away. We can always fix you up somehow.'

'Me?' said Max, as if talking to a half-wit. 'Why me? No, what you could do for me is to look after Mini for a few days until the dust settles. It's all very simple,' he went on conversationally. '*Hylobates moloch* are, as you know, arboreal apes by nature, and therefore a light diet of mixed fruits and flowers suffices, with *unsalted* nuts. Perhaps a raw egg occasionally, but no boiled rice or bread, please. They distend the stomach. Feed her three times a day and put her drinking water in a pan so that she can wet her hand and lick it. She cannot tolerate the stuff in quantity. She will sleep almost anywhere, preferably on a branch, but you will need to provide her with cover against monsoon rains – gibbons are *most* susceptible to chills, even in this climate. But they have a highly-developed sense of territorial integrity. Take her round the garden and show her which are your trees, and she will

46

not run away. She is well-trained, and anyway here is a nylon lead you can use if you absolutely –'

'Wait,' shouted the horrified Ivansong. 'You are one thing, Max, but Mini is another. I can't –'

'But what are you so excited about,' asked Max, throwing up his hands in astonishment. 'She is highly civilised, never any trouble, only asking to be loved, eh, Mini?' He tickled the dark patch at the top of her head.

Ivansong hesitated. 'All right, Max,' he said. 'Things seem to have quietened down for the moment. I've got my car parked in Reuters' courtyard. If she'll go over there with me alone without making a fuss, I'll take her. If not, not. You come to the house tomorrow, and see how she is. But, Max, I can't accept any responsibility for her. I'll just do my best, okay? How do I manage her in the car, anyway?'

'But she *loves* cars, Larry. She adores cars. Put her beside you, and you will see, she will be as good as gold. D'ailleurs elle est *jamais* malade dans les voitures de marque.'

'Well, that's a relief,' said Ivansong. 'Now, then, come on, Mini.'

'Go, go,' said Max urgently, putting the small gibbon on the ground. Ivansong took one of the slim hands and together they set off, Mini looking back sorrowfully at her fat and forlorn master, who stood with his hands anxiously clasped in front of him, watching her walk away. Once in the car, she lay flat on her stomach along the top of the passenger seat in front and closed her eyes resignedly, leaving Ivansong to his thoughts.

There was something wrong about the silence beyond the bronchitic growl of the engine. He switched on the little Japanese transistor radio in the top right-hand pocket of his stained bush-shirt. Slow, limpid Mekinese gong-music. That was ridiculous. There should be. . . *why no announcements?* Why weren't the loud-speaker vans blaring out the news in the streets? Yaksha had the city in his hands, the coup was a *fait accompli* and Sissomak was stuck in Peking. And nobody uttered a word? Ivansong felt the untrimmed hair rising on the nape of his neck, and put his foot down on the accelerator.

He was half-way down rue du Bassac when the machine-guns and bazookas opened up with a coordinated burst of fire somewhere far behind him, and there were two muffled explosions. Ivansong and Mini looked at each other anxiously. God damn it, what a time to be stuck with female *Hylobatidae*, he was thinking, but realised that she might be feeling much the same about him. He swerved into the drive of the house, pulled up sharply, and switched off the motor.

In the distance a machine-gun rattled, and another answered faintly from across the town. He stood precariously on the car seat and was gazing back towards a new and promising cloud of smoke when a voice above shouted: 'It's something frying near the post office. Catch.' He looked up at the balcony in time to field the small flannel that Thinking Lotus, wrapped in a towel dressing-gown, dropped on to him. It was soaked in after-shave lotion and he was mopping the back of his neck with it gratefully when she added: 'By the way, who is that?'

Ivansong explained quickly, taking the gibbon gently in his arms. 'Touching,' commented Lotus. 'But what do we do with it?'

'Look,' said Ivansong hurriedly, 'something funny is going on, and I've got to get back to town to find out what it is, though I've a very strong suspicion. Take her over, will you? I simply must rush, and she's very well brought up, and so on.'

'I can see that,' replied Lotus. 'Very feminine, too, in her movements. She will have a beneficial influence on Mango, who shows a regrettable tendency to want to be a boy. And we can feed her with fruit from the garden, though that will only be the rejects the birds leave us after they have taken their pick, but we cannot have everything, can we? However, just at this moment I have only had the top half of my bath –'

'Well,' interrupted Ivansong, gazing impatiently towards the city, 'tell Ah King to tie her up for the time being, or lock her in the loo, or put her in the fridge or something, just for now. I *must* be off.'

'But I want to hear what has been happening,' cried Lotus despairingly. At that moment, however, their mountainous Chinese amah appeared in the doorway and Ivansong unceremoniously thrust Mini into her arms, leaped into the car, and roared out of the gate before he could be stopped.

He toured the streets slowly and carefully. Everything was the same as it had been one hour before except for the still smouldering wrecks of a scout car and a thirteen-ton AMX tank of the Fourth Armoured Regiment outside the post office. The same soldiers in sloppy green battledress and the same field police in crumpled khaki stopped him at the same checkpoints to glance at the 'Press' label taped to the windscreen and to ask for his passport.

Yet there was a subtle change, as if he were seeing Nava through a looking-glass, as if left had quietly become right, and right left. Sentries barred him from all the key points taken over by the coup-makers, and when he was lucky enough to run into someone of consequence, he learned nothing. He called at the British and American embassies, only to leave more puzzled than before. Those that knew would not speak. Those that spoke did not know, it seemed.

He stopped the car outside the Ministry of Information and switched on his transistor radio to hear a voice repeat monotonously in Mekinese, French and English: 'Everyone must remain in their homes and stand by for an important announcement. The authorities have everything under control and the public is asked to remain calm. There is no cause for anxiety.'

Ivansong switched it off and made his way through the side door of the ministry to the foreign press liaison department, but there was only a clerk on duty. 'I have been told to tell everybody that there will be a press conference in the Royal Palace at six,' the man said. 'Please pass this on if you see any of your colleagues.'

At the entrance of the conference hall in the Royal Palace, a ministerial flunkey in white sharkskin reverentially bestowed on Ivansong a cyclostyled handout, and he sank on to a collapsible wooden chair nearby to study it as other journalists pushed by him to the rows of seats beyond. The release was headed 'Announcement of the Royal Government of Mekong'. Ivansong suddenly knew exactly how it was going to read, and he was right:

'At midday today a group of traitorous rebels and malcontents, taking advantage of the departure for Peking of His Royal Highness Prince Saravane Sissomak, attempted to mount a coup d'état and seize control of the capital in order to abolish the Monarchy symbolized by Her Majesty the Queen Mahaksatriyani. They were led by the notorious renegade Yaksha and his insurrectionist clique, and at first caused some damage and casualties.

'Apprised of this perfidy and the identity of its perpetrator, however, His Royal Highness Prince Norivong Kitay with the full support of His Excellency General Voronikone Keo, Director of Security Services, rallied loyal units of the Mekinese Army, Police and Gendarmerie in order to safeguard the Monarchy and the security of the Realm. After some fighting, the revolt has been suppressed, rebel leaders have been rounded up, and the traitor Yaksha has been shot while trying to resist arrest.

'In the absence of Prince Saravane Sissomak, Her Majesty the Queen has graciously appointed Prince Norivong Kitay as acting Chief of State and has confided to him the task of restoring peace. A state of emergency has been declared, and a series of proclamations will be issued in order to ensure the full cooperation of the general public.

'Long Live Mekong! Long Live the Queen! Long Live Prince Norivong Kitay!'

The hall, with its long, sad velvet drapes and great, grubby chandeliers, was humming with comment which petered out as Prince Kitay led a group of men on to the rostrum from a door at the back. Chairs scraped. The assembled journalists and officials stood up and then sat down again once the prince had settled himself behind the metallic posy of microphones on the long, polished table before him. Ivansong moved further forward and found a seat next to one of the tall windows that gave on to the Mekong.

The straight, stick-like prince, wearing over his ceremonial sarong a white military tunic tinkling with orders and medals and garnished with several yards of gold rope, waited woodenly through a burst of photo flashes, the blinding arcs supporting the television cameras of Charlie Polak and Bernard Kalb lending his still, haughty face and pouting lips a lavender hue.

He then put on a pair of spectacles and read perfunctorily from a sheaf of papers without looking up. The gentlemen of the press had now all seen the account of what had happened on that momentous day. It remained to arraign and execute those rebels who had already been seized, and to capture the rest. Beyond this, it was the firm intention of the prince and his ministers and advisers (he turned briefly to the men on each side of him) to re-establish law and order.

To this end, Her Majesty the Queen had graciously consented to sign a decree authorising the imprisonment without trial of all persons suspected of harbouring hostile intentions towards the Throne or the Government. A curfew was being imposed as from that day, and a comprehensive rationing system would be introduced to ensure that wastage tantamount to sabotage would in future be prevented. Compulsory national service would be instituted and the details promulgated within a few days. . .

Ivansong turned a page of his notebook, but before he could scribble on, the windows rattled briefly and he glanced out across the wide Mekong, quicksilver in the sullen evening light, to see a black plume of smoke rise like a djinn from behind Mount Kham. The Mekinese Reds had just shot down their first twin-rotor Boeing-Vertol CH-46D Sea Knight helicopter, and the Marines had received the first two thousand gallons of their airborne water supply in the form of a sharp summer shower.

'. . . return to the true virtues of our proud feudal and Buddhist traditions,' Kitay was saying, looking at his audience contemptuously over the rims of his spectacles, 'avoiding

51

adventurist experiments in socialistic fads or liberal religions of alien origin, and emphasizing those things that have made us great in the past – respect, service, each man keeping his appointed place, seeking no reward this side of death.

'. . . nonetheless happy to welcome the cooperation not only of my loyal Mekinese ministers, but also of friendly foreign advisers who have been quick to come forward and show their devotion to my person.'

And who might they be? Ivansong asked himself, his eyes flicking past Kitay and the pock-marked face of General Keo and down the line of neat shining little Mekinese in neat, shining little suits. Chuck Strawbury was certainly not in the line-out. But then Ivansong saw at the end of the row a familiar figure heavily disguised in a synthetic alpaca jacket and a grievous bow tie, and realised that Max Alias had moved nimbly during the previous two hours.

8

Calvert H. Eldritch glanced distastefully across his desk when Inqvist and Strawbury sat down opposite him, and sipped gingerly at the coffee his secretary had brought him while he counted to twenty as his grandmother had taught him years before. Years before. But only nine days before, back in the golden era of last Monday week, he had battled with these geniuses and lost. It seemed an eternity ago.

'Dave,' he said cautiously, testing the odious sound as a man may test a rotten plank underfoot, 'you look as if you felt we might salvage something here. Why don't you just cheer us all up?'

'Well, Mr. Ambassador,' Inqvist replied, eyeing his left shoe quizzically and running his gold signet ring over his even, grey crop of bristle, 'it seems to me things have gone pretty much as planned, and we've reason to be reasonably pleased. Yes, *sir*, within reason, of course.'

'Not nervous, by any chance, are you, Dave?' asked the ambassador. 'I mean, there is this little business that we do have Kitay when we played for Yaksha, who was neatly tricked into mounting a false coup so that he could be denounced and clobbered, if you see what I mean.'

'Oh, sure,' conceded Inqvist through his immobile, ventriloquist's mouth, 'but as Robert Burns said, "The best laid plans –"' ' "schemes," Dave' ' "– schemes of mice and men", and so on, you know.'

'Yes,' replied the ambassador grimly, 'but he also spoke of man's inhumanity to man, if I remember correctly, and it seems to me that we are going to get plenty of that here from now on in.'

'I don't see it,' broke in Strawbury, snapping his fingers and crossing one long athletic leg over the other. 'What's so wrong with Kitay, Mr. Ambassador? He's a royal prince and he's the rightful heir to the throne. His achievement quotient may not be statistically stimulating but his patriotic and anti-communist postures are almost traumatically compulsive, to a point,' he went on, warming happily to his argument, 'where his lack of subjective depolarization would permit you to operationalize anything through him if you tried. Well, practically.'

'Quite sure that's not Jesus Christ you have there on the couch?' asked the ambassador mildly.

'Hell, no,' retorted Strawbury, affable and unperturbed. 'If that were Christ, I don't think I'd recommend –'

'Chuck,' interrupted Eldritch, banging his desk gently with a fist that was white-hot at the knuckles, 'Yaksha was a national hero of sorts, but let's say we might have managed to get along with him even so. Kitay, on the other hand, is an anachronistic stuffed-shirt, a stupid, feudal autocrat born five centuries after his time who believes in the divine right of all kings, starting with tyrannosaurus rex. We cannot possibly get along with him and we are in for a great big heap of trouble here, I'm telling you.'

'I still think we've altered the whole course of history in South-east Asia,' insisted Inqvist, shaking his head. 'I concede that things turned out a little differently from the way we planned it, but you cannot make an omelette without breaking eggs.'

'Well now, Dave,' said the ambassador softly. 'Has it ever occurred to you that omelettes are simply edible abortions and not what eggs are for in the first place? And as to our having altered the whole course of history, let me tell you about my first audience with Kitay.'

'You've seen him already?' they chorused, looking at each other quickly, Inqvist metalloid and expressionless, Strawbury raising imaginary eyebrows and blinking his pale lashes once.

'I'm sorry, gentlemen,' explained the ambassador briskly, 'but I had no time to advise you. I was summoned to the palace at one o'clock this morning. Yes,' he paused for effect, 'he summoned me at one. So I came over to the office, called the duty officer, and checked the telegrams first. And there was one just in from Washington.'

He paused again and took another sip of his tepid coffee. 'Gentlemen, I have been instructed by the Secretary after consultation with the President that while I remain accredited to the Queen Mahaksatriyani, our government will not immediately and automatically extend to the regime of Prince Norivong Kitay the same assistance and cooperation that it extended to Prince Saravane Sissomak. Aid programmes will be quietly phased out.'

Inqvist whistled a mindless note between his teeth.

'What is that supposed to make me, I wonder?' asked Strawbury. 'Boy, every man to his own cephalagra.'

'Well, the Pentagon will fix yours, I guess,' replied Eldritch unsympathetically, 'but I think you'll find yourself running down the military liaison mission here.'

'But, Mr. Ambassador,' cut in Inqvist, leaning forward uneasily, 'I had authority to tell Kitay we would give them everything they wanted –'

'Give *him* or Yaksha?' asked Eldritch sharply.

'Well, I suppose I kind of said "you", or maybe "Mekong".'

'Yes, you said "you", all right,' confirmed the ambassador through histrionically narrowed eyes. 'And you also told him that when regimes change, Washington has to "get along with the next guy".'

'But I meant Yaksha, Mr. Ambassador!'

'He took it you meant that just as we would support Yaksha if he ousted Sissomak, we would support him, Kitay, if he ousted Yaksha. I hate to say it, but nice going, Dave.'

'But – why, that rotten, dirty little ape,' said Inqvist between his teeth. 'He gave me his royal promise – he said it twice – his royal promise to put Yaksha in the saddle. How does he explain that?'

'You sound just about as enraged as Major Henry Burney,' commented Eldritch mildly.

'And who's this Major Fanny Burney?'

'Henry – he was her nephew. I'll tell you. He was a British envoy to a mad Burmese monarch about a hundred and fifty years ago, and he persuaded a group of dignitaries who had seized power in the capital to surrender it again, after the king's brother had sworn to him that there would be no reprisals. Once this prince had the city back in his hands, however, he promptly had the five ministers involved slaughtered and the wives and daughters of their leader foully tortured. He treated the outraged Burney's protests with contempt and, despite their former friendship, he never forgave him – and this is a direct quote from one historian – *"for interfering with his royal right to break a promise"*. My italics. Do you get the message, Dave?'

Inqvist nodded, closing his eyes in submission. 'I get the message.'

'Well,' went on the ambassador with a sigh. 'Let me summarise it for you. I was kept waiting forty minutes, received on a cushion, and offered no refreshment or apology or explanation for the call at that hour. The prince went through the usual formalities, and then asked me if I had heard from Washington. I told him I had, and that my instructions would be the

5

subject of an official diplomatic communication through channels, but that I could paraphrase the contents.'

Eldritch passed a hand over his indifferently-shaven jaw. 'I'll say he took it on the chin. He said he had grown accustomed to regarding all Americans not only as brothers, but as *big* brothers. It was in some ways a relief that we were not again trying to overwhelm smaller people with charity and advice. Some, at least, would prefer to avoid being under any obligation, so that they would not have to make the supreme sacrifice of repaying the West by adopting its way of life.

'Mekong had observed recent sociological developments in America and had concluded that it did not need democracy any more than it needed *square-dancing* – yes, he actually said that to me, the old devil. He would not speak of pollution, he went on, but he would say that it was important to see that we did not upset the spiritual ecology of the Mekinese. Are you with me, gentlemen?'

The others nodded, Inqvist morosely, Strawbury as if he found it all rather diverting.

'The prince kindly pointed out that we did not speak the same language even when we did. To us knowledge was facts and figures; to the East it was above all the intuitive *knowing* which could lead to an awareness of the true nature of the Cosmos, as against the world of illusion which we worshipped. As for all the hatred, bigotry and killing that had been provoked by religions from west of India, he would prefer to say nothing – beyond noting that given the human material upon which he had had to work, it was hardly surprising that all Christ's efforts had been crowned with thorns.

'He then spoke of matters nearer to his heart, of the possibility of severing relations with Washington and of turning to the Russians and Chinese for more aid instead. And when I opened my mouth to try to improve the atmosphere a little, he said: "Your Excellency, even though you do not represent a kingdom yourself, you should know that one does not address royalty without invitation." And that was it.'

'Out?'

'Out.'

There was a pause.

'Well,' said Strawbury at last, looking up at the ceiling with a wry smile, 'we seem to have a problem here.'

'It does not happen to be the only one,' Eldritch reminded him. 'There is also the Pentagon's little ploy for "negativizing" the Reds in Nakhara, isn't there? I almost sympathize with Kitay when he talks about us living in a world of illusion and crassly ignoring the true nature of the Cosmos. The military have just given us a striking example of that particular form of idiocy, haven't they? Can't you just see them poring over their maps, jabbing a finger at Hill 520 as the only commanding eminence in the area, and saying "that's where our boys'll go in, they'll have a 360-degree field of fire. What a honey!" It was so obvious, wasn't it?

'Except that while it may be "Hill 520" on their maps, it is the sacred Mount Kham in real life, and the whole surrounding area consists in acres of ancient and priceless temples and tombs which no one dares damage. So they have no field of fire at all, and the enemy has a man-made labyrinth of solid stone in which to deploy.'

'The same applies to him, though,' objected Strawbury, his pale, almost transparent irises sliding across their plastic-rimmed aquaria to pause, motionless, opposite Eldritch.

The ambassador shook his head slowly. 'Even assuming they have the same scruples, the Reds do not have to fire one shot into the Marines on the Mayon. The Mayon is a hedgehog of four-faced towers, and no helicopter can come really low to unload, let alone land. How many choppers have been shot down already while hovering above it, trying to man-oeuvre their supply slings down to the ground at the end of a forty- or fifty-foot wire? How much water has reached those boys, let alone anything else?' There was a silence. Eldritch broke it. 'And of course there's just one other thing, Dave. Any time he wants, Kitay is in a position to disclose that the CIA was behind the man who has now been made the villain of the piece, Yaksha. Eh?' He sighed sadly, lifted his substantial hands and dropped them lifeless to the desk.

'Well, that's all for now, I think. I just wanted to put you in the picture. For Heaven's sake let's keep as low a profile as possible until things straighten out a bit. I don't want any more of this whole deplorable business to get out of this compound than needs to, especially not to the French, and most especially' – he lifted a minatory finger – 'not repeat not to that Latinising son-of-a-bitch Pawkinson-Convoy.'

'. . . and given the close and cordial relationship I have now established with the United States Ambassador,' Nigel Pawkinson-Convoy read over to himself, 'I expect to be able further to clarify the American position – *O damnosa hereditas!* – in a second telegram within a few days when I am recovered.'

'Usual distribution,' he scribbled underneath this, 'and Saving to Washington.' What a hell of a time to be bitten by some bloody bug, he thought, throwing his notes on to the bedroom secretaire and furiously fumbling with the knotted belt of his silk dressing-gown. 'Dolly,' he shouted. 'Dolly, where the devil are you?' Lady Pawkinson-Convoy came out of the bathroom – a dark, small bony ruin of a woman with unsteady hands, strained, bitter eyes, and shoulders bowed down by a heavy rope of pearls. 'Look, Dolly, give this to Miss Cholmoney, and tell her to type it up. I'm going to have a bath and shave now and I'll be visible to the staff in about forty minutes.'

'But the doctor said –'

'Oh, blast the doctor, I'm not dying.' He pushed his way past her into the bathroom, stripped the dressing-gown and pyjamas from a torso that might have been made for a middle-aged gorilla, and stepped on to the scales. Two pounds *up*? But he must have lost weight through the fever, surely? You couldn't trust these damned things. And that reminded him of another annoyance. 'Tell Clarence not to forget to put something in the bag about that confounded weighing-machine,' he added. God, ambassadors would be doing their own laundry next.

The machine on which the British Embassy's diplomatic

bags were weighed before being taken to the airport was out of action. One of the rods connecting the platform to the counterbalancing pendulum and the scale-indicator had snapped, and the staff were making do with a heavy spring-balance until the first secretary could persuade someone to send the necessary spare parts. The Mekinese would not do anything with it. They seemed to think that when something stopped working, it was dead.

'And tell Clarence I'll see him in about an hour up here, and he's to be ready to talk about the school.'

'The school, Nigel?'

'Oh, Christ, yes, the school, the school. He'll know what I mean.' He had better say no more than that. The Khammax project was secret. He watched his wife leave the room, her hard-bitten eyes lowered to her hard-bitten finger-nails, and turned back to the shaving mirror. He ought to have been able to leave much of the business about the school to the military attaché, but he had forgotten more about jungle warfare than a fellow like that would learn in a lifetime. As Major Pawkinson-Convoy detached from 13 Commando, he had spent nearly two years in the Malayan jungle assisting Ching Peng, the Chinese communist guerrilla leader, in the task of making life disagreeable for the Japanese.

He had been fitter then, though. He gazed at himself in the mirror in the same way that he gazed at all others – down the length of his broken-backed nose. Six foot of ugly customer, he thought to himself, taking in the thinning black hair, the sagging cheeks and chin and the fleshy neck, and going to seed at fifty-five if he was not damned careful.

Then he had had to get the flu. How that must have pleased Dolly and his staff. Well, who cared? As that blabbermouth Cicero had said someone else had said: *Oderint, dum metuant.* What did it matter if they hated, as long as they feared? Not that they would have understood that. There wasn't a classicist among the whole lot of these jumped-up ninnies they sent you nowadays from slumland grammar schools and bogus universities knocked up out of breeze-blocks and plasterboard.

59

You did not realise until you were in your fifties that the past was not just the past; it was history – the young pheasants at Prince's Prize when he was first taught to shoot, Winchester and Oxford, Dolly (and her money), the last of the good wars – such things were irrevocably gone, and only to be found between the hard covers of men's minds. The rest was a dreary tale of degeneration and pollution. Graceful learning itself was an object of derision, and his apt Latin a subject for ignorant sniggers. Even Sissomak had joked about it. Only that bloody head-shrinker. . . But Pawkinson-Convoy shied away from the memory. Life had nonetheless had its moments, he reminded himself, sponging off the residual shaving soap. The Indonesians had burned down the British Embassy in Djakarta when he had been there in 1963, the Red Guards had gutted the 'British Office' in Peking when he had been there in 1967, and there had been other similar highlights to his career in Buenos Aires, Cairo, and Baghdad. Finally, the Mekinese had thrown themselves into a round of anti-British rioting a few months before when he had set up two sacred funerary urns on either side of the bronze statue of Queen Victoria that flanked the main driveway within the embassy compound.

He had found the urns in the corner of a small, disused shrine that by some quirk of landshark logic had been included within the bounds of the British diplomatic mission in Nava. But his sacrilegious whim to display them beside the effigy of the late Queen-Empress (whom the Mekinese did not yet include among their gods, bodhisattvas and avatars) had provoked a storm of pious fury, for such urns were reserved exclusively for the corpses of holy abbots and above. Unable to break into the embassy compound easily, the angry mob had therefore set fire to the British Council.

He rose dripping from his bath, and reached for a towel. He was still weak, even trembling a little. But he stood on the scales again to make sure that there had been no mistake about those two extra pounds. No, there had not. The door of the bathroom opened and his wife came in.

'For God's sake, Dolly, can't I even have the blasted

bathroom to myself for five minutes? What is it now?'

Dolly Pawkinson-Convoy sighed and lifted her shoulders. 'Nothing,' she said. 'I just wanted to make sure you were all right. You're shaking, you know, Nigel. You have to remember you're not as young as. . .'

'Oh, for Heaven's sake shut up, woman.'

'Must you talk to me like that?'

The ambassador began running standing still, the towel wrapped around the lower half of his body, the rest bounding and jouncing as he jogged. But he soon stopped, panting. He shook his head with frustration and walked into the bedroom to flop into a bamboo armchair.

'Dolly,' he said at last, 'I'm exercising and dieting as severely as I can. But don't you damned well understand,' he went on, glaring at her and shaking two hairy fists in the air between them, 'that worry leads to eating, and eating leads to fat, and if a man has something on his mind, therefore, he damn well has to spit it out, not keep it bottled up inside him where it merely makes him hungry and put on weight.'

'I thought people lost weight through worry.'

'I'm not *people*,' barked Pawkinson-Convoy, 'and I'm under enough strain as it is, can't you see?' He opened one fist and stared gloomily for a moment at his quivering fingers.

'Then for God's sake take some leave or something,' retorted his wife coldly. 'Because next time I find you huddled on the floor and half-way out of my life, I may remember not to turn off the gas.'

9

Two days later Ivansong sat naked in the pose of Rodin's 'Thinker' and listened attentively to the tape-recorder balanced on the laundry-basket in his bathroom. 'Vocabulary lesson ten,' his own voice instructed him in Chinese, '*P'ochan* – bankrupt; *Hsienchinchiang* – a cash prize; *Yenhu* – to protect, cover – cover as in espionage. . .'

The telephone rang. He stopped the tape-recorder and took the receiver off the wall over his head.

'Ivansong.'

'Oh, Mr. Ivansong,' said a precise voice at the other end. 'This is the chiropodist here. About your appointment. Would eleven-thirty do?'

Ivansong sat quite still for a moment, feeling reality drain out of his body. 'Yes,' he answered, 'I suppose so. Anyway, it will have to, won't it?'

'That's right,' agreed the chiropodist pleasantly. 'Good-bye.'

Oh no, thought Ivansong, not that bloody lunatic. This is where the nightmare begins again, the moment when the dream goes grey and you start to feel cold and it is high time you pinched yourself and woke up. *Greeen!* In person. And 'chiropodist' at 11.30 meant a rendezvous at 'Instant Mekong' by 9.30. He would have to hurry. He bathed and pulled on his clothes and came out of his room. The lounge was empty, and the door to the bedroom-study where Thinking Lotus often worked well after he had gone to sleep was shut. He could get out of the house without telling her about this yet.

He slipped downstairs, only to run into the mountainous

Cantonese amah. 'Good morning, Master, good morning. Master sleep good?'

'Fine, Ah King,' said Ivansong hurriedly, edging past her, 'fine, thank you.'

'Then Ah King happy Master happy,' she offered, smiling and bowing affably. Now where was the big-arsed barbarian devil rushing off to at this hour, for the love of Buddha? But he was already through the door and into a heavy shower. After vainly trying to start The Bitch, he abandoned it for a pedal trishaw and just caught the next ferry over to 'Instant Mekong'. The monsoon rain swept drearily up river before a sudden high wind. Ivansong, soaked to the skin, had the boat to himself.

Once on the far bank, he began to run steadily through the empty tourist trap, head down. He passed the waxwork museum of Japanese atrocities, the giant concrete Buddha with the lift running up the middle and the panoramic view through the eyes. He skirted the miniature Nakhara Wat built for visitors who found the life-size version too fatiguing, the firewalkers' pit and the leper colony, the snake farm and the stilt-houses of the displaced hill-tribesmen. The bonzes who performed a daily ritual for tourists with chanting, gongs, candles and incense for fifty piastres a head sat about disconsolately under the upcurling roof of their cement shrine. They expected no custom in this weather, and paid no attention to Ivansong as he jogged on past the shops of the silversmiths and woodcarvers and plunged into the sample Mekinese jungle, with its plastercast elephants and nylon orchids.

He emerged, dripping, into the last section, ignored the imitation opium den and the model massage parlour, and stopped, panting, outside the House of Mystics. A sign on the door read 'Closed for repairs', and he pushed his way in to find Greeen in a compartment at the back, carefully shaking out a black umbrella behind a table on which stood a heart-shaped planchette.

'Well,' said Greeen, 'isn't this cosy? Sit down. Ever done this before? You put your hands on one side of the board and I put mine on the other,' he went on without waiting for an answer, 'and our unconscious movements make it roll about on its little castors, you see, so that this pencil stuck through the middle writes on the paper underneath. Just the thing for a Freudian slip.'

'Where's Flodden?' asked Ivansong.

'You passed him in the jungle. He'll see we are not disturbed.'

Ivansong gazed at Greeen in silence. He never changed. It was seven years since he had first met him in London. 'Go straight up when you get there,' he had been told, 'he's on the eleventh floor,' and when he had found the address it had turned out to be a grimy old four-storey block in the heart of the City. However, there was a connecting corridor inside that led to a special lift in the glass skyscraper next door. One of Greeen's little jokes – or tests. And Greeen was every inch a joker, with his narrow, sleepy, sea-coloured eyes, his thin smiling shark-like mouth and long jaw, a tall, sallow, sandy man with a pendulous nose and forty-five years of the farce behind him who devoted himself to the business of duplicity and violence with an air of spurious rectitude.

'You really spell your name like that?' Ivansong had asked, politely incredulous.

Greeen had tilted his head to one side. 'Why not?' he had replied simply. 'It's been in the family for nearly 230 years.'

'What was it before that, then?'

'Nobody knows any more. It was after the '45 rebellion, and when the English were hunting down people from clans like Campbell and Macdonald with their usual bloody-minded impartiality, many among the more prudent Scots hid themselves behind borrowed and somewhat unimaginative Anglo-Saxon names. The world is full of Blacks and Browns whose ancestors thought they would be massacred if they stuck to MacGregor or whatever. Well, it's hardly surprising if there were a few simple spelling mistakes among a bunch of benighted semi-literates like that. "How about Greene," I suppose some oaf suggested, "Greene with three Es, just to be a wee mite different?" So I end up Greeen.' And he had then explained why they would be seeing more of each other in the future.

It was dark and stuffy in the palm-thatched wooden bungalow, for the shutters were closed, but Greeen switched on the weak bulb that hung over the table, and they sat down opposite each other, fingers on the planchette, which moved uneasily.

'Well,' asked Ivansong, breaking the silence with a sigh. 'What are you doing here, for God's sake? Hasn't Mekong got enough troubles already?'

Greeen smirked at him amiably for a moment, and then began speaking slowly and precisely.

'Ivansong, we arranged for your transfer to Mekong through your obliging editors as we have urgent business here in which you will participate, and I have to come back to Nava personally in order to put that business into effect.' The planchette quivered but otherwise Ivansong remained still.

'You mean it isn't the Kitay coup that has blown you in?'

'No, the Kitay coup only confirms that we were right to choose Mekong as our point of attack. It's part of the pattern. All over South-east Asia neutralists and non-communists and even staunch anti-communists have for some years been behaving as if their sole object in life was to advance the cause of Red revolution. Look wherever you like – South Vietnam. Indonesia, Cambodia – it's always the same story.'

'And now Mekong.'

'Mekong,' repeated Greeen, and then burst absurdly into song in an ersatz hill-billy accent: 'Oh, Uncle Sam he had a coup, C-I-C-I-Aaaay. And in that coup he had a clown, C-I-C-I-Aaaay. With a coup-coup here, and an Inqvist there, coup-coup, qvist-qvist every. . .'

'Christ, you are the end,' commented Ivansong. 'How do you make all those different revolting noises come out of the same mouth?'

'Sneer if you will,' retorted Greeen, 'but just add up the score for yourself. The Americans have lost Sissomak and Yaksha and they are stuck with a hostile Kitay. Sissomak is in the hands of the Chinese. Kitay, who is hand in glove with that thug Keo, is an insensitive, wooden-headed autocrat, and between them they are going to drive the people into the ranks of the Mekinese Reds, who in turn will now have the popular Sissomak as their champion. Meanwhile, since history teaches that no one can lose the world faster than a military genius, we find that the US Marines on Mount Kham are virtual hostages of the guerrillas. Hey, presto!

'But,' went on Greeen, raising a finger from the planchette, which skidded sharply to one side, 'this is what we seem to get nowadays – communist coups in anti-communist states, anti-communist coups in neutral states, and we always wind up worse off. At first we thought that we owed it to all that *good thinking* the Americans go in for, but there has to be more to it than that.

'So we came to the conclusion that what was required was a really effective penetration operation, not of the Americans, but of the opposition, and we chose Mekong as the scene of the crime for several reasons. First, it was neutral, a sort of no-man's-land in which any number could play, since you had all the relevant western and communist powers represented here. Secondly, three of our local agents have been blown in the past fifteen months and we are not amused. Thirdly, we have an inkling as to who has been responsible for the leak and he is still in Nava. Fourthly, we have a way into Chinese Intelligence through one of their own little bits of business in this country.

'What we want to do now, therefore, is to get our first man in with them as a double agent, and let him hold open the door, so to speak, so that we can feed in a whole damned platoon in time and stand a real chance of finding out what the other side thinks it's up to. Do I make myself clear, duckie?' concluded Greeen, with a smile that almost closed his eyes and revealed a long row of small, sharp teeth.

'What is your route into the Chinese Te Wu?' Ivansong asked suspiciously.

'Well, let me see, how shall we begin?' answered Greeen. 'You have doubtless read about the personable and versatile "swallows" of the KGB, the young ladies trained in

Verkhonoye to bed down intelligence targets, so that they can be comfortably and conveniently bugged and photographed in compromising, even exotic positions?'

Ivansong nodded only slightly, but the planchette jerked violently. Greeen grinned. 'Ironically, these crude devices actually work, like most uncomplicated gimmicks. You will remember, for example, that an effeminate British diplomat named William Vassall was recruited without difficulty by the Russians after he had been photographed naked with a young KGB officer in Moscow (they dearly love a queer, those boys). On another occasion the KGB put a woman on to the French ambassador to the Soviet Union and a handsome young fellow on to his wife at the same time.

'The KGB also tried to snare President Sukarno with a seductive agent working under the somewhat flimsy cover of an airline hostess. And of course our American friends took the sting out of the late Martin Luther King by tapping in on his rather varied love-life and then warning him not to be nasty about the FBI in future. Are you with me?'

'I think I am beginning to wish I had not been born,' replied Ivansong carefully. The planchette trembled. 'Where does all this lead us to, as if I could not make an educated guess?'

'It leads us,' said Greeen, 'to the bridal suite of the Hotel de l'Asie, since we have learned from Indonesian sources that it has been set up as a trap by the Te Wu who, as it were, bought themselves some influence in the hotel when it was expanded. It seems they seduced the Chinese owner by advancing him half a million American dollars through the Bank of China in Hong Kong at one per cent, and granting him a five-year moratorium on repayment even of the interest. Bad business, but perfectly legal. So the bridal suite is bugged to the rafters, and both bedroom and bathroom are covered by cine-cameras operating through one-way mirrors in the ceilings.

'So now what you are going to do is this' – the planchette quivered, but Ivansong held his breath – 'you are going to have yourself a party in that suite with some nifty piece of feminine pulchritude, and you are going to allow yourself to be hooked by the Te Wu when they turn up subsequently to recruit you, complete with pictures of Larry Ivansong and Friend, snapped at a happy, intimate moment during the summer season at Nava. You will then be in position to spearhead our infiltration of the Te Wu, with whom you will have an excellent reputation, for we shall feed you with some luscious lies for them, as well as some rather plain but nourishing home truths. Any questions?'

'Questions, you bastard,' shouted Ivansong. 'No, I haven't got any bloody questions because I'm not bloody well going to do it!' The planchette board circled wildly, both men keeping their fingers hard down upon it.

'Be careful,' admonished Greeen. 'You'll have this thing out of control. And moderate your voice, this place isn't soundproof. You have no choice, and you know why. So what's all the argument about? Now stop bluffing and let us get down to some preliminary details –'

'Are you going to say that if I don't do this you'll ditch my wife's parents?' asked Ivansong threateningly, as they fought to keep the planchette on the table.

'But of course,' replied Greeen reassuringly. 'What makes you think anything has changed between us?'

Thinking Lotus came of a prominent Confucian family of teachers and mandarins whose ancestral home was Soochow. But when the communists overran China, her parents were caught in Peking by the swift advance of the Red armies – and so was Lotus, for she had just joined them after a year at Westfield College in London. Her prudent father, having earlier purchased costly but excellent false papers that converted them into suitably humble proletarians unrelated to each other, then planned for them to escape separately and to meet in Hong Kong. Lotus reached the British colony safely, but her father and mother never arrived. They had been caught, denounced as landlords, stripped of their property, deprived of their citizenship rights, and left to scratch a living as best they could in the Chinese capital.

The false papers became the foundation of a permanent new identity for Lotus, on the other hand, and when Ivansong met her, she was struggling to make a living as a producer in an impoverished émigré opera company, for the Chinese theatre was her first love. Eighteen months later he had married her, to the fury of his masters in London whom he had deliberately failed to inform, for an agent of the service with parents-in-law in Peking was obviously open to pressure and must be regarded as a complete write-off.

It was Greeen who had first discovered from Ivansong that there was nothing now to link Lotus with her family, and who had seen how to turn the situation upside-down. He had arranged for her parents to be given quarters and at least nominal jobs as translators in the office of the British chargé d'affaires in the Chinese capital. Lotus was able to write letters to them occasionally, and these, devoid of any hint of her new identity, were sent by diplomatic bag.

She then became part of what Greeen called 'the Ivansong Act', for she drafted the articles which her husband supposedly wrote, so that he did not have to spend all his time preserving his cover as a correspondent. It was for this reason that she had a separate, locked bedroom-study wherever they lived, and concealed her ability to speak and write straight English by talking it with an erratic mixture of prim diction and yawing idiom that made Ivansong think of a dignified Chinese bride on her first pair of skates. However, Greeen could always undo what he had done for her parents. Ivansong bowed his head. The planchette came to a standstill, trembling, in the centre of the table.

'Wait a minute,' he said suddenly. 'This is all nonsense. Look, Greeen, in the first place, why would I necessarily give way to the Opposition even if they did compromise me?'

'The ground is being laid,' replied Greeen with a small snigger. 'They will have information that you like to play around with the girls but you are rather scared of your wife, and in particular you are scared of her women friends in the "Red Butterfly" secret society in Singapore, who, as you are aware, specialise in knocking off unfaithful husbands in various disagreeable ways, strictly for cash.'

Ivansong knew better than to point out that Thinking Lotus

did not have friends in that fearsome commando. 'But you seem to have forgotten,' he objected happily, 'that the Chinese have no reason whatever to be interested in Larry Ivansong, *bona fide* Far East correspondent of the Worldover Syndication Service.'

'Ah, but they do, you see,' countered Greeen genially. 'Because we've blown you to them for the purpose of this operation.'

'You've *blown me*?' The planchette was saved just at the edge of the table. 'What the hell do you mean you've blown me? What gives you the right to ruin my whole life and perhaps –'

'Oh, come, come,' said Greeen, with a small smile. 'We all have to risk being blown, and most of us can't be sure whether we are or aren't much of the time. Think big, as they say, Ivansong. This is going to be the operation of your career. Plenty of good posts you can hold afterwards – if there is an afterwards – even if you are known to the other side. And anyway, what good have you been doing around here? You didn't tip us off about Kitay, did you?'

'Now, that's hardly fair,' began Ivansong. 'Good God, hardly fair, I said, and look who I'm talking to. I must be going round the bend. But wait a minute, here's something else. Even if they are aware I'm one of us, why should they mount an elaborate ploy to catch me? Why just me?'

'Because we've discreetly let them know you are one of the king-pins in "Operation Standoff".'

'I've never even heard of it.'

'No, but they have now. "Standoff", as far as they are concerned, is a scheme to take our complete Far East network away from our existing stations and confine it to a new system of unofficial residents working under local cover. And you are to be our unofficial resident for Mekong, they have been led to believe. So you see, Ivansong,' went on Greeen, 'notionally, you really do have things to tell them that they think they ought to know.'

'And where does the girl-friend come from?'

Greeen shrugged. 'As far as we know their arrangements are

rather amateurish and haphazard compared with the Soviet Union, where they do these things properly. They have two or three girls on tap here, but they are not trained agents, just whores – professionals in their own right, of course, I won't say a word against them in that respect, but not primarily in our line of business as such. It doesn't really matter though. You get Lotus out of Nava on one pretext or another, and I'll guarantee that some cut-out from the Chinese – Max, maybe – will be throwing you one of their performing birds within days.'

'Max Alias?' asked Ivansong, startled.

'Who else? Anyway, the girl then gets you into the Hotel de l'Asie, chums of the Chinese on the management switch you both to the bridal suite on some excuse, and the mikes and the lenses do the rest.'

'And of course when it comes to professionalism,' said Ivansong, the planchette skittering drunkenly across the table, 'you're the ace. It's the first time I've ever heard of anyone blackmailing someone to go and get himself black-mailed by someone else. You must be particularly pleased with this caper. It puts you right up there among the top ten pornocrats.'

'Blackmail,' echoed Greeen contemptuously, looking as mean as a seamstress with her mouth full of pins. 'Ivansong, the whole world is run on blackmail. Were you under some curious impression that it was run on love? It's all a matter of mutual threats and extortion with menaces. That's what fixes the relationship between parent and child, worker and manage-ment, law and lawbreaker, man and his masters.'

'God Almighty,' murmured Ivansong, despairingly.

'Certainly,' confirmed Greeen, misunderstanding him, 'among others. You make a covenant with whatever deity you believe in whereby you promise to behave if he does what you want, but at the same time he holds the threat of hell over your head. Who's blackmailing who when a millionaire philanthropist has a twinge of conscience and endows a hospital – or is it mutual blackmail? Take a second look at the social security and national health, the boons and bonuses

6

of the world, man's humanity to man, and you'll find the bulk of it all is inspired by two little words: "or else".'

'Ah, you dear fellow,' said Ivansong. 'It's the way you tell it. I can hardly keep back the tears. You know what I think of you as a humanitarian and a philosopher.'

Greeen lifted the planchette, and screwed his head around to see what the pencil had traced during this stimulating half-hour. 'Oh yes, I know,' he said with a predatory smile at Ivansong. 'You've spelt it all out here in words of four letters.'

10

Ivansong found he had little time to reflect on his latest problem in life when he arrived back in Nava. All morning the Sea Knight helicopters had been clattering through a mist of rain over Nakhara and hovering above the towers of the Mayon to ease the water bladders and the barbed wire slung on long hawsers below them to the damp yet thirsty Marines on the ground, but the visibility was bad, the terrain steep and narrow, and much of this fell into the hands of the gratified enemy. When the Marines moved lower down the hill to enlarge their perimeter and wire the Mekinese Reds out, therefore, they found to their annoyance that the Mekinese Reds were already there and busy wiring them in.

By the time Ivansong had joined other correspondents on the fringes of the Nakhara complex, the Marines were reacting to this turn of events by trying to break out of their cordon on the crown of Mount Kham instead of shutting themselves up inside it. But although the weather had cleared the Sea Cobra gunships sent to cover them could only wheel impotently above and watch the men on the ground being driven back, for not one was authorised to empty its three-thousand-pound load of death and dilapidation on to the sacred stones of the battlefield. Kitay had disdainfully refused to commit any troops to a relief operation. Instead, he had instructed the head of the Mekinese Delegation to the United Nations to protest to the Secretary-General about the barbarous vandalism ruthlessly perpetrated by armed American intruders on the site of one of the world's greatest cultural treasures.

By five Ivansong was back at his house and accepting an anchovy-paste sandwich from Ah King beside the sunlit swimming pool. 'I know Master like,' beamed the fat old amah amiably. How could these red-haired brutes eat that filthy muck, not to mention the piddle and milk they called tea? No wonder they stank so much. She giggled corpulently as he took two more sandwiches, and Ivansong gave her a conspiratorial smile, the lines biting deep into his face. How could they ever do without the old bitch? It was true she was capable of putting Camembert cheese and raspberry ice-cream together in the refrigerator, or spraying the whisky glasses with insecticide to get a good polish on them for a party, but she was absolutely loyal to Thinking Lotus. She spoiled Mango, and she filled the kitchen with the revolting odour of the boiled fish-heads to which she was addicted, but who was perfect?

Ah King waddled over to Mango and whispered some coarse comment in Cantonese about the cut of Ivansong's swimming trunks, but Mango was busy petting Mini in the shade of a tulip tree. Suddenly the gibbon skipped over to Ivansong and Lotus, grabbed three Osborne biscuits from a tin on the low, marble table between them, and fled back to the haven of Mango's arms, nibbling suspiciously. The amah chuckled her way off to the kitchen, and Mango shrieked with joy. Lotus gave her a wink over her Chinese newspaper.

'It is truly marvellous,' she said with a luxurious little sigh against the faint crepitation of war from across the river. 'Every little beast in the world lives in harmony with both himself and the bloodthirsty universe, free of sin and moving with the flow of nature. Only Man is the sad little joke, the circus dog stumbling about on his hind legs at the crack of his own conscience.'

'Joke?' queried Ivansong. 'With that malignant growth he carries about in his head? Think of the morass of misery into which we have been irresponsibly misled by four millenia of brilliant brains.'

'Well, either way,' said Thinking Lotus, 'here is a good example of the exquisite fun they have.' She turned her local Chinese weekly newspaper around and pointed to an article on the front page. 'There will be much flapping in the dovecotes now,' she went on. 'You see, Chou En-lai is only listed number four in the Peking politburo, which all the keenest intellects must read to mean that he and those other gentlemen the experts so courteously call the moderates are going down, and the villainous extremists are on the way up. Except.'

'Except what?' asked Ivansong, but at that moment a breathless Ah King arrived.

'Good fliend come,' she cried happily to Ivansong, and added to Lotus in Cantonese: 'A black-arsed barbarian carrying his balls cupped in his hands, he's so pleased with himself. Never seen this one before.'

'Ah King,' scolded Thinking Lotus, 'you are not to talk about our doubtless distinguished visitor in that informal manner.'

'Just thought you ought to know,' remarked the amah, affronted, and sailed off as they heard a voice approaching in full lugubrious song:

Dans une tour de Londres, là-haut, là-haut,
Dans une tour de Londres, il y avait prisonnier,
Il y avait un pri-son-nier. . .

'Max Alias,' explained Ivansong, as the gibbon teetered across the lawn and leaped to the shoulder of the métis, who had come into view carrying a small basket wrapped in fancy paper and tied with pink ribbon.

'Ah!' roared Max, kissing the ape resoundingly on both cheeks, 'la jolie laide elle-même, hein? And what mischief have

74

you been up to? Don't try to hide anything. Larry will give the game away. Larry, has she been. . . Oh, excuse me, Madame,' he said, as he caught sight of Thinking Lotus. Ivansong performed the introductions.

Mango walked solemnly up to Max and, staring speculatively at the basket, said firmly 'Oh, look, a present. It must be for me. What's in it? Is it one of those. . .?'

But Max shook his head, eyebrows raised. 'My dear child,' he replied reprovingly, 'this is a gift for our adorable Mini. Many people give presents to pretty little girls. I give presents to ugly little apes.'

'Is it one of those dear little bears which run on batteries and drink gin?' asked Mango, following her own inscrutable line of reasoning.

'Bear?' echoed Max. 'No, you cannot give her a bear. And if you have a teddy bear, you had best not let her play with him, because little gibbons are like song birds. They are always very jealous of their home, and if they think another animal is trying to move into it, they do not sing, they bite. You understand, *petite*?'

'*Petite*,' repeated Mango slowly and thoughtfully, trying it on the taste-buds, and Max gave Mini the parcel. The gibbon tore it open gently, discovered a monstrous bunch of imported black grapes under all the wrapping, and raced up the tulip tree with it.

'Isn't she greedy?' shouted Mango with delight. 'You know, she already stole the biscuits at tea-time and ate an anchovy paste sandwich (but she didn't like that much) and Mummy is going to make her a little dress, won't you, Mummy, and then we're going to –'

But no one was listening, for Max had swung abruptly towards Thinking Lotus. '*No* dressing up, I beg you, please,' he said excitedly, 'and I must also ask you to be good enough, Madame, not to feed her biscuits. They are bad for the teeth, and besides, genus *Hylobates* do not require a carbohydrate diet. Flowers, fruit, nuts, seeds, grasses, leaves, roots – all the things that are good for us, yes, those the gibbons eat. Excess of dough, sugar, fats, all the unhealthy things we consume in such outrageous quantities, no, gibbons do not.' He shrugged, 'They are not so foolish, of course, for the simple reason that they are gibbons, not people.'

'Relax, Max,' advised Ivansong, 'and sit down while I get some drinks. Lotus loves them all, and no one is going to put Mini into a muu-muu.' Max Alias slumped on to the grass, lit a limp Gauloise which he fished out of a pocket in his gaudy golden shirt, clicked his fingers to bring the gibbon to him, and quietly took Thinking Lotus in. What was the secret, he wondered? How did these Chinese women already *dans la trentaine* keep their figures? She was like a girl in those black pyjamas, teeth brushed, hands washed, and all deliciously ready for bed. But, *merde*, she had the head of a female Red Guard with that severe schoolgirl Cleopatra-cut and pale, cleansed face. Not a woman to get into a fight with, and perhaps that was a good thing.

'And how is it we have not met before?' he asked Lotus curiously.

'I only came down with Mango and the amah a short time ago. And this is my first visit. Larry, of course, has been here often.'

'And will you be living in Nava for long?' he asked with genuine interest.

By the time Larry returned with soda-water for Max and a manhattan for himself, they were deep in conversation, Mango and Mini sitting between them and turning their faces almost in unison from one to the other as the talk was patted back and forth.

'She is a stranger from Borneo,' Max was saying, 'but here they are good to animals. They believe Buddha passed one reincarnation as a white elephant, and who can kill even an ant if it may be his own grandmother reborn? You are certainly familiar with the principle of gaining merit by bequeathing animals to temple sanctuaries, and you have perhaps already heard of the Feast of the Beasts which falls quite shortly?' He took his soda-water from Ivansong with a nod.

'I see you have made your peace with Kitay,' said Ivansong,

shaking the ice in his glass so that it tinkled and he could look down at it as he spoke. 'Does that mean that your position is stable again and you want Mini back?'

Max picked up the gibbon, which stood on his fat thigh and put one arm around his neck protectively. 'Kitay, c'est un salopard,' he replied succinctly, regarding her with fond canine eyes. 'I work for him as I worked for Sissomak, who was in many ways a cretin. Moi, je m'en fous pas mal de toute la bande. I would not trust either of them further than I could shout from a gibbet. What is the difference? They are all men, anyway. So I would be happier if you would keep the ape a little longer, yes? Until we see what is going to happen. Alas, my little Mango,' he added, looking down on the small Chinese doll who gazed back at him primly, her hands folded in her lap, 'such a shame you have to grow up into a girl when you, too, might have been a gibbon, eh?'

'Girl,' scoffed Mango. 'I'm not going to grow up into a girl. I'm going to grow up into a millionaire cowboy with a two-way wrist-television and a formula car with bazookas in the headlamps.'

When Max finally left, with many last words of motherly advice about Mini, and Ah King had coaxed the millionaire cowboy off to the bathroom, Thinking Lotus said: 'Now give me that drunken cherry out of your glass, and tell me why your friend so particularly likes his monkeys stark, staring naked.'

'You cunning little oriental,' murmured Ivansong, his face lengthening in a half-suppressed smile. 'So you saw what really hit him on a bruise – the idea of dressing Mini up.' He gazed at the hollow blue sky for a moment, remembering.

Max (began Ivansong) was a paleozoologist originally, and when this happened he was doing some work on prehistoric monkeys in the Coriandra mountains of North Mekong. The site of his dig was a rock fault on a remote escarpment, and he was only just in finger-tip touch with the nearest village of hill-tribesmen, the last tenuous link in the supply chain that brought him his canned food and wine and Gauloises bleues from the outside world. He lived in a native hut on stilts, his only companions were a young, long-tailed macaque and a sack of books, and he was a happy man.

Being a métis, however, Max was afflicted with a burning desire to prove that he was no native himself. He had heard that Englishmen dressed for dinner in the jungle, and he therefore reserved his loose-cut cotton shirts and his sweat-stained French shorts for work up country and for whoring about town. When dusk came at the dig, he would take a shower, lay his folding-table with a cloth, clean cutlery and a polished glass, and cook his evening meal. Leaving the food to simmer, he would then change quickly into a badly-cut linen suit and sit down to eat like *un gentleman*.

It was his companion who first suggested to him the idea that he might turn it into another gentleman. One evening the monkey, having watched him closely for some days, laid a fork and knife opposite to him and, perching on a ration box which it had drawn up to the table, drummed on its surface for civilised food. From that moment onward, Max undertook the social education of Cigar the macaque.

As the months passed, Cigar learned to wear with dignity the undistinguished examples of bespoke tailoring that Max contrived from old clothes of his own and forced upon him, and in time he could knot his own tie, wield knife and fork with the brutal efficiency of your average Frenchman, and sip his wine with an elegance worthy of Maxim's.

Not finding Cigar much of a conversationalist, however, Max took to propping a book up against the water bottle at mealtimes, and it was in this way that he was seduced by the Taoist classics. The world of artificial form and manners seemed more absurd with every chapter he read, and he began to realise that preoccupation with caste and success and wealth was no more than a nonsensical chase after an illusion. All that mattered was to act naturally and spontaneously, as an ear hears a sound without listening for it.

To the intense chagrin of Cigar, therefore, Max ceased to bathe and dress for dinner, to put the check cloth on the table and lay out the accoutrements of French gastronomical culture. Instead, he slopped around in sandals and shorts,

78

spooning his *singe* out of a jagged tin and drinking his wine straight from the bottle. At first the macaque cooked for both of them, but he later gave up laying two places, and simply set out the gleaming cutlery and the glassware and napery for himself in the evening.

Max was about to start teaching Cigar how to be a macaque again when three young French civil servants from the provincial capital arrived at the site one evening, just as the sun was setting. They found a heavily-bearded and pungent Max squatting on the lowest branch of a tree in his underpants and eating a hand of wild bananas, while in a wooden bungalow nearby a monkey, dressed casually for dinner in white ducks and a bow tie, sat alone at a well-appointed table sniffing critically at a cork drawn from a bottle of Beaujolais. Ivansong went off to recharge his glass. Night was falling, and it was quiet across the river. 'Poor monk,' said Thinking Lotus unhappily when he returned. 'What happened then?'

'There's not much more to tell. The three Frenchmen thought it would be a great joke to make Cigar drunk, so they gave him a tumbler full of some cheap brandy which they had brought with them. Cigar put on the comic music-hall act of all time and finally raced up a huge teak tree with uncertain but prodigious jumps, missed his hand-hold somewhere near the top and crashed to the feet of the wildly cheering audience, all in one piece but no more than that.

'Max went berserk, and managed to inflict grievous bodily harm on all three of his compatriots. He then burned his French passport, joined Yaksha's anti-colonial rebels, but ended up with Sissomak. Curtain.'

'No wonder he does not mind whether he is working for Yaksha or Sissomak or Kitay,' said Lotus, after a pause. 'He must have fallen madly out of love with the three billion images of God. Or does he have a wife?'

Ivansong shook his head. 'He's just a friendly, warm-hearted misanthropist. He doesn't mind who he sleeps with as long as he can pay them, and he doesn't mind who he works for as long as they can pay him. And his real boss at the moment is not Kitay or Sissomak, anyway, it seems. It is the Chinese Te Wu.'

'Just so,' said Thinking Lotus, nodding, 'a man of integrity. I am glad I did not misjudge him.'

'Man of integrity?' exploded Ivansong. 'What kind of a – ?'

'Pooh,' interrupted Lotus, 'I trust we are not going to get one of those lamentable occidental dissertations about honour and glory on only two drinks. Look, Larry, look at that tree over there,' she pointed to a tall shrub covered with fragrant while flowers. 'Some people call it a false jasmine. But it is a genuine false jasmine, Larry, not a false false jasmine made out of paper or plastic. It is a tree of integrity. It plays its appointed role in the admittedly somewhat curious scheme of things. So does your friend Max.'

'Yes, and so does your false wig with the genuine hair, I suppose. You're not trying to tell me that your devious Asiatic mind. . .' Ivansong's voice faded out and then in again '. . . Lotus, what happens if you make love with that wig on, will it stay put? I mean –'

'Why do you want to know?'

'I'll tell you later. Will it?'

'Come and find out.'

'What? Now?'

'Larry, if you do not bite life first, life will bite you. *Now!*'

I I

I

Thinking Lotus was packing rapidly and talking all the time to cover up her hatred of partings: 'Why four slippers? I have not got enough feet. I really do have too many old clothes, Larry. The trouble is that you have to dress up so much when you are poor. When we are rich, it will be simpler, even if we do have to work harder.'

'You always say you have nothing to wear even now,' objected Ivansong, sitting on her case and snapping it shut.

'Then I must simply get together a parcel and give some deserving woman nothing to wear,' retorted Lotus. 'Larry, will you be all right?' she asked, turning to blink at him mournfully. 'I have given Ah King very strict instructions about you and about feeding you properly, as well as Mango and Mini. None of that paper soup or those deep-frozen card-board vegetables you so dote on. And I have made you out a lovely long list of nice things to keep you busy –'

'Everything will be fine,' cut in Ivansong hastily, anxious not to see this masterpiece one moment before he had to. 'Don't forget me, that's all.'

'There is only one moment in life that I forget you,' said Lotus simply, 'and that is entirely your fault anyway.' But as Ivansong softly kissed her, they both heard an inanely reproachful tenor voice coming up the drive below:

Monsieur, Monsieur, vous oubliez votre cheval,
Monsieur, Monsieur, ne négligez cet animal. . .

'Max,' breathed Ivansong. 'This is great. Now we very literally play it cool. But you will have to go to the airport alone, by taxi, okay?'

'Do not worry,' said Lotus, clinging to him briefly and then slapping him smartly on the backside. 'I shall send Ah King for one at once.'

Ivansong found the métis already conferring with Mini over a bunch of small pink bananas but, as he approached, the grey gibbon leaped for the bare and bony jacaranda in the front garden. It was from here that she restaked her claim daily to 171 rue du Bassac by hooting ritual defiance each dawn at the other gibbons who presumably owned the adjoining territories.

'You have heard the news?' asked Max gaily, treading the butt of a Gauloise into an adjacent bed of blood-red cannas. 'Mais c'est pas mal, mon pote. Kitay has declared Sissomak a traitor and a war-criminal, and he is to be tried *in absentia*. Yes, Sissomak, it seems, abandoned the country after instigating communist students to burn down the Thai embassy and allowing the Mékinois rouges to occupy the sacred precincts of Nakhara. He is now in league with Mao Tsetung in Peking and is plotting the Chinese colonisation of Mekong and all South-east Asia. He has embezzled state funds, says our new leader, he has sabotaged the economy, he – oh, I tell you, he has committed all the crimes in the instruction manual.

'Comme j'adore tout ça!' he went on, in an ecstasy of malice. 'The university is to be closed, many students have been arrested, and once again the troops and the *flicaille* are coming out in force. Quelle bande de fumistes! Sissomak was one thing, but this one,' Max raised a finger and an eyebrow in unison, 'this one is a real numéro, His Royal Highness Chao Luk Norivong Kitay, and I remain yours truly his most grovelling serf, his – how do you say it? – his most cringing churl.' He bowed elaborately like a stockinged French courtier, to the astonishment of Mini and an open-mouthed Mekinese taxi-driver who jerked his Renault to a halt almost at their feet.

Ivansong had no time to comment before Lotus swept out of the house, wearing a light raincoat over a cheongsam with a tight two-inch-high collar that kept her head imperiously erect. She came over to greet Max unsmilingly, as Ah King bullied the taxi-driver into putting her cases in the boot.

'You are both going somewhere?' asked the métis, looking from one to the other with alarm. 'But what about Mi –?'

'I am flying to Singapore alone,' interrupted Lotus. 'I have a property there that cannot be neglected, and I must see that everything is all right with my house and my servants, and I have business friends whom I have to talk to. Somebody has to look after things. Well,' she glanced at her watch, 'I must be going. Larry,' she held up her cheek and he touched it chastely with his lips, 'please behave yourself. This is all going to take some time. I have said good-bye to Mango. Look after her properly. I shall write if I need anything. Ah King has her instructions, so there should be no problems. Good-by, Mr. Alias.'

She walked proudly to the taxi as if to the guillotine. Ivansong forced his feet to remain where they were. The taxi swept past him and he raised his hand in a grim salute. Then she was gone.

There was an uncomfortable silence. 'For God's sake let's have a drink,' Ivansong burst out suddenly, and led the way indoors and upstairs, leaving Max to follow thoughtfully in his footsteps, his hand to his unshaven chin.

'I thought you owned your house in Singapore?' Max began.

Ivansong handed him a glass of soda-water, and savagely punctured a can of beer so that the froth shot over his batik shirt. 'Of course I do,' he answered, 'but you'd hardly think it, would you?' "My house, my servants, my property, my tenants",' he mimicked. 'Really, things can be absolutely bloody, can't they?'

'But, forgive me, Larry,' Max said slowly. 'But when I met her the other day your wife seemed so. . .' he left it in the air, shrugged, and made a baffled face at himself in a small Chinese mirror over the rattan drinks trolley.

'Oh, yes,' retorted Ivansong as if he were chewing bitter almonds, 'she can be all sweetness and light, but you ought to have had enough to do with Chinese women to know that they are as tough as old boots underneath and as bossy as the devil. Bossier. Sometimes, I wonder. . .' Ivansong sighed, raised his hands, and then dropped them limply, 'Hell, what's the good.'

'You are not actually – ?'

'Breaking up? Heavens, no, that would be more than my life would be worth with some of the friends she's got around. Ever had any dealings with the secret societies in Singapore? Well, never mind. In a way it's a good thing she's gone off just now, as a matter of fact.'

'Why just now?'

'She doesn't know it because the letter only arrived this

83

morning, but my head office in London is foisting on to me some pet woman-reporter of theirs who's on a swan through the Far East and wants to see Mekong on the way. They argue that if she's just passing through, she may be able to write things afterwards that I couldn't send from here as resident correspondent without getting myself kicked out or jailed or shot or something. Given Kitay, I must say they have a point. It's a damned nuisance though. I've never met her and she's probably some frightful old frump. But I'm glad my wife will be out of the way for a while, because you know the other thing about Chinese women?'

'Fiendishly jealous?'

'Fiendishly jealous.'

They both sighed. 'Now tell me more about Kitay,' said Ivansong.

Two hours later Max le Métis stumbled ashore from a Mekinese pirogue at the plank landing-stage of the Peninsula of Ten Thousand Years, and made his way down the path that ran like an aisle through a vast silent audience of Chinese tombstones liberally incised with characters in gold or red and decorated with faded photographs of the deceased. At Stonecutter Village itself the stillness was broken only by the musical chink of chisel on granite and marble, the whirr of an electric polisher, and soft Chinese singing from a radio in the Teahouse of the Tranquil Fish which changed abruptly to 'Here comes the Bride' played on a wurlitzer. Gravestones and rubbish-bins were companionably stacked up beside the open workyards, where men in shorts and tattered undervests hammered away with exquisite precision at the raw rock. A sexagenarian in bathing shorts swept out a small golden temple dedicated to the Goddess of Mercy.

A storm had flushed out the sky, leaving it pale and lucent, and the children had come into the muddy street to play again. Max pulled a bag of poisonous-looking boiled sweets from his trouser-pocket and began distributing them as he walked among their small upturned faces, but the little microphones concealed about them picked up no more than had those hidden among the artificial flowers on some of the graves near the entrance to the village. All that the tape-recorders yielded to Short March was a thumping chorus, sung in a contented tenor:

Encore une boiteuse, s'en allant au marché, ohé!
Elle portait sur la tête les seins à plein panier, ohé!
Les seins allaient, balli-ballant,
Les oeufs allaient, cassi-cassant,
La boiteuse allait, boiti-boitant. . .

Max broke off, turned abruptly into one of the workyards and, passing through the shop behind where an old man with an abacus and a strapping youngster with a bottle of sarsaparilla both looked up sharply and then ignored him, knocked four times on the door at the back. He had to wait while Short March shut up the radio room above, swung a hinged section of wall into place to mask the entrance, and came down into the 'office' to let the métis in, his cat in his short, strong arms.

The otherwise bare room contained an old-fashioned rolltop desk with a Japanese transistor radio on it, a trestle table flanked by wooden chairs, a small safe, and a coloured calendar depicting the month of June as an underdressed Hong Kong sex-bomb candidly photographed from ground level. There was a thermos flask on the table, and Short March poured weak green tea into two thick tumblers. They sipped in silence, while he stroked the Siamese queen.

The cat put up with this for a minute and then jumped to the floor to wash its hind legs.

'What is her name?' asked Max.

'Name?' queried Short March in his granulated bass voice, 'we don't give cats names. We shout "Miao-miao" and if they think it's food, they come. We leave name-calling to you barbarians.' The seal-point stopped its ablutions and gazed up at him, sleepily narrowing its eyes.

'They have the whole thing wrong, you see,' he went on, pointing accusingly at the animal. 'Take this one. She belongs to the black gang of modern revisionists who think the class war is already won and all we do now is take the pickings. Yet at the same time she treats me as a bourgeois deviationist who's trying to curb her fundamental right to rebel by poisoning her with the sugar-coated bullets of a welfare society. You can see the basic ideological contradiction, but how do you rectify a cat? Very well, milk. Now let me switch on Radio Peking for the sake of form and then we can talk. What is your news?'

While insistent waves of rough-edged martial music and girlish voices expanding on the relative merits of the Russians and Americans as implacable enemies half-drowned their conversation, Short March took a punctured tin of milk from his desk and poured a little of it into a saucer for the cat. Meanwhile Max told him that the wife of Larry Ivansong had left for Singapore, Ivansong himself seemed a little scared of her, and the marriage was fraying badly at the edges.

Short March grunted. 'We have two reports,' he said, suddenly prim and sparing in his speech. 'The first confirms that Ivansong will be a key man in this Operation Standoff. His importance as a target is therefore established. The second confirms that in his Singapore home he and his wife work and sleep in separate rooms and only communicate by internal house telephone, that they are on bad terms, and that this much frustrated man would like to break away and form a more satisfying friendship elsewhere, but, as you say, he is afraid of her.

'She is suspected of having Lesbian tendencies, and is known to be very close to certain ruthless members of a secret society of women called the Red Butterflies. Our background records on this society are considerable. There is no doubt about its potential to frighten – not to say to mutilate in a most disagreeable fashion – fornicating husbands and faithless lovers alike.'

'Ah, but that is excellent, that is just what I needed to know,' Max said with specious enthuiasasm. 'Thank you very much. And now I wonder if I might ask for a small adv –'

'*Thank you?*' echoed Short March indignantly, 'What is this "thank you"? "Thank you" is merely a sound, like a belch. Do not think you can earn money just by making noises. We judge by actions. Have you a satisfactory girl on hand?'

As they discussed the details, their voices dropped, and Radio Peking supervened.

'. . . the feudalistic bourgeois-reactionary Kitay and his clique of landlord-capitalists,' a silvery voice told them in polysaturated English, 'are being utterly defeated by the ever-strengthening armies of the Mekinese Liberation Front which has been striking heavier and heavier blows and scoring brilliant victories against the enemy.

'Large forces serving the aggressive plots of the American Imperialists in their criminal invasion of Mekong have been completely cut off and decimated near Nava itself. Meanwhile in his frantic efforts to stave off inevitable defeat the Imperialist puppet Kitay has ordered the arrest and execution of thousands of students and workers, and is requisitioning the land of all medium peasants. This has aroused the just anger of the masses, and they are now flocking to the forces of His Royal Highness, Prince Saravane Sissomak, who will shortly return to the liberated areas of Mekong to lead personally the people's struggle against the American Imperialists and their feudal running dogs.

'The news of this excellent revolutionary situation has been greeted with mammoth demonstrations throughout the People's Republic of China. In Shanghai four hundred thousand soldiers, workers and students today massed in front of. . .'

2

'. . . the Royal Palace of Nava to hear a proclamation read out personally by His Royal Highness Prince Norivong Kitay,' intoned an unctuous male voice from Radio Mekong. 'In this proclamation, His Royal Highness Prince Norivong Kitay declared the Kingdom of Mekong to be in a state of war. The National Assembly has been dissolved and, in the name of the

7

Queen, His Royal Highness Prince Norivong Kitay will henceforth rule by decree. There will be total mobilisation of national resources. The whole country will fight until the renegade Sissomak, who has been condemned to death *in absentia*, is totally defeated. . .'

Ivansong lay back contentedly on the opium couch, rested his head on the wooden pillow, and kept the pocket radio close to his ear. The Opposition had certainly not wasted any time, he reflected. Thinking Lotus had only been gone three days, but Max had already made the first move and now he was in the thick of things. Through a crack in the curtain he could see into the next compartment and make out, by the dim, flickering lights of Madame Phnom's establishment, the bare buttocks of the métis rising and falling with a sort of blind compulsion that went well with the news of what Kitay was doing to his country.

'. . . His Royal Highness Prince Norivong Kitay has conpemned the United States of America for unwarrantable interference in the internal affairs of Mekong. One plot to overthrow the monarchy has already been unmasked, thanks to the vigilance of the Police and Security Services under the direction of His Excellency General Voronikone Keo, and has led to widespread arrests. The government solemnly warns the public that prompt and vigorous measures will be taken to stamp out any conspiracy that is aimed at sabotaging the authority of His Royal Highness Prince Norivong Kitay. And that concludes. . .'

Ivansong sighed, and thought he heard an echo.

'C'est fini, chéri?' asked a voice softly, beyond the curtain. Ivansong switched off the set. He had won the first round.

It had begun earlier in the day when Max had called at the house to see Mini, and to suggest that he and Ivansong dine together. Ivansong had written and cabled a one-thousand word situationer on Mekong by six, and was feeling purged and virtuous as he parked The Bitch outside the Hotel de l'Asie and walked into the bar. Max would only drink tomato juice, but called for a well-chilled outsider for Ivansong which made him feel less virtuous but even better.

He was sipping the second of these when he became aware that a three-dimensional girl with a rough mop of blond hair, carnivorous blue eyes and that opulent gloss to the skin whose secret is known only to old ivory and young Frenchwomen, was standing looking at them from the wrought-iron grill that masked the entrance. She appeared to be dressed in nothing but a plain blue silk frock and a pair of white shoes, and her generous mouth widened suddenly into a smile as he stared at her, for Max had also looked up.

'Jacqueline!' cried Max, ecstatically. 'But when did you get back? I thought you were in Saigon? Come, come and have a drink. Let me introduce my very good friend, Larry Ivansong. Larry this is Jacqueline Cannabière, the most gorgeous girl in Indochina. You are still the most gorgeous girl in Indochina, I trust?' he asked her anxiously.

She raised one well-tended eyebrow at him, wiggled her haunches almost imperceptibly, and sat down. Larry said: 'Bon soir, Madame,' to which she at once replied with all the verve of a music box, 'but you speak wonderful French, Monsieur. Have you lived in Mekong long?' And it had gone on like that. Jacqueline – 'Please, Jackie, all my friends call me Jackie' – had drunk a Cinzano and Ivansong another outsider, and they had then moved to a cosy table with a little red lamp on it at the 'Casse-croûte', which was Nava's smallest and best restaurant.

Jacqueline Cannabière proved a formidable and explosive conversationalist when involved in Gallic bouts of mutual indignation with Max Alias, but this all trickled away into sugary infantilities when she turned to Ivansong: 'But they tell me London is very beautiful, and, furthermore, you can buy so many things so much more cheaply than in France. And I just adore the Queen. She is so *dignified*. And the prince, so handsome. Ah, the English, I have always admired. . .'

So Ivansong for the most part remained silent, his longish nose dipped morosely into his glass of Rosé d'Anjou, until towards the end of the meal he felt a set of bare toes fix themselves firmly over his flies, and signal, just twice. He glanced up, startled, to find the blue eyes blazing with concupiscent mischief and noticed for the first time how sharp and white the lady's canines were as she opened her mouth to push her tongue, ever so slightly, between her truly excellent teeth. She then turned back to Max and went on rapidly: 'Quant à moi, je trouve ce j'm'enfoutisme tout à fait dégoûtant. . .' But she did not remove her toes.

When she withdrew and Max studied the bill, the real struggle began.

'But it is obvious she likes you, and she is a very talented girl and generous,' protested the métis. 'What is the matter with you? Qu'est-ce que c'est que cette plaisanterie-là?' he went on without stopping, turning fiercely upon the maître d'hotel. 'Two bottles of the rosé? We only drank one. Do you think I am a tourist or something?' The maître d'hotel beat a dishonourable retreat, and Ivansong replied:

'You seem to forget that I am married, Max.'

'Married,' spat out Max contemptuously. 'Quelle bêtise! Is that supposed to be some sort of an excuse? What is this – more of your Anglo-Saxon hypocrisy? Cupboard love of God Almighty? How does marriage prevent you from behaving like a man? And don't speak to me of moral laws, I beg you. If I had my way, the Ten Commandments would be transscribed into a quiz: "Thou shalt not commit adultery – *true or false*?"' He counted his change and left a minuscule tip on the tray. 'You don't have to create a scandal by taking her home – you just spend an agreeable and edifying night in the Hotel de l'Asie.'

'And she looks as hard as nails underneath all those curves,' objected Ivansong, as she started back down the aisle, hips rippling professionally.

'As to that, I shall refrain from making any odious puns about good screws,' countered Max, 'but I can assure you this girl can exorcise your fears of your wife or the devil or both if you give her a free hand – so to speak.'

Fighting a stubborn rearguard action, Max insisted that they go on to Madame Phnom's plush smoking establishment for a pipe or two, but even when they were stretched out on the polished wooden beds amid the sweet, heavy fumes and began exchanging enigmatic glances by the soft light of the opium lamp, Ivansong still preserved his sense of proportion. Jacqueline finally gave him a long curious look, shrugged, and said 'Good-night, *darling*' in English. She then beckoned to Max, and the pair of them went into the next cubicle, where they continued to talk in harsh whispers.

'Business is business,' said the girl simply, and held out her hand.

'But you have done nothing!' expostulated Max.

'Peuh,' she retorted elegantly, 'the incompetence of the English is not my responsibility. You made a deal with me – payment in full, however it turned out. Faut pas faire de chinoiseries avec moi, Max!' But Max did not believe in giving a girl something for nothing, and that was why, a few minutes later, he could be observed through a gap in the curtain, sadly exacting payment in kind. He was depressed. This repetitious copulation with La Cannabière was against his principles, a case of *déjà vu*. And why did Ivansong have to be so difficult?

On the next day, however, Felicity Clipstream and the Swinging Chick flew in from Hong Kong, and his affairs began to look up.

12

I

The Bitch grunted curtly as if in a drugged sleep when Ivansong turned the ignition key the next afternoon, for the battery was almost flat again. In consequence he was late at the airport and the Cathay Pacific Airways jet had already landed when he almost ran into the concourse, cursing and patting his pockets to make sure that he had not forgotten his wallet. He saw Chuck Strawbury talking to a big American air force general with a complexion like milk-powder and slightly shaking hands who had evidently just arrived, but before he could even catch his eye and wave, a carrying voice straight out of a West End musical sang to an imaginary dress circle, 'Oh, *you* must be Larry Ivansong, or have I made a most *frightful* boob?' and he turned towards it, his mind stripped for action.

She wore a small straw hat wrapped in a Brigade of Guards tie, large amber sunglasses, and a mop of dyed silver hair with matching fingernails. Her face was heavily painted and powdered for the non-existent limelight, her white knitted mini fitted her too closely for anyone's comfort, and from its hem a smooth golden expanse of presumably Eurasian thigh and calf led down to vertiginous high-heeled boots. Her earrings were golden fish with rubies for eyes, she had a bloodstone ring on her right hand, and a small silver sack hung from one slender wrist.

'No,' said Ivansong with the sudden smile that cut sharply into his lean face and set his eyes sparkling. 'No boob. How did you know it was me, though?'

'Oh, my dear, your picture is plastered all over our advertising blurbs. Don't they ever send them to you? I must say I think that's rather squalid of them. I take it they did at least let you know all about me?'

'Yes, no slip-up there,' answered Ivansong. 'Suzy Lee Flowerclass, spinster?' She nodded and said 'Mm-mmm' encouragingly, and held out her hand. 'Then we're all set.'

He found the porter with her two white imitation pigskin fibreglass cases, and took her out to the car. He was just slamming the door on his side when a second female voice breathed almost in his ear, 'I say, excuse me, but can you tell me if they have a hotel bus for the Asie and where I would find it?' He looked up out of the driver's window at a long, leggy young woman with a school-girl fringe, round horn-rimmed spectacles and small neat features. She wore a combination of chocolate-coloured tunic and white blouse that could have been a fifth-form uniform, but she had the roughening voice of a thirteen-year-old boy.

'Is that your luggage?' he asked dubiously, gazing down at a huge and shapeless canvas bag beside her.

'Uh-huh,' she replied laconically, and reached down for it with one preternaturally long arm.

'Well, then, I'll give you a lift. We're just going to the Asie ourselves. You don't mind?' he asked Miss Flowerclass.

'But of course not,' she trilled, 'we were on the same plane together,' as if it had been some costly college for the daughters of gentlemen.

'Come up with us if you can squeeze in,' said Ivansong to the long, brown girl. 'As my wife so proudly boasts of this death trap, we can *nearly* seat three people in front.'

They bunched together and introduced themselves. The young woman told them her name was Felicity Clipstream. She had been working for the International Wild Life Foundation in Central Sumatra but had come to Mekong to follow up a highly improbable report that orang-utan had been sighted in the Coriandra Mountains. She wanted to look into it, and to persuade the Nava government to protect the apes if the story proved to be true.

'People are foul, you see,' she said briskly. 'What they do is to find a mother with babies, shoot the mother, and carry off the young alive. A baby can be sold for anything up to two thousand pounds in America or Europe. So they're dying out. Pigs!' she concluded ambiguously, and lit a king-size filter-tip cigarette with a tarnished zippo lighter.

'How frightfully *squabby*,' sympathised Miss Flowerclass, and Miss Clipstream gazed at her with a mixture of gratitude and disbelief. 'What do you do?' she enquired almost nervously, 'or is it awful for me to ask?'

Miss Flowerclass explained, adding, 'and now do forgive me if I talk two words of shop with Larry, won't you, Felicity – it is Felicity, isn't it? I think that's simply marvellous. Call me Suzy, won't you, angel, though God knows it's really the *bottom* as names go. Larry, darling, I know it's a ghastly fag but I hope you're not absolutely furious with me for barging in here like this. I'm just going to do a few secondary pieces and I promise not to be an insufferable nuisance. Am I forgiven? And what in the world is *that*?' she continued, pointing one silver nail at the impressive stone lingam framed by the Siva Arch at the intersection of Chulalok and Boulevard Cardamom. Ivansong told her.

'I say, how utterly gorgeous,' gurgled Suzy Lee Flowerclass, waggling her hips gently in her seat. 'I ought to be asking you all sorts of dreary things about the political situation, instead of which we're back on *sex* already. Absolutely typical.'

'Work will be no problem,' Ivansong assured her. 'I have a series of background interviews more or less lined up for you, but you can always change the schedule if you don't like it.'

'I am sure it will be perfectly fabulous, my dear. But what about *playtime*?'

Ivansong explained that Nava was somewhat subdued at the moment, but the Feast of the Beasts would start on the Fourth of July, when the American ambassador would also be throwing a masked party to celebrate Independence Day. 'It should be good,' he said, 'and I shall fix an invitation for you. Incidentally, Miss Clipstream –'

'Felicity, for what it is worth.'

'Felicity, I'm sure the British Embassy could get you in too. We don't have many visitors other than correspondents, and after all beasts are your business, aren't they?'

'Yes, that's just it, beasts are my business. So what about *playtime*?' echoed Miss Clipstream, with a quick shy grin and a glint in the eye behind the strong lenses of her glasses.

At the Hotel de l'Asie, Suzy Lee Flowerclass produced a Hong Kong passport and signed the register, but put a long warning finger on the top button of Ivansong's crumpled jacket when he suggested showing her up to her room.

'Darling Mr. Ivansong,' she murmured, with a small wriggle of the shoulders, 'of course I'm sure it would be scrumptious, but I think we'd better observe the decencies for a bit, don't you?' She patted her silver hair fastidiously. 'After all, we've only just met, remember? Suppose I see you in the bar here, say at six?'

Damnation, Ivansong cursed silently, as he drove home to see Mango and Mini and change. He still had not had her alone to himself for a single moment. Then he grinned into the driving mirror, which looked back at him askance. But she did look positively stunning. And what a name, for God's sake. *Flowerclass*. Where in hell had she acquired that?

'Madame, please forgive me for asking you,' Max said two hours later, sipping his soda in the hotel bar. 'but how do you come by your very unusual name?'

They had hardly sat down when, to Ivansong's mingled fury and excitement, the métis had walked in and joined them uninvited, shouting 'Boyesse' at the nearest little wait-ress and ordering drinks all round. Ivansong had fortified himself with an outsider, but Miss Flowerclass had demanded a hell-and-high-water, and then instructed the bewildered barman how to make it. 'Quite simple, really, my dear man. Take two jiggers of vodka and a jigger of port, add just a *teeny* touch of angostura bitters and a slice of lime, put in the ice and then just top up from the tap.' When it came she sipped it, pronounced it heavenly, and turned her cryptic dark glasses on Max.

'Suzy Lee Flowerclass? Oh, that's terribly straightforward. You see, Mummy was married to a Shanghai Lee who was filthy rich but killed by the Japanese during the war, poor dear, and so she moved down to Hong Kong. She was most awfully emancipated and western and all that sort of thing, and she'd managed to bring out some of the family fortune so she was quite well off. But she did love her tipple, and one gay evening just after the war she got a bit tiddly and sentimental at some thrash given by the Royal Navy about which she remembered quite astonishingly little afterwards, and three months later, it seems, I began to make my presence felt.' She giggled happily.

'Well, the pretty pickle of it was this: the party was thrown by two or three frigates moored side by side the way they do, and the poor sweetie couldn't even remember afterwards which of the bloody ships was responsible, let alone which of the bloody officers. But they were all Flowerclass frigates, so you see the nearest she could get when it came to the birth certificate was –'

Her laughter matched her hair, Max noticed. Qu'elle était bizarre, mais qu'elle était mignonne. And Larry was falling for her. The situation had possibilities. 'What happened next?' Ivansong was asking.

'Oh, Mummy was marvellous. She sent me to a super school in England where I learned reading, riding and the facts of life, and then died in Formosa. I had an itch to write, and I needed a job, so I went into training with Worldover as a reporter, and finally they agreed to my doing this swan through Asia to Tapei. I say, might I have another of these amusing things, do you think?'

Ivansong ordered more drinks all round as Felicity Clipstream strode over, clutching a large imitation crocodile handbag with both hands. 'Hullo,' she said. 'I say, may I . . . I mean, would it be awful of me if I sat down with you for a little. I don't feel like drinking alone and I don't know anyone here yet.'

'Of course not,' said Ivansong, and introduced Max. 'What will you have?'

'What's that you're drinking?' she countered, looking with faintly greedy interest at his glass.

'It's an outsider – a hundred-to-one dry martini.'

'Really? I think I'll try one of those,' she said, brightening, and thereafter never looked back. 'Moi, je parle un peu le français,' she assured Max a little later in a strong Oxford accent.

'So I hear,' replied Max hastily in English, 'but what else do you do? Miss Flowerclass is a journalist, so is Ivansong. I am a professional *flâneur*. What is your guilty secret, Mademoiselle?'

Miss Clipstream took a gulp of her subzero martini, and lit a filter-tip cigarette. 'Me? I'm a – an unprofessional loser,' she replied with a downturned smile. 'Why do you dye your hair silver?' she asked Suzy Flowerclass without malice. 'Would it do any good if I dyed mine, do you think?' One long arm went up to her head and she ran a few fingers through her fringe.

'Only if you're Pisces, darling,' answered Miss Flowerclass. 'Personally I think it's a lousy colour, but I was born in the twelfth sign of the Zodiac, the Fishes. Hence these,' she explained, touching her earrings. 'I'm madly superstitious, and the lucky things for Pisces people are silver, bloodstone, and number seven.' She took a long black cigarette holder from a small bag and screwed a king-size Kent into it. Ivansong watched her, fascinated, as she lit it, and when her hand fell casually down alongside her exposed flank, he linked his fingers gently with hers. This furtive little byplay did not escape the attention of the observant Max Alias, who gaily ordered another round of drinks and a plate of toast and taramasalata.

By nine-thirty they had agreed that it was too late for a conventional restaurant, and Ivansong was soon driving them along a shack-lined road from which the rice-fields stretched away on either side. The bubble of The Bitch's engine drowned the intermittent firing from across the Mekong (contrary to normal practice, the Americans were trying to bring in supplies by the light of flares) and the two women, having found something in common, sang 'My father was the Keeper of the Eddystone Light' together, sweetly but a little out of tune. The car pushed its way into a small village crowded with taxis and motor-trishaws, and, after parking it on the grass verge, Ivansong led the way past two night-clubs staffed with taxi-girls from some of the worst houses in South-east Asia, and into 'The Bogus Snake'.

The 'Snake' was a high, sprawling Mekinese bungalow thatched with palm and supported on short stilts. The bar and bamboo stools, and the rustic wooden tables and benches in the barn-like restaurant were ill-lit by imitation oil-lamps which hung from the walls and rafters, but the adjoining dance floor with its two whimpering guitarists and pounding drummer was flailed by psychedelic lashes of colour, as torn Chinese umbrellas suspended from the ceiling twirled to let through blinding reds and greens and yellows and purples from the clusters of bulbs fixed above them. Behind the dance floor was a door on which was painted simply 'The Rope', and underneath that, 'Members only'.

The restaurant was almost suffocatingly full of smoke and people, and a young Mekinese in an open-necked dress shirt worn outside the trousers suggested they have a drink while waiting for a table. Two men already leaning on the small bar proved to be Charlie Polak and Catullus Yip, half-hearted introductions were exchanged like throw-away lines, and the waiter returned to say there was a table for six free, and would they all like to share it?

As soon as they were settled, and had ordered their drinks and chilli crab *à la mékinoise*, which was the *plat du jour* and therefore uncomplicated, Suzy Lee Flowerclass murmured throatily, 'Mmmmmmm, I adore this sort of joint,' as if she were tasting a marron glacé, rose to her feet crying, 'Come on, men, I'll take on any three of you,' and dragged Ivansong to the dance floor. She then put on such an astonishing performance of boneless virtuosity to the heavy thrumming of the cats in the background that others edged back to watch this miniskirted vision of silver and white and gold as she waggled and bounced and shook, her hair flying and her dark glasses swinging incuriously from side to side. Opposite her, an exhausted Ivansong gave way to Charlie Polak, and Polak to Yip, and then mercifully the music sank sighing to a halt as if the batteries had run down.

It was at this moment that Miss Flowerclass caught sight of the door to 'The Rope', 'My dears,' she sang out to her three partners. 'What on earth happens behind that incredibly sordid little sign?' and began weaving her way towards it.

Cat took her gently by the arm. 'No, Suzy, not in there,' he said in his soft, pseudo-American burr. 'They don't like it.'

'My God, what goes on, then, darling?' demanded Miss Flowerclass, 'unrivalled scenes of orgiastic debaucher –?' she stumbled over it, and Ivansong cut in. 'Be a good girl, and come quietly,' he said firmly. And they led her, docile but

98

still glowing, back to the table, where an interesting sight met their eyes.

Max and Miss Clipstream were locked in close argument, their outside elbows on the table so that they could turn and stare at each other almost at squinting range. Felicity Clipstream was shaking her head slowly and incredulously, as if at a mental defective, while Max tapped his soda-water impatiently on the table.

'How can you say such a thing?' she was protesting, her eyes gleaming behind the schoolgirl spectacles. '*Pongidae* are infinitely more intelligent than any gibbon, and the orang-utan can be quite extraordinarily astute. You have only to read Barbara Harrison's account of how a young orang in Sarawak first listened to a nest of flying insects through a hole in a log, then enlarged the hole with his teeth, then tried poking it with a twig that was too thick, then whittled down the twig, then pushed – yes, could I have a quick dry martini, do you think?' she added, turning briefly to answer Charlie – 'to realise how cunning they can be once they grow up.'

'Pouf,' replied Max contemptuously. 'Quelle histoire. The facts are they are slow, and they are dying out in consequence. They do not adapt, and their sense of territorial defence is deficient.'

'Oh, balls,' cried Felicity Clipstream. She clapped a hand to her mouth, but immediately went on, 'Just because a Sumatran siamang can hoot like a Flowerclass frigate turning to starboard. . .'

Max laughed, and Miss Clipstream took off her spectacles and grinned up at him. Now Max had noted before that when a myopic woman removed her glasses, the unfocused eyes sometimes took on a lost look which could be curiously excit-ing to the male, since it aroused the protective instinct yet simultaneously seemed to express blind lust. So like an intelligent pongo digging a twig into a wasp's nest, he leaned forward and kissed her softly on the lips.

'Boy, are you the swinging chick,' commented Charlie Polak admiringly, his warm eyes on Suzy Flowerclass. 'Would you by any chance be free for a cultural evening tomorrow? There's so much I'd love to show an intelligent girl like you. Have you visited the Golden Pagoda within the palace precincts, where the frescoes depict in minute detail the twelve circles of hell? Or how about the *Ramayana*, danced to music from the royal orchestra? Or maybe a real traditional Mekinese evening starting with five large dry martinis and dinner at the "Casse-croûte"?'

'Sounds positively delicious,' Miss Flowerclass smiled, but her dark glasses were looking the wrong way, for the crab had arrived, piping hot and crepitating in a brown earthenware pot.

Charlie sighed ruefully, 'Okay, I get it. Well, you can't wrong 'em all. Hey, waiter, give us a bottle of that Chassagne Montrachet 1964 of yours, well-chilled, but not out of your god-damned icebox. Listen, Suzy, take my advice and don't try any games with the Rope Club over there, because those boys have to be handled with care, this side up.'

'Oh, Lord, you don't mean it's for *queers*, do you?' asked Miss Flowerclass in a bored voice.

'No,' laughed Charlie. 'Look, let Cat here tell it. He knows the set-up better than I do.'

'Okay,' said Cat seriously, slowly tearing apart half a crab with his hands, 'Take these names for a start. Many Hindu-Buddhists believe that the world as we each see it – subjectively – is what they call *Maya*, and *Maya* is an illusion. The true Cosmos is One, and since you are of that oneness, you have no separate ego. You only exist in relation to everything else. But as long as you continue believing in the individual self, you are chained to selfish emotions, passions and ambitions, and these in turn chain you to life, so that you will go on being reborn until you can finally shed the whole hallucination. That's the state they call Nirvana. You with me?'

'Sweetie, I'm hanging on by my ears. It reminds me a bit of

Satan taking Jesus Christ to the top of a mountain and offering him the world, *of all things*. Do go on.'

'Well, the world exists, of course, because having an illusion is not seeing something that is not there at all, but seeing something that *is* there wrongly. So they always tell folks that it's like looking at a rope and mistaking it for a snake. The rope is the real, undivided universe; the snake is the illusion.'

'So this outside restaurant "The Bogus Snake" is the mirage,' said Suzy Flowerclass, 'and the Rope Club through there is the reality. But how come?'

'Drugs,' explained Polak, sampling the Montrachet and nodding to the waiter. 'The short cut. They think they've got God over a barrel.'

'That's it,' agreed Cat. 'Mostly grass and soft stuff, mind you. Quite a few people who can cope look in from time to time, even weekend warriors who aren't really hooked at all. Like me. But I was once asked to act ground control on an LSD session – you know, be the one guy that stays sober, so to speak – and the manager here is a real garbageman, uses anything. They call him Flakey, though, because he usually connects with cocaine, and he seems in some extraordinary way to be able to take it or leave it. Well, with Sissomak trying to clean the place up, they were always afraid of getting themselves burned by the fuzz, so they're an edgy lot, if you get me.

'And there's another thing'. Cat dipped his hands into an enamel finger-bowl, and took a hot towel from the waiter. He paused until the man had gone. 'There's some kind of connection between the "Rope" here and the young monks at the foot of the central tower at Nakhara Wat who play doorkeeper to the Paramahamsa Bonze. Those kids are on ganja or something, and they get their supplies here. Maybe they get more than that. I don't know.'

'But, my dear Cat,' protested Miss Flowerclass, 'you're surely not suggesting that young Buddhist monks are juvenile delinquents, are you?' and her voice rose dizzily to the rafters.

'You get good and bad monks, the way you get good or bad

anything,' remarked Ivansong. 'There are monks who still teach that the world is flat and Buddha was born from his mother's armpit. There are monks who don't understand the meaning of the Pali or Sanskrit texts they mumble, but who will change your *karma* for you for cash. Some of them smoke and talk during sacred ceremonies, and others cheat, booze and fornicate. What do you expect? There are 45,000 bonzes in this country alone. They can't all be angels, even if many are.

'Talking of which,' he went on, 'what do you say to one for the road after we finish this, and then hitting the hay? It's getting on, and these girls only flew in today.' Miss Flowerclass flashed an almost invisible smile at Ivansong and Miss Clipstream's slightly damp hand quivered suddenly in Max's, but by the time they were on the road, two in the front and two in the back, there came over all of them an irresistible urge to sing.

When they reached the Hotel de l'Asie, Felicity Clipstream stood beside Max and watched a little nervously as the other two walked into the lift, her tongue moving slowly across her upper lip.

'Well?' she turned to Max brightly and took a deep breath. 'Why not come up just for a night-cap, since you don't drink? After all,' she added with one of his own Gallic shrugs, her long arms hanging limply at her sides, 'what's the good of the International Wild Life Foundation if it doesn't give you an international foundation for a wild life?'

Once they were alone in her room, Ivansong kissed Miss Flowerclass and neither spoke. Uncounted time afterwards he went into the bathroom, turned on the taps, and they sat side by side, each with a towel around the waist, while the bath ran itself behind them.

'But why did you dye your hair silver, instead of just buying a blonde wig?' Ivansong mumbled, nuzzling a delectable little mole on her arm, 'it will be very embarrassing all the time you are waiting for it to get back to the normal colour.'

She lifted his head and looked squarely at him. 'Do not frown,' she said reprovingly. 'It gives your eyebrows fallen arches. It is a wig.'

'You dyed a wig? What on earth for?'

'Is it not obvious that was the obvious thing to do?' replied Thinking Lotus softly, below the sound of the rushing water. 'No one would normally dream of dyeing a wig silver, so no one would dream that my dyed wig was anything but my own hair. And when I do not want the silver hair any more, I take it off and bury it or burn it. Then no one can possibly imagine I was ever *that* girl wearing *her* hair. Even you did not detect it.'

Ivansong looked at her thoughtfully. 'Clever, these Chinese,' he said, shaking his head.

'You do not know just how fantastically clever, *dawling*,' retorted Lotus, giving a bad imitation of herself imitating Suzy Lee Flowerclass.

Ivansong grinned. 'I'm glad you got the passport all right. Having disreputable friends comes in useful sometimes. I wouldn't like to see you trying to get past a Hong Kong immigration officer with it, but this one was just for the Mekinese, I suppose?' She nodded. 'What a name, though. What happened to the original owner?'

Lotus shook her head wryly. 'I suppose she went down with the ship – or ships.'

They emptied the bath and, as the water ran out, talked of Mango and Mini and future tactics, but when they started to refill it in order to go on speaking in safety, someone banged on the wall fiercely and a muffled, agonised voice shouted, 'How many baths do you reckon to take between midnight and dawn? Are you a bloody mermaid or something?' This was a situation for which the intelligence manuals had not provided a solution, and so Ivansong reluctantly dressed.

'Have you got the book?' he asked her before he slipped out of the door. She reached over to the bedside table and triumphantly held it over her head. 'In Chinese,' she whispered. 'It was sold out in English.'

A few nights later Ivansong opened his own copy. The town and the house were asleep. A half moon rode high in the blue-black heavens, and he lay naked on the springboard of the swimming-pool, a scotch-on-the-rocks resting coldly on his stomach, the underwater lighting shimmering on the surrounding trees. He had not accompanied Miss Flowerclass to her room that evening, but merely reminded her that she, too, must do her homework. Tomorrow was D-Day, the Fourth of July.

So far so good, he reflected. Moreover the hour he had most dreaded seven days ago had proved to be the easiest thirty minutes of all. It had begun when he had asked Thinking Lotus whether she could wear a wig in bed with him, and she had replied 'come and find out – *now*'. He had suddenly faced the immediate prospect of having to tell her about Greeen, and to suggest that if she could wear a wig when they made love here, she could wear one if they made love on camera in the bridal suite of the Hotel de l'Asie. His own wife, therefore, could be his compromising sleeping partner, and the whole blackmail ploy would be secretly defused from the start. He would have the game in his hands, for the simple reason that the Chinese and Max (and the unmentionable Greeen) would quite erroneously be thinking that they had it in theirs.

He remembered lying beside her, the wig still firmly in place, the evening sun filtering weakly through the curtains of his bedroom-study like some frustrated voyeur, and thinking deliberately in words as he did on such occasions: 'I must now warn my wife that if her parents are to remain safe, she must either connive at my sleeping publicly with some whore paid by the communists, or put on a wig and play the lead in a blue film herself, disguised as my pick-up.'

Then, before he could indulge in any further futile ratiocination, he had said, 'Sit up, Lotus, I want to tell you something,' and had plunged into it, using the first words that sprang into his head. When he faltered to a stop she leaned over and kissed him.

'Larry,' she said finally, with a small shake of her bare shoulders, 'this frightens me because of my parents, and it must not go wrong. But Greeen does not know how much he does not know, and we are never going to enlighten him. You' – she raised a cautioning finger – 'are not going to play the bedtime game of clouds and rain with any other harlot but me. So,' she put a maidenly hand over her breasts, 'me it is.'

Ivansong heaved a great sigh of relief. 'But you do realise that, well, the whole thing will be photographed? God knows who will see the pictures before we are through, and they will go on some file in Peking. I mean all this business of appearing like a tart –'

'Well,' said Lotus, 'it could be argued that there is nothing wrong with this ancient and popular profession – certainly no more wrong than plain fun between boys and girls. Since when has frivolous self-indulgence been more virtuous than honest toil honestly rewarded?

'But in any case,' she went on, gazing at him incredulously, 'do you imagine for one moment that I would risk the peace of mind of my parents in order to preserve my lily-white honour by not sleeping with my own husband? Twenty-five centuries ago Confucius spoke with his students about the supreme virtue of filial piety, and ever since then girls have sold themselves into some of the nastiest beds in history for the sake of the family.

'So when I rape you in this room, that is just ignoble pleasure, but when I suffer a fate worse than death from you in the bridal suite of the Hotel de l'Asie, that will be noble self-immolation, and it will rightly be on the record, not just for background.'

This was too much for Ivansong, but a little later, and a little breathless, Thinking Lotus continued her dissertation.

'It is not you that should be concerned about my finer feelings, but me about yours, do you not see? It is fastidious man who loves softness and fragrance and sweetness and grace, the fragile, the silky, the peaches-and-creamy in women. And women? There is nothing *nimby-pimby* about women, my love, or had you not noticed? They are the grosser sex. They throw themselves into the arms of great, coarse, hairy, sweaty, impatient, importunate rogues in rut, and the harder the better. It all goes most suitably with their earthy destiny – the mens and the morning sickness, the birth and the placenta, the dirty diapers and the rest of the bowl of cherries.'

'Go on,' ordered Ivansong with a smile, 'you intrigue me strangely.'

'Finally, Larry, do not forget that the Chinese theatre is my subject, and we shall turn this into a delicious and anonymous Peking opera. If we can so arrange matters that our thousand and one nights will all fall on the Fourth of July, I shall wear a bizarre wig, and we shall both perform in our animal masks. We shall put on a technical performance, not a romantic one, and the whole thing will be meaningless *Maya*, sex the illusion instead of love the reality. As long as you do not give way to any messy four-legged emotions, there will be no cause to be shy. And anyway what we have done two thousand three hundred and forty-eight – no, forty-nine – times before God we can certainly do once or twice before Man.'

Ivansong's eyes widened slowly, and he thumped the bed with his free hand. 'Wait a minute, I think I've got something,' he said. 'Do you remember that couple in London who made a film showing forty different ways of making love in about eighty minutes? It was in 1970, I think, and –'

'But, darling Larry, you are not as young as –'

'Christ, Lotus, they didn't finalise every contract, or initial every clause, or however you want to put it. It was a practical demonstration, not a suicide pact. They were illustrating the positions described in the. . .' Ivansong snapped his fingers. 'Damn it, that's what we must do. Get hold of the *Kama Sutra* and study it so that we coordinate properly.'

'The *Kama Sutra*?'

'Yes, you know, the Indian Manual of Love. It's a terribly proper work, something like that thing the Foreign Office circulates so furtively on how to address a letter to a Papal Nuncio or seat twelve at dinner. I can certainly get a copy in

French here – that is, in the unlikely event that the British Council doesn't have it in English.'

'Indian Manual of Love,' purred Lotus softly, 'the words are very beautiful.'

'So is the music,' Ivansong assured her.

They had then worked out their initial strategy. Thinking Lotus would leave for Singapore as Greeen had instructed, ostensibly on family business, and then fly to Hong Kong. There she would acquire not only suitable clothes and a blonde wig for her new part, but a copy of the *Kama Sutra*, and a lost, stolen, strayed or forged passport which artistic if mercenary Chinese friends in the underground travel business could certainly supply. She would return to Nava as a roving correspondent for the Worldover Syndication Service, and they would play it from there.

Ivansong sat up to sip his drink, leafed through the *Kama Sutra* for a minute or two, and then settled down to absorb its pedantic instructions systematically and in their correct order, in accordance with the Otto Furst system of memorisation – the Close position, the Squeezed position, the Entwined, the Mare, the Raised, the Wide Open, the Pressed, the Half-Pressed, the Bamboo Cleft, the Nail, the Crab, the Packet, the Lotus, the Revolving, the Leaning, the Cow. . .

Ivansong yawned. It all sounded far too much like hard work.

13

The residence of the United States Ambassador to Nava was at that time within the American compound on Boulevard Chulalok, an ageing but well-preserved French colonial mansion with a central staircase that swept up to a vast reception room extending over the portico. But on this evening of the Fourth of July the guests were assembling on the spacious lawn, and drinking their first painfully cold martinis by the wavering light of big flaring kerosene torches supported on metal poles.

Ivansong joined the line of arrivals, wearing his one dark silk suit and a domino across his eyes designed to give him the appearance of a rather tall short-eared owl, for this was also the first day of the Week of the Beasts and the Eldritches were combining American Independence with the local custom of holding an animal masquerade, and guests had been encouraged to wear masks.

'Have you ever done any square-dancing, Mr. Ivansong?' asked Mrs. Eldritch in her flat little voice, a plump pheasant of a woman with the grip of a lightweight boxer and tired, cornflower eyes.

'Often,' Ivansong smiled. 'But not the kind you mean.'

'Well, you may find yourself doing so tonight,' said his hostess. And by God, how right you are, he thought. He wandered over to a waiter, collected a large glass full of ice cubes with a faint bouquet of scotch about them, and began to circulate in search of his latest love.

He soon caught sight of a silver head in the thickening mob, and as he drew near heard a voice rise like birdsong above the surrounding silhouettes. 'My dears, I simply don't know how to thank Max Alias,' Miss Flowerclass was saying, 'he's been absolutely angelic over this. I mean, they would have had me out on the street, but just when all was lost and this fiendish little man at the desk was telling me I had to vacate the wretched room by midday and they had no alternative accommodation, Max came up and insisted on calling the manager and making really quite a scene, really.

'And so I ended up in the bridal suite – *terribly* grand – for a ridiculous figure too, I might add' – she whispered something hoarsely that he could not hear – 'and you should just *see* it, it's positively ravishing, with mirrors and pink lights and marvellously naughty old wallpaper from Nakhara, and simply a morass of deep lambswool carpets, and the bed. . . Well!'

As he pushed his way towards her he saw that her mask was a pair of narrow dark glasses framed in wide silver wings fashioned to resemble the face of an exceptionally sly and untrustworthy cat. Before joining her, he decided to get himself a second drink, only to hear more familiar voices on his right.

'But *Hylobatidae* are precisely the same as your precious orang-utan in this respect,' an exasperated voice was saying. 'Oestrus occurs about every twenty-eight days and approximately half-way through the menstrual cycle. The baby is born thirty weeks after conception. Unlike your feeble females among the orangs, however, the mother is about the same size as the father. Birth is therefore not a problem. But where is your drink? Boy! Over there,' called Max. 'Did you say something, chérie?'

Felicity Clipstream shook her head, and just continued to look at him steadily in the flarelight. She was wearing no mask, and suddenly Ivansong realised that she had no need to do so as he took in the round eyes countersunk behind the horn-rimmed spectacles, the small neat head, the tall slim frame with its elongated arms, clothed tonight in a tobacco-coloured dress of coarse linen. Max Alias had found the ultimate in gibbons.

'Elle est sensationnelle,' Max said to him in rapid French as he came upon them. '*Sensationnelle!* Who would have believed it? But she will kill me at this rate. Look at my hand, I ask you. Trembling already.'

'Still talking about the sex-life of gibbons?' asked Ivansong in English, his long face deceptively solemn.

'Mince alors, mais cela dépasse tout,' protested the outraged métis, but Miss Clipstream turned to Ivansong and announced firmly in her high, hoarse voice, 'Well, as a matter of fact, Larry, you know, I've finally come to the conclusion that sex is really rather *nice*.'

'Evening, Ivansong,' He turned to find the British ambassador behind him. 'Good evening, Sir. Miss Clipstream, may I introduce –' 'We've met,' said Nigel Pawkinson-Convoy curtly. 'I want a word with you if I may,' he added, and walked away, cutting Max Alias and the gibbon girl dead.

The ambassador led Ivansong off to the edge of the party, and they stood with their backs to a floodlit ornamental lily-pond.

'Someone ought to tell that stupid creature not to get mixed up with that bounder – what's his name? – Alias,' he said in the clipped and precise tones he always used before he lost his temper. 'Fortunately, I gather she is only staying a few days. She had some damn fool idea about going up into the Coriandra Hills looking for monkeys, but I soon put a stop to that. Now what about this woman from Hong Kong your office has sent here?'

Ivansong felt the tension drain away through the ends of his fingers as it always did at the beginning of a fight.

'What about her?'

'Is she staying long?'

'That will depend on my London office and her own plans.'

'I think not. I want her out of Nava. She seems to have been behaving like some sort of a tart already, from all I hear. Tell your people to recall her or something.'

Ivansong did not reply, but he had seen a large, familiar frame genteelly filching a martini from the tray of a passing waiter, and he called softly: 'Charlie, the ambassador has just described our colleague, Miss Flowerclass, as some sort of tart – on pure hearsay, of course. What's your view? You've at least met her.'

'Met her?' answered Polak with a slow smile. 'I am one of the two dozen guys who have been trying to lay her without success since she arrived. Does that answer the question?'

'Do you usually use language like that to senior diplomats, Polak?' asked Pawkinson-Convoy, his large brown eyes flaring like hot coals.

Polak considered him for a while. 'When I choose my words,' he said at last, 'I make a distinction between infants of tender years and middle-aged civil servants. Maybe that's where I've been going wrong. And if I'm Polak to you, Mr. Ambassador, you are Pawkinson-Convoy to me, Pawkinson-Convoy.'

'And does your ambassador invite you to receptions to insult the heads of missions of friendly states, may I ask?'

'Does your government pay you to offend the accredited representatives of powerful international news media?'

'By God,' laughed the ambassador mirthlessly, suddenly furious, 'the terminology you grubby newspeddlers find for yourselves. So that is how we are supposed to describe the drunks who gather around the world's bars writing inaccurate rubbish about wars they haven't got the guts to go within a hundred miles of, eh? And now get out of my way, both of you, because I've no intention of listening to any more of your damned insolence.'

Ivansong and Polak changed their positions slightly, and the ambassador found himself wedged into one of the little stone bays or curlicues that gave the fountain its ornamental shape.

There was a moment of shocked silence, then Polak said slowly and quietly: 'The percentage of foreign correspondents killed in the Korean and Indochina wars was higher than for the soldiers themselves. On their behalf, let me state with all due reverence, sir, that I don't, for one, stand for that kind of crap from little birds in gilded cages like you.'

'By Christ, I'll make you pay for that,' snapped Pawkinson-Convoy, 'you're going to wish you'd never been born.'

'It wouldn't be the first time,' remarked Polak, with a slight smile.

'Look,' said Ivansong, 'let's keep this thing within bounds. What Polak means about gilded cages, I think, is this –'

'I don't give a damn what he means,' broke in the ambassador. 'Have you both gone raving mad?'

'What he means,' continued Ivansong patiently as if there had been no interruption, 'is this. We're a profession that has its faults like any other, but we operate in circumstances that no one else is asked to accept. When a soldier moves, all his basic needs are looked after by a vast administrative tail that gives him leave, clothes him, feeds him, transports him to where he has to go, arranges where he will sleep, tells him what to do next, and supplies him with doctors and drugs if he gets hurt or falls sick. And it can hardly be said,' he added blandly, 'that a diplomat works under more difficult conditions.'

He paused and looked at Pawkinson-Convoy with distaste, but the ambassador's eyes were now fixed, almost hypnotically, on one of the kerosene torches nearby.

'Now take the correspondent. A war or civil war or a riot or a coup d'état in some Godforsaken hole he may never have been to before brings an urgent cable from his editor saying "go". He has his camera, his typewriter, and such money as he prudently keeps on hand for these hilarious occasions and he just takes off. He starts without transport, and if he gets a seat on a plane, it may not be able to land because of the crisis, whatever it is. If he lands, he may not even be able to get out of the airport because of the shooting. He has no logistical backing, nothing faintly resembling the pillow-breasted nanny of an organisation that every GI Joe Soap or junior embassy clerk can count on.

'He is in stiff competition with his colleagues, and he takes risks not for Queen and Country or Old Glory and the American Way of Life, but for getting the story and seeing five hundred words of his copy on page three. If somewhere along this accident-prone line he slips, and it never reaches his paper or radio station, then he has done it all for nothing.'

'How very heroic,' sneered the ambassador in a non-committal voice as cold and quiet as the grave.

'Heroic?' echoed Polak contemptuously. 'Heroic correspondents?' he laughed, 'How you'd love them, wouldn't you? Your idea of a British reporter is one who writes what British ambassadors tell him, and who makes his way to the top by never speaking ill of the living.'

Polak paused and looked at Ivansong, who looked at the ambassador, who was once again gazing fixedly at the torch as if he were deaf with rage. Polak shrugged. 'Therefore kindly damned well watch your step when you talk about us to our faces, will you, Mr. Ambassador?' he added. 'Not being a diplomat, I don't go in for all that sesquepedalian glossolalia some of you are so fond of. I like to tell it in sentiments of one syllable. So forgive me if I conclude by calling a shit a shit, won't you, Your Excellency?' He walked off casually to pick up another drink.

'I advise you to do nothing rash,' began Ivansong coldly to the Ambassador, but at that moment Mrs. Eldritch came over. 'My, there you are,' she said to Pawkinson-Convoy, 'why, I've been looking for you all over, Nigel, and so has Dolly. We're going to start the square-dancing. No, don't worry, not everybody,' she went on as he sighed heavily and worked his face back into an expression of polite resignation. 'The American community now has its own little company, and they want to dance for you all. Those who would like to can just try later,' and she led him gently away.

A badminton court at the side of the main lawn had been floodlit for the performance, and the more courteous among the guests now gathered around this to watch, while Mrs. Eldritch clapped her hands and the fiddlers and dancers dutifully assembled, the girls in full skirts and frilled petticoats, their partners in check shirts. The caller, a short, freckled young man wearing a black tie and red cummerbund, appeared at the edge of the court with a microphone, the dancers formed themselves into two squares, each of four pairs, and faced each other expectantly. Then the fiddlers struck up, and under the astonished gaze of the Mekinese guests the badminton court sprang to life in obedience to the controlled ravings of the microphone:

> Now all join hands and circle to the left,
> The pastry's rising, so make it deft,
> Swing your partner and promenade so,
> Allemande your corner, do a do-si-do,
> Grand right and left, till you've weaved that ring,
> Then first and third to the centre and swing. . .

During the clapping, a waiter came around with a trayful of champagne and, as Ivansong reached for a glass, the little finger of his free hand was taken, and he found Miss Flowerclass at his side. 'Mmmmmm, bubbly,' she murmured.

'I say, isn't it just too scrummy, I mean champers and square-dancing on the Mekong, I simply *worship* that sort of thing.'

'Well for God's sake don't go and join in,' urged Ivansong, 'or we'll both be thrown out.'

> Couples balance, couples swing,
> Give a left-hand ride to that pretty little thing.
> Balance in, balance out.
> Then do-si-do your honey right about.

'Why, what's happened?' whispered Miss Flowerclass.
'The British Ambassador thinks you're a tart.'
'*Squabby* little man.'

> First pair out to the couple on the right
> Circle all, and keep it tight.
> Now break the ring, allemande your corner...

When it came to an end, and everyone had been served with champagne, Calvert Kirkwall Eldritch took the microphone, walked to the centre of the court, and said simply, 'Your Excellencies, Honoured Guests, Ladies and Gentlemen, I invite you to remove your masks, and to drink a toast to Her Majesty the Queen Mahaksatriyani and the Kingdom of Mekong,' whereupon all the lights at once went out. The Mekinese Reds had sabotaged the main power station.

There were hardly any flares at this end of the garden and Ivansong lost Miss Flowerclass in the murmuring semi-darkness, from which familiar voices abruptly emerged just in front of him.

'And the situation is worsening, Monsieur,' grated General Keo, speaking slowly in French. 'The main highways are constantly cut now, petrol is in short supply, and we may even have to reduce the rice ration. Between ourselves, Monsieur, the key to the crisis is to hand, but the tragedy is that we cannot grasp it.'

'How do you arrive at that, Excellency?' replied a metallic burr in transatlantic plume-de-ma-tante.

'But it is simple, Monsieur, with due respect to your gallant country and its great Gallic traditions, and to our century-old links. We need full American support, and for that we must be prepared to give our full support to the Americans. Between ourselves, that can never, never happen as long as Prince Kitay is our chief. Nonetheless, sooner or later, someone must hold out the hand of friendship to the United States in order to save Mekong, Monsieur l'Ambassadeur.'

'Ambassador? But there is some mistake. I am not an ambassador.'

'Mistake? But you are surely Monsieur Bercy-Mouchoix, the French Ambassador?' cried Keo, in a suitably startled voice. A cigarette lighter flared, and the General's black eyes, although still as those of a basilisk, appeared to dance to its yellow flame.

'No, General, I'm Dave Inqvist. We've actually met before, but you may not –'

'But of course, Monsieur Inqvist,' answered Keo in sturdy enough English, 'I am sorry. A foolish mistake. The darkness, you know. But, I beg you, please forget what I just said. I am afraid it may have sounded a little indiscreet.'

'Hell, no – I mean negative to that, Excellency,' broke in Inqvist, as he lit a Camel and his mask-like face flashed briefly into view. 'On the contrary, maybe we could discuss this problem sometime in peace and quiet. It seems that, as Plato said, democracy passes into despotism. Let's face it. Mekong is hardly a model of freedom as things stand right now, and we Americans believe firmly in the rule of the people, and in allowing all citizens their sacred inalienable human rights. That's fundamental.'

'Monsieur Inqvist,' murmured Keo, lighting a Philippine cigarillo greedily so that his pock-marked face with its cowl of lacquered black hair emerged in a pulsating glow, 'I am above all an admirer of the American way of life, and I also believe in the firm rule of people, while allowing them their sacred human rites . . .' Blood sacrifices? You never knew with these inscrutable Americans. But it was best to humour them.

They wandered away, but as Ivansong started to follow to

hear the rest of the joke Suzy Flowerclass tugged his arm, he hesitated, and they were lost in the sea of black shapes around him.

French Ambassador? Ivansong laughed silently to himself. With an American accent you could perhaps cut with a buzz-saw provided it had been properly maintained? But Keo was not really funny – he was a gangster and a pimp and a pusher on such a scale that he was now a national figure loaded with honours, a coward and a bully who would be frightened to death if he met himself on a dark night. If Washington turned in that direction, Mekong could become even more explosive than it was now.

By this time the servants had brought out a few lanterns and Ivansong was able to find champagne for Miss Flowerclass and himself, but as the diminutive Mekinese waiter held the tray up to them in the capricious light, a large form backed into him clumsily and four glasses fell to the ground. The waiter swung the tray up adroitly to save the rest, and the form grabbed two of the survivors, one in each hand, while treading the victims into the turf.

'Terribly sorry,' said a slurred voice, 'but thank God for his manifold mercies, especially these two. Can't see a damned thing around here. Wherethehellsthauxiliarylighding?'

Ivansong could just make out the big, pale US Air Force general he had seen with Strawbury the day he had driven to meet Suzy Flowerclass, and now the general caught sight of her silver wig in the semi-darkness.

'Well, Chrissakes, didn't I see you at the airport the other day, sweetheart?' he asked.

'My dear,' replied Miss Flowerclass calmly, 'how can you possibly remember? You're already far too sloshed on all this divine bubbly.'

'Yes I did, though,' he said, 'saw you too,' nodding to Ivansong, and swaying slightly. 'Here,' he turned to a small solid shape beside him. 'This one's for you.' It was accepted with a murmur. The general took a gulp at his champagne.

'I was talking about our boys up there on Hill 520,' he said. 'It's just another example of the absolute inhumanity of letting politicians fight wars. Those guys are short of every damned thing, and shortest of all of water, and our choppers can't get near them. Now you fight a war or you don't, and if you do, you leave it to the professionals and you don't pull any punches. I mean what's all this goddam nonsense about a crummy lot of carved stonework? Anyone would think it was the Vatican. Anyway we agreed in Vietnam that even socio-political targets like schools and hospitals could be bombed when occasion justified. Men's lives are at stake because politicians fool around playing patacake – half a battalion of men, and maybe they are only Marines but they're still Americans.'

'What's your answer, then?' asked Ivansong.

'Simple,' replied the voice, accompanied by a slight gurgle as the last of the champagne went down. 'We shoulda put a proper firebase down in the first place if we intended to do the thing at all. Get a C-130 in to roll out a 15,000-pound daisy-cutter and flatten the top of the hill so's you got yourself the beginning of a proper landing zone, then bring in your artillery and you're in business. The point is we should've been ready to go *all out*. The hell with all this superstition that's going around about sacred monuments and holy hermits holed up in them. Instead of taking the obvious decisions, everyone is running around consulting gurus. We even got our own tame American guru here – Chuck Strawbury.'

He paused, and thought flickered just beyond the corner of Ivansong's mind. But the General was now run in. 'Mind you, I got nothing against Chuck. Now there's a case in point again, in fact. Ecological warfare. Dammit, we finally come up with this Beanstalk refoliant seed that grows so thick and fast that we could choke up China's entire agriculture, or roll out a whole gigantic wiring-system of impenetrable tropical jungle that would block off all of the communist half of South-east Asia. But the panty-waists in Washington say no. Jesus, if –'

But Ivansong, clutching the hand of Miss Flowerclass tightly to keep her quiet, was thinking sardonically: just so, Chuck, so you had a team working on a refoliant bomb that was going to bring riches and happiness wherever it was dropped, salving the wounds of Mother Earth and the bruised conscience of the great American public. How would you explain this one away, the refoliant that can suffocate a country into submission with vegetation? The indispensability of opposites? There is no peace without war?

The floodlights came on over the court, and as they stared frowning at each other in the glare, the general noticed that the small, solid shape beside him was not, as he had vaguely supposed, one of the embassy attachés, but a stocky, square-faced Chinese. 'Well, I'll be damned,' commented the general, nonplussed.

'Good evening, Mr. Lee,' interposed Ivansong. 'This is Mr. Lee Tian Kwang,' he explained, 'one of the leaders of the Teochew community in Mekong.' He introduced the others, and Short March shook hands all round with a series of small, grave bows.

At this point a waiter arrived with more champagne, a microphone squealed angrily as the American ambassador trod on its lead by mistake, and the toasting was resumed. Since Prince Kitay had pointedly cut the reception, General Keo spoke gracefully on behalf of the Mekinese, raising his glass to the President and people of the United States, enlarging on the wonders of democracy, and recalling with reverence the contributions to civilisation as a whole made by such great Americans as George Washington and Arnold Lincoln – a quick whisper from an aide – *Abraham* Lincoln, of course.

Ivansong again caught the quick movement just beyond the corner of his mind that the word guru had earlier provoked, but it vanished as it had come. Guru? Lincoln? Benedict Arnold? He shrugged.

By now the general was drinking scotch-on-the-rocks, and apparently in a patriotic mood. Suddenly he noticed that Miss Flowerclass had not taken off her cat-mask during these solemn ceremonies and, his blood stirring with alcohol and outraged national loyalty, he leaned forward and said 'Lady, this is American Independence Day and on this distant enclave of American soil I must ask you to take off your fancy dress when the President's health is drunk as a markerespect. And what's more,' he added with a slight belch, 'you can take that wig off, too. Because it damn well is a wig, isn't it, damn it?' And he swallowed the rest of his drink in one gulp.

His voice had risen commandingly, and many people were looking at them, including, Miss Flowerclass saw to her horror, the British ambassador. The plump Mrs. Eldritch moved swiftly towards the group on nimble feet, whispering 'Please, Miss Flowerclass, it is quite all right. It is quite unnecessary,' but just as Ivansong closed his eyes with relief, Pawkinson-Convoy came forward and said smoothly but precisely: 'I am sure that as a British guest Miss Flowerclass would be glad to atone for any negligence that the general might have construed as slighting to her American hosts.'

Suzy Flowerglass ignored him, but turned to her hostess and, throwing her voice to the amphitheatre, sang: 'That was really adorable of you, Mrs. Eldritch, darling, but if it is all right with you I will, in fact, make myself comfortable, you know.' And while Ivansong ran a hand through his own wilful mane and wondered wildly how to stave off the impending disaster, she gently took off the cat-like dark glasses and the silver wig to reveal a pair of placid blue contact lenses and a smooth helmet of hair the colour of polished copper.

14

Miss Flowerclass, who had removed the contact lenses in the car and put her silver wig and cat-domino on again, led Ivansong into the bridal suite by one long, slim

9

silver-tipped hand and pressed the button marked 'Love'. The erotic frieze on the long wall opposite the great oval bed crept furtively into view when the hidden lights glowed, and she crossed to the heavy maxicurtains that masked the windows to draw them open by their cord. High up on the sixteen-storey block beyond the gardens of the Hotel de l'Asie, a huge, rotating neon sign spelt out the words 'Hamsa Hilton' in red, orange, green, blue and violet, drowning the bridal suite in a whirlpool of psychedelic light and turning Miss Flowerclass into a strange, submarine goddess. She then raised her two arms sinuously above her head as if about to dance a *pas de deux*, but simply let her sole piece of clothing fall to her feet.

A full minute later Ivansong made his first movement, as if someone had snapped their fingers in his face. He started to breathe again. From this beginning, he progressed rapidly, tearing off his clothes like a star late for an opening performance, walking towards the vision in the middle of the room, and taking it gently but along all its length in a first, slow embrace. The silent orchestra struck up. The ballet opened.

'Now you are not to do more than too much,' whispered the goddess, as they rolled softly on to the bed, and stretched out tautly against each other.

'But this game is for adults of all ages,' protested Ivansong. 'Anyway you should be on my right, and I want to feel those old China hands of yours creeping. . .'

'All in good time,' murmured the goddess. 'Only contempt breeds familiarity.'

'On the contrary, it's simply a question of learning to grow bold gracefully,' hissed Ivansong. 'No, look, you're starting wrong. You should be crossing your thigh – no, the other one – that's it – you know, I think perhaps we should have had an undress rehearsal for this.'

'Do you suppose we are on camera?'

'Of course, now for the second take, you have to get your feet – here –'

'Look out, you're slipping.'

'No, it's all right, something got caught for a second – get your legs over my shoulder. There. No, no, *both* shoulders, you nut.'

'But that isn't right, Larry. At this point my *right* leg should be down around your *left* thigh, and we should be sideways to each other.'

'Nonsense! Both your ankles should now be –'

'Shush, you're making too much noise. Oh God, my feet are all thumbs.'

'It's all right, we made it. Now, raise your legs high in the – no, watch it, you'll have me on the floor. That's better. Better. But what are you doing now? You know the next part, the Half-Pressed Position, you have to keep one leg straight out and bend the other back against your chest, and then move into the Bamboo Cleft.'

'What bamboo cleft? No, what we do now is I roll on to my stomach and put my hands against the. . .'

'Rubbish, you've got it all wrong. You want the *right* leg horizontally out wide, and the left foot on my – no, you, you . . . on my *shoulder*, that's it. Now you know the next bit, the Nail.'

'The nail?' queried the goddess, by now distinctly worried. 'You mean the finger nail.'

'No, don't do that, for Heaven's sake. For the Nail you move your *left* foot from my shoulder, keeping your right leg out horizontally, and put it on my head.'

'*On your head?*'

'On my head,' repeated the vexed Ivansong in a fierce whisper, 'can't you remember anything? And for Heaven's sake don't laugh, because that can get us nowhere fast. Now, next you bring both legs down and cross the thighs – what's the matter? You seem to be losing your grip completely. That's better – and just about in time. Now get both legs – yes, that's it. Christ, don't do that, you'll rupture both of us.'

'I like this one,' the goddess murmured contentedly in his ear a little later, 'it really feels like naked aggression. What do they call it?'

'Don't you remember? It's the Revolving Position. But we can't stop here, we forgot the Crab.'

'The Crab?' Ivansong felt the goddess tensing.

'Yes, we'll have to go back,' he said softly. 'Now get your legs off me, move them round gently, one by one – that's it, that's it – and leaving everything otherwise *exactly* where it is, slowly tuck your feet into your stomach'

'Tuck my feet into my *stomach*?' queried the astonished goddess with a sudden convulsive giggle

'Oh, Hell, now you've done it,' moaned Ivansong. 'Cut.'

Fretfully he declined the kiss of life and lay beside her, panting. 'Look,' he whispered with biting patience, 'let's at least get the next part right. What's the matter with us, anyway? Heaven knows what Vatsayana would have said if he had seen that performance.'

'Who's Vatsayana?' asked the goddess timidly.

'The chap who wrote the *Kama Sutra*.'

'O, no,' contradicted the goddess gently. 'That was a Mr. Malla. He's got his name on the cover of my copy of the book.'

'Kalyana Malla wrote a manual of love called the *Ananga Ranga*, not the *Kama Sutra*,' hissed the exasperated Ivansong, and then stopped dead. There was a moment of stifling silence. 'Oh, no. Oh, no. You *didn't* buy the *Ananga Ranga* in Chinese by mistake? You haven't been going according to . . . while I've been faithfully following the *Kam. . .*' his voice trailed off, and she turned an enchanting posterior towards him and buried her face in a pillow.

'Have we got much more to do?' she asked a little later.

'No, it's not a question of *Da Capo*. We've broken the back of it,' whispered Ivansong. 'Now all you do is follow my lead, okay?'

'Okay.'

No wonder he had seemed so incomprehensible to her, rattling off instructions there like the caller in a square dance, thought Ivansong. . .

'What are you mumbling into the small of my back?' asked the goddess later still, as they successfully performed an intricate manoeuvre which Vatsayana had in fact recommended should first be tried in water. But as she turned to his lead, his rhythmic murmur took on meaning:

> Give a left-hand ride to that pretty little thing
> Balance in, balance out,
> Then do-si-do your honey right about

'Do-si-do your. . .' gasped the goddess. 'I will do-si-do you,' and she rolled over him choking with laughter and pulling him after her, until they both collapsed on to the sprung sheepskin rug beside the bed. 'Oh God,' she panted beneath him, her breasts heaving, 'the bed pushed us out, and I really cannot blame it.'

She stopped suddenly, and slipping off her mask, dropped it beside them. The bed now shielded them from the psychedelic display of the Hamsa Hilton, but by the glow of the concealed lighting in the bridal suite Ivansong saw the mischief in her eyes change slowly, liquidly, to a tender question. He felt her moving again under him as her lips parted softly and she whispered, 'Larry? Make love, not sex, yes?' The room was very still, transfixed in time.

'Once more, with feeling,' he agreed.

15

1

'Don't forget your interview with General Keo at ten-thirty, you red-headed temptress,' murmured Ivansong, bending over the bare shoulder of the somnolent Miss Flowerclass and kissing her warm cheek briefly. 'And I hope you realise that after last night you'll have to wear your dark wig for weeks if you want to become an honest woman again.'

'Not if I dye my own black hair black again,' replied Miss Flowerclass luxuriously. 'Just want to sleep a *little* longer, angel. They warned me Mekong was no picnic, but they never said it was going to be a honeymoon.'

Ivansong closed the door softly behind him, pulled down his crumpled jacket, ran a hand over the bristle on his face, and made for The Bitch, which started up perversely as soon as he turned the ignition key. He glanced across the river before pulling away. Under a glazed, ochrous sky the jagged cap of the Mayon on the summit of Mount Kham was ominously silent, for the rattle of the American choppers and the defiant roar of concerted fire from Chinese-made AK-47 automatic rifles had died with yet another military dream.

Matters stood much as Ambassador Eldritch had foreseen and the US Air Force general had implied. It was impossible for the helicopters to juggle their dangling supply slings down among the stone teeth of the landing zone quickly enough to avoid being shot up like captive kites at the end of their own wire hawsers. Deliveries had therefore stopped, and the dehydrated Marines were too short of ammunition to hit back at the enemy, even if their concern for the archaeological treasures around them had by now become somewhat blunted.

Laying smoke had proved costly and ineffective, and the unorthodox attempt to fly in supplies at night by the light of flares had led to the usual futile fumbling in the half-dark. A plan to plaster the belt of banyan between the Mayon and the ring of ruined monuments around the foot of Hill 520 with napalm or jelly was abandoned for fear of incinerating or suffocating the Marines just above it. And, after careful reflection, the President had declined to sanction saturation bombing of thirty-five square miles of the world's greatest architectural wonder in a neutral country against the wishes of its government and people. There was only one thing left: the Marines must break out.

Ivansong drove home thoughtfully through streets in which Mekinese troops were listlessly putting up new strong-points of sandbags and barbed wire. Mango and a smiling Ah King greeted him happily on the doorstep, and

Mini hooted defiantly from her perch on the jacaranda tree.

'Master get back safe,' beamed Ah King, 'what want blekfus?' These red barbarian whoremongers, they couldn't go five minutes without it, by all accounts. What filthy holes and corners had he been poking into during the blackout last night, the concupiscent turtle?

'Not too frightened when the lights went out?' asked Ivansong, bending down to take Mango in his arms.

'Pooh,' said Mango, 'why do you always forget I am six now, Daddy? Is it because I had a different mummy and daddy when I was born and so you didn't akshually see me come popping out? And when's mummy coming home?'

'Very soon, I hope,' replied Ivansong. 'I have a feeling we need her around here.'

He started a limping discussion with Ah King on the running of the household, but thought better of it when she indicated in her ataxic English that he should mind his own barbarian business and keep out of her kitchen. Feeling she might have been a little sharp with him, however, she went on to hint that they were glad to have him as the family rice-winner. 'You like do anything, you do anything,' she told him magnanimously, waddling about with a saucepan in her hand. 'You want eat, eat; you want drink, you drink, like our house really your house. We very happy you here.'

After breakfast he shaved and bathed and typed a story on the Kitay predicament, speculating that the Americans might try to replace this stubbornly anti-western usurper, and on the Mayon predicament, speculating that they might even bomb the complex of ruins that ringed Mount Kham in order to free the trapped Marines. He sighed. It was all so much guesswork. The truth always seemed just out of reach.

Ah King brought his coffee, but it gradually grew cold as he systematically slackened his body and mind where he sat, sending the waves of relaxation down from head to toe each time he breathed out, and feeling the knots twitch loose, the nerves unstring, and his face grow numb until he did not know whether his mouth was open or shut. It was as he reached that point where the whole being quite wrongly feels light enough to float off that a corner of the curtain parted.

Ten minutes later, he crossed into the bedroom-study of Thinking Lotus, rummaged in her pile of uncut Chinese newspapers, and finally found the despatch indicating that Chou En-lai had fallen to the fourth position in the politburo in Peking. Then he returned to his own room and looked through a file of Sissomak's last few pronouncements about China, ending with a verbatim account of his short statement at the airport before he left. In contrast to all its predecessors, this one made no mention of 'my good friend, Mr. Chou En-lai'. On the other hand, Sissomak had said that he wanted to consolidate the friendship 'between myself and the present and *future* leaders in Peking'. Speaking of his decision to go to China at that moment, he had added, 'Let us say it was written in the stars.'

Now, reasoned Ivansong, sitting back in his chair and putting his large sandalled feet on his desk, this could mean that Sissomak had been shown the press report and had gone to China because he feared that 'his good friend' the Chinese Premier was losing ground and that he had better start cultivating other leaders if he could. But 'it was written in the stars'. Sissomak had not moved on the evidence of a press-cutting. He had consulted the Paramahamsa Bonze. And the Bonze had advised him to go – perhaps even unconsciously reinforcing the reasons suggested by the news from Peking.

Or consciously? For there was something else to be considered.

Ivansong hit his furrowed forehead with the heel of his hand. Why had it not struck him before? He remembered being in Luang Prabang, the royal capital of Laos, when communist guerrillas had almost surrounded the city and could have seized it with a snap of the fingers. But they had not done so, for the body of the late king still awaited cremation in an urn filled with formaldehyde (some said mercurochrome) in the palace, and not even the Laotian communists dared rouse the *phis* guarding it by committing sacrilegious violence. The *phis* would disperse when the dead monarch was burned, and then – but not until then – everyone could relax and start fighting again.

Yet the devout Prince Kitay had dared to mount a double coup and to have Yaksha and his followers killed while the body of the Bonze-Superior lay pickled in a funerary urn awaiting incineration, and the *phis* protecting it were still earthbound. He could not possibly have risked the wrath of powerful spirits outraged by such impiety had he not been reassured by an equally powerful seer that all would be well. And that seer must have been the Paramahamsa Bonze, whose short list of clients was known to include the royal prince.

So what have we got, thought Ivansong? The Bonze may have been responsible both for sending Sissomak to Peking and for encouraging Kitay to seize power in his absence. But who in hell wanted Kitay? Except Kitay.

There was only one thing to be done. Ivansong passed his hands through his already rumpled hair, ran a cable form into his typewriter, and punched out with his two index fingers a service message to his office in London, asking for a summary of the life of Lincoln.

He then tucked his cables into the pocket of his blue and white Hawaii shirt and went out to the car. At Kitay's gate he dropped three letters which had been mistakenly delivered to him by the barefoot postman, and then drove on to the telegraph office. In the square outside, loudspeakers were announcing the execution of a mixed bag of suspected communist traitors and supporters of the renegade Yaksha, the dissolution of the Cabinet, and the imposition of the death sentence on anyone caught speculating in petrol or peddling rice coupons. The air itself was sullen, the faces around Ivansong morose.

'When I see a day like this in a country like this,' said Charlie Polak, clapping Ivansong on the shoulder, 'the first thing I do is to send my unnumbered millions out to a numbered account in Switzerland. Then I ask New York for more dough.'

'And what comes after that?' asked Ivansong, winking at Cat who stood beside the American.

'A drink, and lunch . Lesgo, keeds.'

Over lunch at the 'Taverne Font-le-Baume', Polak said: 'I was just telling Cat here about our little shindig with Pawkinson-Convoy last night . I'm still sorry I led you into it, Larry. No repercussions? He could order the whole embassy to boycott you, a son of a bitch like that.'

'He can't do anything,' replied Ivansong , shaking his head. 'He's the one who has to avoid unpleasant repercussions and bad publicity, not us. We gentlemen of the press create them. Remember?'

'Well, I'm glad to hear it,' remarked Polak, serving them all with wine. 'How's that swinging chick of yours? Now there's someone I really would like to show the shape of things to come. Okay, okay,' he smiled deeply, seeing the chilled expression on Ivansong's face, 'no hard feelings on my side if I can keep control of myself. I'll leave them all to you.'

'The thing about swinging Suzy Flowerclass,' said Ivansong, making up his mind, 'is that she does give me breathing space to get on with one or two little ideas that I never had time to get around to when I was here on my own for Worldover. As a matter of fact' – he pulled his chair closer to the table and cut into his escalope – 'I'd quite like to talk to you two about what's uppermost in my thoughts right now.'

'What's that?' asked Cat, cautiously.

'The Bonze.'

'*The* Bonze?'

'Yes. You see, the way I see it , he seems to be influencing affairs willy-nilly. Look. We know three things: he advised Sissomak to go to Peking in the first place. He is also consulted by Kitay. And Kitay took advantage of Sissomak's departure to seize power. See what I mean? Is it all coincidence? Or what?'

Polak whistled softly between his teeth and around a toothpick which he now pointed at Ivansong. 'But who would want that creep Kitay in power?' he objected. There was a pause while they examined this chicane. 'Still, I'm interested. Do you know that in 1964 the Pentagon made a special study entitled something like "Witchcraft, sorcery , magic and somethingortheother in the Congo and implications for military operations", more or less? Seems the mumbo-jumbo led to a lot of double-crossing between the Congolese government and the rebels. I remember it because Fulbright questioned the value of the report. What's your idea?'

'Only one. Get to see the Bonze ourselves. I know it's difficult, but I remember Cat saying the other night that there was some channel to him through the Rope Club. What do you say, Cat?'

Catullus Yip rubbed a hand across his meagre moustache. 'Well,' he began doubtfully. 'You know we've tried one ploy – okay if I tell him about it, Charlie?' Polak nodded and half closed his eyes to light a Camel with a book-match. 'We got to the bottom of the steps of that central tower where he lives in Nakhara Wat, and when those acolytes of his appeared, we offered them a straight bribe. Dough. Plenty of it. Cash in hand. And, dammit, they refused it and started to get pretty unpleasant and so we took off.'

'Which was funny, when you come to think of it,' interpolated Charlie, 'because if ever I saw a lousy bunch of crumbs that had fallen way down from the Master's table, they were it, despite their bald heads and yellow winding sheets and bare feet and the whole *stik*.'

'Anyway,' Cat shrugged, 'that was that. You don't have to worry about the Reds. They won't do anything to stop you, as far as we know. Your problem is with those pious little bastards.'

'Yeah, but Larry may have something. There's always a point at which the two great cultural influences of modern society – the groovy and the gravy – must meet. Maybe we were offering cash in the wrong quarter. Maybe we should try dealing with that Flakey guy in the Rope Club. He gets high on any garbage, but he's no monk. He's still in business, and there's only one kind of business in the world – money. What's he really like, Cat?'

'Oh-oh,' Cat raised a warning hand. 'He's split right down the middle, that one. He's for money, all right. That's one side of him. But the rest is way out. He can't stand squares, and in his book Woodstock was practically cubic. You proposition him, and as soon as he realises it's only a one-shot deal and he's not going to make real dough out of you, he'll throw you right out on your ear. In that world he walks, just two feet above the ground, we don't even exist except as unprocessed paychecks. He could get you to the Bonze all right. But why should he?'

They thought this over while the waiter brought the Camembert. 'How about this,' suggested Ivansong finally as Charlie Polak poked it with his finger. 'We can dress to impress. We haven't got the beards or the beads. But what about the patter?'

'You mean all that like-I-said-that's-the-whole-bit-man stuff?' Cat shook his head. 'He gets that from everyone in the Snake. That won't even get you into the Rope.'

'But supposing,' Ivansong was feeling his way, 'no, listen to this, supposing we made that all sound as square as Queen Victoria when unamused, like, like. . .'

'Like Eisenhower preaching a sermon on the falling domino theory as applied to sin?' threw in Polak dreamily. He thought about it for a little while. 'Cat, could you get us into the Rope? I mean, you kinda belong, don't you, even if you don't hang around there deep fried, southern style, and like Momma made you?

'Flakey is no mouse,' said Catullus Yip carefully, 'but maybe, if we took it slow.' So after the coffee arrived, they began to plot seriously.

2

The Rope was a combination of shrine and bar. The drinks were at one end, and a candlelit altar to Harihara, framed in gold and strewn with blossoms, was at the other. The air was drugged with incense and pot and the heavy perfume of wilting frangipani. Sweating profusely and straining his eyes in this dim, suffocating chamber, Charlie Polak saw that it was flanked by a row of curtained cubicles along one wall, and decorated with a mixture of Nakhara rubbings and mind-expanding daubs in fluorescent paints.

Flakey was a tall apparition in a yellow habit and fashionable accessories, including thonged sandals, a rosary of wooden beads, and a small carillon of cowbells hanging from a longer chain around his neck. Above this confection there rose incongruously a slightly decadent Greek head – a toque of curly blond hair, a high forehead, and a long face into which a lipless trap of a mouth had been cut.

'Whosis, Cat?' he asked at once with lazy menace in an almost imperceptibly sour Sydney accent, eyeing Polak up and down. 'Like the threads don't look that groupy, man, and we don't go for squares, not so's you'd notice.'

'Jackson,' said Polak to Flakey, his brow furrowed, 'I don't frisk all the kedgeree. Wherefore chant like a flamingo? I see you're on the swerve, okay, the ghetto reeks of candy, and you got the old roseola on your near fore,' he added, pointing to the puncture-marks on Flakey's left arm. 'So why all the *dragoon*?'

'How's that?' asked Flakey, his mouth falling open.

Cat explained gently. Polak was a cosmo. His friend was the same. Cat did not go for it himself.

'Who's the friend, friend?'

Cat told him. Could he come in too? Flakey's small lizard-eyes flickered with interest. 'What's this cosmo scene?' he asked cautiously.

'They'll tell you, I expect,' answered Cat, and seizing his cue went out to get Larry Ivansong.

'Trunk,' commented Ivansong, looking around disapprovingly and raising two hands in greeting to Flakey. 'Irreconcilably omphalic. This strip is stabbed full of lichen. You get the frowze on your canal?'

Flakey shook his head silently. Lichen? Frowze?

'Well, since I'm no phoenix for the helio – pulse, wheels and raffia, that's for me – so how about a murder ink on the stones?'

'Look, man,' protested Flakey, trying to assert himself, 'like I don't know what your hang-up is, but this is no love-in for freak-outs. We can switch you on, as you're friends of Cat, but like I don't dig you, see, and until I do you don't get with the action, and that's the whole bit.'

'Blasco,' Polak told him compassionately, 'since you are all strata and we never dragged the old knee, so it's hard for us to lash. "Hang-up, love-in, freak-out? Switch on, dig, action? Whole bit?" Given that's strictly from spats, and tags you off. As the circus is full of jacaranda, each one doing his that, and either you're gasman or idiom. And, Jackson, you're as gasman as a cummerbund, a real *dragoon*, despite the high hush and the ivy.'

'Peel it twice,' agreed Ivansong a little maliciously. 'As he muffs me frugal. The murder ink, Jackson. And Polak wants a gettysburger. No sesame.'

It turned out that Flakey disposed neither of Kaoliang rice wine drained from marinated squid nor fresh minced ant's egg that day, but he warmed to his two new acquaintances out of sheer curiosity.

'The cosmo is a devotee of *advaita*, of course,' explained Polak kindly. 'And now I'll try and put this in plain old-fashioned language for you: the basic principle can be seen in those trick pictures which change according to the way you tip them or alter your own position.'

'Your Snake and Rope image is all macassar – sorry, kind of off-beam and square,' took over Ivansong, eyes scintillating. 'A cosmo adjusts both himself and the Illusion until he perceives Reality, just as a man manoeuvres his head and the painting he holds in his hands until he sees it in the right light. But of course it's the light that really does the manoeuvring, not the man or the painting.

'Lichen, swerve, candy, zest, they can help you get in position, do your that. So can raffia – you got any girls here? – or mink and ivy for the boys with cottage feet. But to get down to the nitti-*vritti*, you can know without any of that, like when you're saddled.'

'Saddled?'

'Yeah,' cut in Polak, 'working, pregnant, got to keep upright. But you do your own wield and yield here, huh? You're what you'd call the boss-man in your quaint archaic way?'

Flakey nodded.

Polak leaned over the bar. 'So how would you be interested in a little freight for the void?'

'Freight?'

'Yeah, protein. For doing nothing. What did they used to call it? Bread, you know, dough.'

It was like fighting a guerrilla war, for Flakey swerved and eluded every time they tried to ambush him and pin him down to a promise. In the end he said:

'Look, like I told you, the Bonze is something else. For a slice of the bread and your pledge' – he looked a little sheepish here – 'to come back and shoot me that cosmo vocabulary of yours and the rest of the jazz, I'll send you with a guide, but it's on the understanding, man, that you're not looking for any cutprice forecasts. You just want to talk cosmos with him. And there's no guarantee at al the guide can get you through. Okay? I still say you ought to let him try and fix an appointment.'

'No deal,' said Cat, 'since we're saddled, see? We may be shoved off to Vietnam or Indonesia or Tokyo tomorrow.'

Flakey went out to the back of the barn-like 'Bogus Snake' and after five minutes reappeared with a dignified young Mekinese monk in saffron robe and sandals. Cat returned to Nava, but by four-thirty Polak and Ivansong and the monk, who was carrying a wickerwork suitcase, were walking through the empty outer courts of Nakhara Wat in semi-darkness and a silence broken only by warning bird-calls, for a tall thunder-head of monsoon cloud dominated a scowling sky and all was still on Mount Kham to their east.

'Five more minutes with that damned cosmic lingo,' murmured Ivansong, 'and I would have given out.'

'You're so right,' agreed Charlie Polak softly, throwing away a cigarette butt, 'it was beginning to wear thin as the skin on an applestrudel already. I've never sweated so much in a bad cause in my life. Like what did you do in the Great War, daddyo?'

'Paid my taxes,' answered Ivansong, 'which is what we are

going to do now.' He called to the monk to stop, and then gestured to him to come with them behind a crumbling stone lion, covered with lichen and small, agile lizards. The monk looked at them doubtfully for a moment, but complied.

'We want you,' said Ivansong slowly, 'to take us straight up the steps of the Paramahamsa Bonze. We do not want you to make us wait at the bottom with his guardians while you go up first.'

'What is difference?' asked the monk suspiciously in brittle English.

'This,' answered Ivansong, and held up a wad of American ten-dollar notes, fastened with a rubber band.

'Monk may not touch money,' observed the monk severely, turning his bald head away.

'And he shall not,' retorted Ivansong, bringing from behind his back a muslin bag, begged from the kitchens of the 'Taverne Font-le-Baume'. Placing the bills inside it and pulling the strings tight, he looped them over one finger, and held the pouch up to the monk. 'Well?'

The monk looked from one to the other, smiled slightly, and sliding his own index finger through the strings, took it with a small bow.

3

At the foot of the great, blocked-out steps that led up to the highest tower of the temple-tomb they were stopped by the three guardians of the Paramahamsa Bonze, but after the guide had spoken a few words to these and given each one a nondescript paper packet which he took from his wicker suitcase, they were allowed to pass.

Polak and Ivansong struggled up after the trailing hem and the dusty sandalled feet of the monk, until, breathless and soaked in perspiration, they reached the platform before the entrance to the tower. The Paramahamsa Bonze sat cross-legged just inside the archway to his small antechamber, gazing blindly out over the pewter waters of the Mekong, his heavy-lidded eyes wide open, his small lips pursed, his head illuminated in the ominous unnatural dusk by the unseen fluorescent light above him.

'What is the meaning of this intrusion?' he asked quietly, as the young monk put his hands together in greeting, bowed low, sank to his knees, and kissed his feet.

'Flakey send them,' said the monk, nervously. 'They are disciples, but new sect. They wish to learn from lips of most venerable Paramahamsa Bonze if they in error, or in right Way.'

Polak and Ivansong bowed and placed their hands together in greeting, gazing in astonishment at the legendary moon-faced guru with the great pendulous ears of Buddha which alone had marked him for many as an avatar, a heavenly incarnation to be reverenced across six countries. He had spoken English in the plummy accents of a stage-butler.

Ivansong added quickly: 'We seek your wisdom, great teacher, for the march of science and of modern medicine challenges our belief, and we would know whether indeed we possess the truth that is diamond' – he paused for a second – 'or only the illusion that is silica,' and he looked earnestly into the limpid eyes of the Bonze.

The eyes narrowed and clouded, and the Bonze said: 'I see,' in a matter-of-fact voice.

'I also, happily' answered Ivansong, a smile cutting painfully into his thin face.

There was a long silence, during which no one moved. Then the Bonze heaved himself to his bare feet. 'Come,' he said, with a sigh, and rolled his huge figure through the anteroom and into a big stone-walled chamber beyond. Polak and Ivansong followed, leaving the young monk outside.

A row of open embrasures gave on to a steep fall down the south side of the man-made pyramid, but the grey light these now admitted was supplemented by fluorescent strips around the high walls, which were covered with thick Mekinese tapestry representing the splendours of Nakhara. A large teak bed with a deep Slumbapillo mattress like a somnifacient club sandwich had been set up in one alcove, while others

10

contained respectively a small refectory table and chairs, a candle-lit altar, a kerosene refrigerator, and two sleek little Mekinese girls sitting side by side on a bench, dressed in high-necked silk blouses, embroidered sarongs, and small golden sandals. The chamber was carpeted with native rugs, and carved red and gold cupboards and chests stood against the walls, but the low tables and tabourets of oriental taste in the middle of the floor were interspersed with comfortable rattan chairs more lenient to the tender Caucasian haunch.

The Bonze subsided with a sigh into one of these, waving his guests to two others, and then clapped his hands. 'Tell you what, my dear,' he said fondly to one of the girls who sidled up to him. 'Let's have a bottle of the Laurent Perrier Cuvée Rose Brut and a few smoked-salmon sandwiches. Not too heavy with the lime and black pepper, now, and see the bubbly is well chilled. Remember what I said last time, eh?' and he patted her avuncularly on her small but noticeable bottom.

Ivansong and Polak looked at each other like men peering through a sandstorm. 'For an ascetic,' began Polak tentatively, 'I would have said you did yourself rather well. How do you square all this'– he waved his hand around hesitantly – 'with the holy role of the Paramahamsa Bonze?'

'Without any difficulty at all, my son,' replied the Bonze heartily smacking his small red lips. 'And it is quite evident to me that your religious education has been sadly neglected for you to ask such a question. Let me enlighten you. First, take the title by which I am known. The Paramahamsa is a supremely sacred goose that can drink the milk out of a mixture of milk and water and leave the water behind. In other words, it can immerse itself in the impure material world of illusion, yet come out of it only with the pure essence of heavenly truth.

'Now the Lord Buddha condemned over-indulgence in discipline and asceticism as misguided, for he himself only found enlightenment after he had ceased his long stint of self-denial and had eaten his first square meal. One such as I therefore finds that his way to Nirvana may lie in accepting the world instead of renouncing it, by learning at first hand what is the illusion to be rejected and to salve from it only the spotless reality, as the Paramahamsa salves the milk. Talking of which,' he added, swivelling his brown eyes and great flapping earlobes around in a quest for service, 'where's that pink champagne?'

There was a puny explosion from behind a door at the back of the chamber, and soon one of the Bonze's little attendants came undulating across the floor with a tray containing a foaming bottle and three glasses. The Bonze poured a little, tasted it delicately, his little finger extended, pouted, nodded, and served the other two. The second girl brought a plateful of open smoked-salmon sandwiches and handed them around with a fixed smile on her ivory face.

'But where does all this come from?' enquired Polak, 'if I may ask, that is.'

'From friends, from disciples, from the grateful who have found my advice sound, from a devout populace.'

'And all channelled through Flakey,' added Ivansong, comfortingly, stretching out his legs and regarding one dusty black sandal critically.

'Indeed,' intoned the Bonze, his lids half-lowered as he gazed at Ivansong. 'All who look after my simple needs or those of any other monk earn merit in Heaven. I therefore cannot refuse to take what they offer without depriving them, whether we speak of fine princes or friend Flakey. And remember this: the Cosmos is one, and the unifying factor is the all-pervasive essence some call God. God, therefore, is in all men. Buddha is within us. So if we reject the material temptations of the world in a deliberate attempt to *become* Buddha, my sons, we are simply denying that we are Buddha already. What's more, we are selfishly trying to better ourselves as individuals and so yielding to the pernicious illusion that the ego exists. Finally, striving is prompted by greed and ambition, which is wholly worldly. To struggle to gain Nirvana, therefore, is to lose it, for to strive for goodness is no more holy an undertaking than to strive for riches.'

The Bonze drained his glass, bit into a salmon sandwich, and said a little indistinctly through the bread: 'And there is another point. Self-denial creates undesirable urges and frustrations. It is surfeit that brings equilibrium, self-control, and the ability to open the mind to higher matters.'

'Didn't I read that in the Paramatta Sutra?' asked Ivansong.

'You may have, my son, you may have,' agreed the Bonze with a slight monastic belch, pouring himself more champagne. 'The Japanese Mahayana scholar-priests cultivate wine, women, song and good food in suitable quantities. They know that we must above all desist from an orgy of self-abnegation,' and he began refilling their glasses. There was a reverential pause while the others digested this already predigested meal, like two profane goslings being fed by a sacred goose.

'You mentioned the wonders of science and medicine, my son,' observed the Bonze, suddenly, turning his brown eyes appraisingly, almost coldly, on Ivansong.

'We are worried,' replied Ivansong slowly, 'because we cannot decide whether they must be counted among the things that take us nearer to Nirvana, or that hold us to this world.'

The Bonze gave Ivansong a long searching look, heaved a fat sigh, resettled himself in his chair, and called one of the girls to recharge their glasses. 'The matter is quite clear,' he said in his fruity way. 'These wonders of medicine must be embraced. There must be no futile renunciation. Let me tell you a little story.' He took a sip of champagne and put a plump bare arm around the minuscule waist of one of the girls. 'I had this – this colleague, so to speak, in West New Guinea – Indonesian West Irian. He was not only a social worker with some knowledge of medicine, but a man of great holiness, a Rumanian, or it might have been a Czech, converted to Hinduism. He conceived it his duty to do something for the wretched stone-age natives they have in those benighted hills down there, and he set off with his own money and some funds he got from a foundation somewhere to live among these people, doctor them, bring them the blessings of hygiene, teach them to count and read and suchlike.

'Well, it seems he settled in one particularly remote and

impoverished village and for a while all went smoothly.'
The Bonze took another sip and gave the girl a little squeeze.
'But then his conscience began to prick him, because they
were all so poor and sick. So he started to give things away –
his tents and camp kit, his cans of food and water-purifier,
his supplies of cloth, and then his sewing-machine, his tools
and medicines and medical instruments, then his bedroll and
his canvas boots and mosquito netting, his books and his
patience cards and transistor radio, and finally he handed
around his socks and underwear, sacrificed his last shirts, his
brush and comb and toothbrush, until he had nothing but a
pair of faded jeans, and these he traded for a coarse bit of
native cloth just to put around his poor old loins, so to speak.'

'Jesus, they must have worshipped that guy,' remarked
Polak, impressed in spite of his thirty-seven years on the
greatest jungle survival course of all.

'But he couldn't do anything more for them,' objected
Ivansong, 'and he had nothing more to give.'

'Oh yes, he had,' contradicted the Bonze lifting his finger
warningly, 'one thing. And they took it.'

'Took it? You mean his loin cloth?'

'Loin cloth?' The Bonze laughed derisively. 'No, not his
loin cloth. His body, of course. They ate him, son, they ate
him, bones and all.'

Ten minutes later Charlie Polak asked, 'But if you indulge
the physical senses, like you imply, how come you can
prophesy so accurately, as everyone says you can. Doesn't
that need some kinds of disciplinary exercises, meditation,
and all this stuff?'

'Of course, my boy,' answered the Bonze. 'Glimpses of
eternity come only from prolonged contemplation. You would
hardly expect me to foretell the future on a bottle of champagne. But as I sat in the lotus position before you arrived,
the spirit of that which is to come did move me.' He stopped
abruptly, and they were silent.

'What was it?' Ivansong asked at last.

The Bonze looked out of the embrasures and over the
darkening river, and their eyes followed. The first lights were

on in Nava, including a flashing neon sign that Ivansong knew read 'Hamsa Hilton', and his heart beat a little faster. Lightning flickered, but no rain fell.

'A new threat hangs over this sad land,' the Bonze almost sang in soft tones. 'Pale and deceitful men with smooth tongues and sly means seek to take from Mekong her one jewel in the waters. If they succeed, death and disaster will overwhelm her.'

There was another short silence. 'I don't get it,' said Charlie Polak.

'You will, you will,' said the Bonze, but when pressed further and asked for his life story he only yawned prodigiously. Finally, they rose to go.

'In these dangerous times,' Ivansong remarked to the Bonze carefully and distinctly, 'you would surely do well to remain here, where you are safe, I should think.'

The Bonze looked at him without expression. 'Just so,' he replied evenly. 'I shall be here. But should you speak or write ill of me, you will not get beyond the foot of my steps again.'

'I don't get it,' repeated Charlie Polak, shaking his head, as they crossed the courts of Nakhara Wat on their way towards the landing stage beyond, and the first heavy drop of rain burst on the back of Ivansong's hand. 'Why in hell did he ever let us into that inner sanctum of his with the booze and the gladioli and the rest of the orgy? He could easily have yakked away at us outside, assuming he wanted to talk at all. The world thinks he's an ascetic, and he shows us the whole goddamned bordello. It just beats me.'

'Well,' replied Larry, 'for one thing he answered that in philosophical terms, didn't he? To know white, you have to know black, and all that argument? For another, no one can deny his weird ability to foretell the future. It's been proved over and over again. And then we may think he ought to be an ascetic, but the ordinary people around here don't necessarily. He's the Bonze with the big Buddha-ears. He's a holy man and so he's expected to do everything in a special way, not to behave like an ordinary mortal.'

Charlie shook his head as they stood on the jetty. 'For Mrs.

Polak's little problem child, it still does not square. What's this stuff about someone stealing Mekong's jewel, anyway?'

'I don't know what that meant either.' Ivansong bit his lip, feeling guilty. But he resisted the temptation to tell Polak why the Bonze had admitted them to his inner chamber so readily. His first reference to the wonders of modern medicine and the difficulty of distinguishing between the diamond of truth and the silica of illusion had opened the door. For at that moment the Bonze knew that Ivansong knew that the famous Buddha-ears were a fraud.

16

I

When Ivansong drove home from the bridal suite two mornings later, he found two cables from his London office waiting for him, one asking for a quick seven-hundred-word profile of General Keo, and the other summarising articles on Lincoln published in *The Times* of 3rd March, 1926, and 11th October, 1943. There was also a letter from the Mekinese Ministry of Agriculture instructing him to register the household for rice-rationing at temporary hutments set up in the grounds of police headquarters.

Ivansong shouted for breakfast, tore off his clothes, and plunged into the bathroom. But he was not quick enough. As he finished shaving and was about to climb into a cold tub, the telephone rang and he sat down resignedly on the lid of the lavatory.

'Mr. Ivansong? Oh, this is Voitures d'occasion Nava. That green Citroen Quinze you were interested in, the 1951 model, the owner will be here at eleven-thirty to demonstrate it and discuss terms personally if you decide to buy. We shall merely take our commission. Will that be convenient?'

'Well, it'll have to be, won't it?' replied Ivansong.

'That's right,' agreed the voice cheerfully, and rang off.

There was a long queue at the rice-registration counter, and Ivansong could only edge forward, towering over the diminutive Mekinese around him and fuming impotently in the unrelenting sun. The mood in Nava was sulky. Kitay was hitting out with nervous brutality at every shadow of opposition, for Radio Peking had claimed that Sissomak was already back in Mekong and operating from headquarters in a 'liberated area'. At last he was given his cards, and, pushing them into a pocket of his bush-shirt, made for the used car market on the opposite side of Boulevard Siho and next to the blackened skeleton of the Thai embassy.

The market was divided into two halves. One side was a boneyard of expired wrecks, sad crocks of automobiles that had once throbbed with life but now lay broken, deflated and still. On the other, glossy panels and gleaming chrome reflected a hundred blinding suns from the blue sky above, for here serried ranks of proud and polished roadsters stood poised upon white-walled tyres.

Every now and then a group of mechanics, cigarettes drooping from their lips, would drag one of the senile wrecks into a workshop at the end of the firebreak that divided the quick from the dead, and in time she would emerge, speedometer rejuvenated, paintwork tarted up, and all that remained for the market manager to do was to put a price on her – 'modèle de luxe: 100,000 piastres' – and have her wheeled over to the lines of the living.

As Ivansong parked The Bitch on the side of the damned, and strode towards the little box of an office that stood among the saved, he saw Flodden immobile beside a sagging but game Renault and knew that Greeen had already arrived, for it was five minutes after 9.30. Tall, his body falling to his feet like a carefully ruled rectangle from the straight, immovable shoulders, Greeen's wooden-faced myrmidon gave no sign of recognition. As far as Ivansong could remember, he never had, and he only seemed to open his pouting, petal-like lips when his master asked him a question. Why did he still carry an old World War Two Luger? 'I sort of like the balance, kindastyle,' he had explained briefly to Greeen.

When not wanted he stayed in his room and read thrillers with a puzzled look in his close-set eyes, or listened to Bartok or Schönberg on his stereo, lying fully dressed on his bed with his feet crossed, his huge fingers intertwined on his chest. At one time Ivansong had suspected a nameless relationship between Greeen and his shadow, but he had discovered that every Saturday night at ten Flodden would set off for the nearest brothel, where the girls would receive him with a mixture of fear and lust that had its own curious scent.

'Well, there she is,' said Greeen, coming on Ivansong suddenly from behind the office. 'Isn't she a gorgeous creature? And goes like a bomb, you know. Very little on the clock, too.'

'What the hell has the clock got to do with it?' asked Ivansong, 'and why can't we meet openly?' he went on as they walked among the silent cars to look at the Citroen. 'After all, you've blown me to the Chinese.'

'And they'll keep it to themselves, I am sure. Not always tasteful in their techniques, but sound in their security,' Greeen remarked approvingly. 'It's the Americans and above all the French that we have to worry about. In this game God may protect you from your enemies, but you have to save yourself from your friends. We can meet socially, but plotting, like sex, is still cosier in private. The ambassador doesn't seem to like you much these days,' he added with a long amphibian smirk.

Ivansong ignored this and put his hand on the bonnet. 'You warmed her up, you bastard. You'd know I'd want to start her from cold. No approach from the Chinese yet, by the way.' He opened up the engine and banged his fist against the radiator. There was a faint tinkle. 'Rust,' he commented accusingly, 'rust like rats in the rafters.'

'Not yet?' queried Greeen, startled. 'But you had your

screen test three nights ago. What the hell does Max think he's doing? Why hasn't he got moving? Now, come on, don't start taking off the distributor cap, fair's fair, after all.'

Ivansong turned back from the engine to look at him, his mind temporarily dazed by a sudden flash of insight. 'I see,' he said slowly, 'so Max was not duped into setting me up after all, was he? You actually fixed everything with him in advance, didn't you? And he was knowingly working for you as well as for the Chinese all the time.'

'Natch,' replied Greeen, looking like a surprised satyr. 'Rather neat, don't you think? Max and you are two halves of a DA operation – your half on our side, his half on theirs – and, as every funfair con man knows, two heads are better than one every time when they're on the same phoney coin.'

'Well, why the devil didn't you let me in on it?' asked Ivansong angrily. 'How do you come to tell him about me, but not me about him? And if he's a double agent between you and the Chinese, why didn't you use him in the first place for the whole penetration operation? Why bring me in at all?'

'Peevishness will get you nowhere,' admonished Greeen. 'I'll switch her on and you can see how she ticks over. Lovely, isn't she?' They listened together for a moment in silence. 'Look, Max is the wash-and-wear type. When it comes to sentimental loyalties he goes in for those non-returnable paper hearts. You can't count on him. We know he works for the Chinese and ourselves. But for who else besides? And paradoxically the other objection is that at the same time he actually has a code of honour. Unlike us, men with no allegiances need one. He agrees to infiltrate you into the Te Wu for us, and he agrees to trick you into the hands of the Te Wu for the Chinese. Fair exchange, and just depends how you word it. But he won't cheat the Chinese by giving us information on Te Wu operations, or how could we trust him not to give them information about ours? That's going to be your business. He has his limits, so we have ours. We never told him you knew you were going to be photographed and framed. He thinks it's all going to come to you as a nice surprise.

'Wake up, Ivansong. Can't you see that you could both only be relied upon to play it straight if you didn't know everything about each other? As soon as you get a security short-circuit and double agents giggling among themselves, someone is bound to give the game away, and Max is not the only Chinese spook in the field.'

'Why tell me now, then?'

'Makes it easier for you to submit to blackmail from Max if you know he's in fact acting for us. What are you staring so closely at that door for? It's all good cellulose paint. Don't kick it, for God's sake, man.'

'Yes, a respray job. The panel's been beaten out here and there's fresh welding. What ran into it, a tank-transporter? Here, have a look at this.' He slipped Greeen the Chinese newspaper cutting about Chou En-lai's demotion in Peking.

'Bingo,' commented Greeen quietly, and turned towards Ivansong, faint interest dawning in the long sleepy eyes. 'You know, I'm beginning to think that one of these days you'll very nearly pass muster. What put you on to this?'

'I'll tell you when you tell me why you care.'

'How *devious* you are,' sighed Greeen, 'but, all right, the fact is that the boffins in London think this may be a Haiching caper.'

'Who or what are the Haiching?'

'The HCKC, of course, the Haiwai Chingpao Kungying Chu.* Who else?'

'Overseas Intelligence Supply Agency? What do they do?'

'You don't know? What do they teach you back at the schools these days? The Haiching is a disinformation department of the Te Wu in Peking specifically responsible for misleading Chinawatchers. They are the jokers who put out fake photos, juggle with orders of precedence when listing the names of communist leaders, start rumours about shifts in power, nuclear development, Sino-Soviet bickering, anything you like. They've had the pekinologists declaring Mao dead, blind, gaga, a victim of Parkinson's Disease, and replaced by ninety-nine doubles. Would you like to give her a run?'

* Not to be confused with the Haiwai Tiaocha Pu, of course.

'But why does London suspect that this news about Chou En-lai may be their dirty work?' asked Ivansong with growing excitement as they eased out on to Siho and headed for Highway Thirty.

Greeen shrugged. 'It's too sudden and it doesn't fit what are laughingly known as the established facts about the Chinese power structure.'

'Then it could be a trick to lure Sissomak away from Mekong and into Communist China?'

'My dear Ivansong,' Greeen held up his hands in mock horror, 'your fantasies are between you and your psychiatrist. Where on earth would that get us or anyone else?'

'It gets us,' replied Ivansong, suddenly taking the Citroen up to eight kilometres an hour, 'to the Paramahamsa Bonze.' As he began to tell Greeen of his doubts and of his meeting with the piously self-indulgent swami, he applied the brakes, and after sidling for thirty-five yards along the highway, the car came gently to rest. They were on a quiet stretch of road, overlooked only by two or three mop-headed sugar palms that vaguely reminded Ivansong of Miss Flowerclass with her wig on at the party on the Fourth of July. He took a chance and switched off the ignition.

'Look, dear boy, I'm not a superstitious man myself,' said Greeen. 'I always cut out "What the Stars Foretell", but only to enjoy reading it one week later. However, the Bonze is a holy man with undeniable clairvoyant powers, and the integrity of a guru of his standing can hardly be questioned, even if he did advise Sissomak to go to Peking.'

'Well, now you do the looking,' retorted Ivansong, and produced the cable from his London office about Lincoln. 'This is the sort of thing I have in mind.' Greeen took the cable, which read after a short preamble:

IGNAZ TREBITSCH OTHERWISE IGNATIUS TIMOTHY LINCOLN BORN HUNGARY 1879 OF DEVOUT JEWISH FAMILY STOLE SISTERS GOLD WATCH TO FINANCE TRIP TO ENGLAND AT EIGHTEEN CONVERTED TO CCC OF EEE AND BECAME CURATE APPLEDORE KENT STOP LATER LEFT CHURCH TO WORK FOR SEEBOHM

ROWNTREE CHOCOLATE KING AND AT THIRTY WAS ELECTED LIBERAL MMMPPP FOR DARLINGTON STOP SPECULATED HEAVILY BORROWED TENTHOUSAND POUNDS FROM ROWNTREE BUT WENT BROKE STOP IN NINETEENFIFTEEN ATTEMPTED EXTORT MONEY FROM ADMIRALTY FOR DUBIOUS ESPIONAGE EXPLOITS BUT CAME UNDER SUSPICION HIMSELF AND FLED TO AMERICA WHERE TRIED GET HIMSELF RECRUITED BY GERMAN SECRET SERVICE STOP WAS EXTRADITED ON CHARGES OF FORGERY AND ENDED WAR IN PARK-HURST PRISON STOP DENATURALISED 1918 EXTRADITED FROM BRITAIN AS UNDESIRABLE ALIEN AND WORKED IN EUROPE AS SPY FIXER PEDDLER OF SECRET DOCUMENTS ETC BEFORE FLEEING CHINA STOP CONVERTED TO BUDDHISM BECAME BUDDHIST MONK CEYLON AND TRIED LAND LIVERPOOL 1934 AS QUOTE ABBOTT CHAO KUNG RPT CHAO KUNG UNQUOTE STOP WAS ARRESTED AND DEPORTED CHINA STOP DURING SINOJAPANESE WAR REPORTEDLY DIRECTED JAPANESE FIFTH COLUMNISTS IN TIBET STOP DIED SHANGHAI NINTH OCTOBER 1948 PARA OF BUDDHIST PERIOD TIMES THIRD MARCH 1926 SAYS LINCOLN UNDER FALSE NAME TANDLER STAYING SMALL BUDDHIST MONASTERY CEYLON LIVING SIMPLE LIFE IMPRESSING ALL WHO MEET HIM WITH GRASP PRINCIPLES BUDDHISM AND PALI LANGUAGE STOP HOPE THIS USEFUL BESTEST EDITOR

'Hmmm,' said Greeen thoughtfully, stroking the side of his face and then running his fingers over his sparse, sandy hair. 'Can't you see him in his saffron robe, holding them spellbound in Colombo? And you think we've got another like him on our hands?'

'Think? I know,' said Ivansong. He opened the bonnet, unscrewed the radiator cap to peer into the steam, and then glanced at the oil filler. 'Oil slick in the water, and smoke from the oil. This bloody thing has a cracked cylinder-head. A pretty pair you make, you and Trebitsch Lincoln.

'Now listen.' He leaned in through the window. 'The Paramahamsa Bonze drew on about five different schools of Hindu and Buddhist thought yesterday to produce a chop suey of an argument proving that the way to Enlightenment and Nirvana lay through pearly teeth and pink champagne,

But he took Parramatta for a Buddhist text when in reality it's a town in New South Wales. He used the typical ruse of the "negative example", beloved of Chinese communists as well as of hypocritical book censors who excuse themselves for reading what is deviationist or dirty by saying they have to study the bad in order to be able to recognise and reject it. And finally, those much-worshipped Buddha-ears of his are a swindle.'

'How on earth could you know that?'

'I spotted them. Take up plastic surgery as a way to a higher and nobler life, Greeen, you might find it rewarding too.'

'Ivansong, Ivansong. Hasn't it occurred to you that millions have reverenced those ears, great ministers have bowed before them –'

'Christ, great ministers will believe anything. Look Greeen, I know what I'm talking about. I'm a deuteranope dichromat. Just look at the play on this steering wheel. I ask you.'

'Deuteranope what?'

'Dichromat. I'm colour-blind. I was turned down for the Navy for it, which is why I'm in your mucky paws today.'

'Never mind the obsequious asides. If you're colour-blind, your sight is defective, and you can't see as well as other people. So how could you notice something that *normal* men have not?'

'Well in the first place,' replied Ivansong, 'a colour-blind man often has much keener vision than an *ordinary* specimen. He will see things from further away, and he can often detect camouflage. But that's not all.

'Have you ever been tested with an Ishihara Pseudo-chromatic Colour Chart? They're in book form, and on each page there's a multicoloured circle like a mosaic of tiny dots. But where you might see only a jumble of colours without any distinctive design to them, I might see the figure "45" standing out quite clearly. Why? Because I am red-green colour-blind, sensitive to red but weak on green. That means that I cannot easily tell two colours apart if the difference between them depends on the green component in one of them, the green light-waves. So my eyes may connect up what look to you like quite meaningless sets of dots of different hues because to me they've all got something in common – they all look reddish. And in that way I get a red "45" where you get nothing.

'Now most colour-blinds have a green-red problem,' Ivansong went on, as they headed back towards the town again. Blue colour-blinds are very rare –'

'My God, and I'm letting you drive me?'

'Women and children first. Don't panic. We go by the position of the lights, not the colours,' soothed Ivansong, as they roared through a red. 'Normally, I don't believe even I would have got on to the Bonze, and it's possible that many colour-blind people have been quite close to him and remarked nothing odd about him. I think what did it was the neon. You see, he was sitting cross-legged under this archway, with a light from a fluorescent fixture falling directly on to his head and face. No one with ordinary sight would have noticed anything strange, but for me the blue neon must have accentuated the smooth pink scars and I saw them as two darkish lines.'

Greeen was attentive now and did not even object when Ivansong pumped the accelerator, to be answered by a protesting thump from behind them.

'Transmission death-rattle,' murmured Ivansong shaking his head mournfully. 'Now, you know what those Buddha-ears are like. The top part of the ear is large but unremarkable – helix, tragus, antitragus normal, nothing specially hallowed up there. But the great, long lobes of the Buddha, that's where the godliness comes in. Well, the scars ran vertically down the side of his face, exactly opposite each lobe, and when I got a chance to look more carefully, I saw that there was a matching scar running down the inside edge of the hanging lobe itself. So you can see what was done. This man had what are technically known as descending lobes originally. His ears tapered down the side of the face and petered out without coming to a separated lump at the end. Many people –'

'Spare me the elementary police manual recognition data,' interrupted Greeen languidly, 'and mind that blasted dog.'

Ivansong spun the wheel, as if on a steam-yacht, and they

swerved slightly. 'This man had simply had that long section cut away from the side of the face to make a separate hanging lobe.'

'But it would have been little more than a pointed piece of skin,' objected Greeen.

'Exactly. So then they pumped in silicone – you know, the way they give fallen women back their three dimensions and transvestites a second cleavage – and after, say, three months, there you are. Our man from Nirvana.'

'What a vulgar, blasphemous swine you can be, to be sure,' purred Greeen, 'But I see now that your mention of the "illusion of silica" might well have distressed him. Well, this has been most entertaining, but everything palls after a while. Shall we get back to Voitures d'occasion Nava?'

'There's one thing more, though,' added Ivansong. 'He made a prophecy last night.'

'What was that?' Green yawned theatrically.

'It went like this,' Ivansong thought for a moment. ' "Pale and deceitful men with smooth tongues and sly means seek to take from Mekong her one jewel in the waters. If they succeed, death and disaster will overwhelm her." No idea what it means.'

'Haven't you, by God,' said Greeen softly, suddenly attentive again. 'Well, I suppose that's one thing to be thankful for in a merciless world. But this time you've convinced me that we must check on the holy joker. Let's have his description.' Ivansong gave it, and Greeen jotted it down without further comment.

When they reached the car market Greeen pointed silently to an empty space among the wrecks on the left, and Ivansong drove into it. Greeen got out carefully, surveyed the car from end to end, and using his handkerchief, wiped one of the zeroes from the price chalked on the windscreen.

'That's funny,' mused Ivansong, looking around, 'I could have sworn I left my – hey!' he shouted deafeningly, and set off down the lane that divided the buyers' and the sellers' market, 'that's my bloody car you've got there. What do you think you're doing?' He was just in time to rescue The

Bitch from pitiless men within the rehabilitation centre who were about to spray it sky blue. As he drove her slowly towards the entrance, he came upon Greeen and Flodden, who were standing silently side by side, watching him.

'Don't call me, I'll call you,' said Greeen.

Ivansong looked at him disdainfully.

'By the way,' asked Greeen smoothly, giving him a quick glimpse into the long, dangerous reef of odontorhyncous serrations behind the thin-cut sandwich of his lips. 'Why didn't you fall for the first girl Max threw at you?'

'She wasn't married,' replied Ivansong. 'I have my code of honour too, you know,' and drove off to lunch with Suzy Lee Flowerclass.

2

He found a slightly drawn Miss Flowerclass shaking extra tabasco into a large bloody mary at the bar of the 'Bodega', a small restaurant opposite the enclosure for the royal white elephants on the rue du Bassac which served Chinese Basque food. He sank into a chair beside her and ordered a whodunit.*

'I simply adore you when you look hot and sweaty and your hair falls all over the place, Mr. Ivansong darling,' she said, 'but now I know what goes into achieving that effect and, devastating though it is, I think I prefer to be lazy and cool.'

'You look quite stunning,' protested Ivansong, smiling into the unfathomable dark glasses and taking in the carefully arranged tangle of silver hair, the Aztec miniskirt and the golden limbs. 'Is everything moving along all right? I had a cable from the office this morning, by the way, and they want me to send them a short profile of Keo. How did you get on with him?'

'But, my dear, they're all the same, these people, and quite

---

* Equal parts of whisky, vodka and gin, a fresh lime, a few drops of angostura, and one dissolving Vitamin-C tablet. Ice and water to taste.

frankly I'm beginning to find it not only grim but positively exhausting. I'm on the run all day, and in more senses than one. They will try to fill me with propaganda and booze and then rape me, and it doesn't matter where the hell we happen to be. The last one was that *tatty* little Minister of Aviation, in a *helicopter*, if you please. And this afternoon I'm seeing the President of the Family Planning Association in a *houseboat*, of all things. I thought I was going to be safe with the colonel commanding the Women's Auxiliary Army, but she turned out to be a blasted dike.' She threw up her hands. 'Oh well, never mind my problems, sweetie. Let's order.'

'Don't worry,' Ivansong reassured her quietly. 'You have no appointments after today – none that I've fixed, that is – and you may be able to get away earlier than you think.' After lunch he dropped her at the Family Planning houseboat, waved crossed fingers at her as she reluctantly walked the plank that connected it to the quay, and drove slowly along the waterside towards home.

It was a clear afternoon, with a fresh breeze blowing. On a river of ruffled silk, two small boats appeared to have collided some distance off shore, and their respective occupants were gesticulating at each other. Ivansong noted with interest that one was Greeen, the other Max Alias. Well, thank Heaven for that, he thought, perhaps now we shall get some action. He called at the Ministry of Information to empty his press-box of government handouts, and went home to be subtly disagreeable about General Keo in seven hundred well-chosen words.

He had just finished typing his last take and was wondering whether to have a drink before going down to the cable office when he heard a bawdy ballad approaching:

> *Ah, ma mère, ne gueulez pas tant.*
> *Nous allons couper la bite au sergent!*
> *Mais avant de la lui couper,*
> *Nous allons la lui attacher. . .*

It stopped as Max came upon Mini at the foot of the

jacaranda, put down the three packages he was carrying, and took her gently in his arms. 'Alors, chérie, ça va toujours? Pas de cafard? Well, well, it won't last long now, and you can come back to Papa. Mango,' he called. 'Come out, come out, ma p'tite, I have something for you to dress up and pull to pieces.'

Mango, in workmanlike dungarees, arrived breathless from around the corner of the house, and Max pointed to the largest of the packages. 'As I am a very important type who cannot come creeping to your door at some satanic hour on the seventh day of the Feast of the Beasts to give you this,' he said, 'you will have to open it now.'

Mango tore away the wrapping and pulled out a life-size Kuddlytoy Silver Gibbon. Mango and the outraged Mini both hooted in unison, one with joy, the other with proprietorial fury, but Max kept a firm grip on his charge. 'You had better take it inside,' he urged Mango, 'Mini thinks it is trying to steal the house and garden.'

'Oh, thank you, thank you,' shouted Mango with eyes like black stars in a white sky. 'Come on, Mister Socrates,' she cried. Let's go upstairs.'

'Who's Socrates?' asked the bewildered Max.

'That's *his* name, silly,' laughed Mango, pointing at the less agitated of the two gibbons, and then disappeared indoors with it.

Max was calming Mini as Ivansong came out with his pocket transistor radio in his hand. 'Assez de ces histoires,' he was saying sternly. 'You have not been forgotten. If we give a Mini to Mango, what do we give to Mini, eh?' And lifting the paper bag that still remained on the ground, showed Mini the mangosteens within. The little gibbon seized the bag and was up in the jacaranda in four seconds. Max shrugged, and Ivansong led the way into the back garden where they settled down opposite each other, one to his soda-water, the other to his scotch. For a full minute Max Alias gazed at Ivansong expressionlessly from under half-lowered lids, and then flicked a large flat envelope across to him. 'You see, no one has been neglected,' he murmured with a soft smile.

Ivansong caught the envelope, but raised his hand in warning and switched on the radio. 'The news,' he said, and began leafing through the sheaf of photograph stills that he took from the envelope as the oleaginous voice of the announcer seeped out into the air.

'. . . The first phase of the programme for Land Restoration is now completed, 984,756 peasant smallholdings have so far been given back to the 545 proprietors who originally owned them, and the smallholders themselves have everywhere expressed their delight at this return to our traditional Mekinese system of benevolent landlords. It is in accordance with the same principle that His Royal Highness Prince Norivong Kitay has today confided monopolies for rice-rationing, petrol distribution, opium control, the gold trade and similar key activities to suitable nominees of his choice . . .'

Ivansong surreptitiously pinched his arm hard, and felt the blood drain satisfactorily from his face as he switched off the radio and looked silently and steadily at Max.

'How much?' he asked at last.

'Larry!' protested Max, spreading his hands beesechingly. 'What kind of a person do you think I am? I thought we were friends. And now this.' He shook his head sorrowfully and clasped his hands in front of him. 'I am shocked, mon vieux,' he said gazing blankly into Ivansong's angry eyebrows. 'Truly shocked. Money? It is an insult.'

'Then what's the point of this – this filth?' Ivansong barked at him, tapping the prints (some of which were really rather good, he remarked to himself). 'You'd better come out with it right away, because I've half a mind to chuck you and your dirty pictures into the swimming pool, you – you swine, you.' He started to rise to his feet.

God, what do I do next? he thought frantically, conscious that Max Alias was putting on the better performance of the two. I wish I'd studied the stage, like Lotus. What a bloody charade. Why hadn't Greeen told Max that he was in on the whole thing and expecting Max's approach? Or maybe he had? You never knew with Greeen.

Quel théâtre, Max was thinking. If only Greeen had brought

Larry into the plot we would not have to sit here behaving like a pair of amateur hams in a nineteenth-century melodrama. But perhaps Greeen had? Larry was acting so badly that Max suspected he knew exactly what it was all about. That *salaud* Greeen. The only consolation was that the shark-faced puppet-master himself was not sitting in the front row laughing his head off.

'Larry, Larry,' said Max, waving Ivansong back into his chair to his immense relief, 'I just want you to do me a small favour and meet a good friend of mine who wishes to ask you a few questions, maybe from time to time.'

'Oh, so that's it, is it, you lousy bastard?' retorted Ivansong loudly. 'You sit here drinking my – my soda-water and all the time you're a bloody nark for some stinking spy network, are you? Didn't anyone ever tell you that blackmail, especially this sort of obscene blackmail, is the most loathsome human activity after coprophagy?'

Merde, Ivansong, but you're overdoing it, thought Max. 'That is absolute nonsense,' he objected aloud, with a contemptuous shrug. 'The blackmailer himself is innocent. Blackmail is founded solely on the guilt of the one who is blackmailed.'

'You sound as if you've had some experience of this ugly game,' sneered Ivansong villainously, feeling unsure of his script.

'Certainly,' said Max Alias, 'and it takes all sorts, you see. Now you remember when President Sukarno paid an unofficial visit to Mekong – the last occasion, I mean? Well, he was not asked to stay in the state guest house that time because he had earlier shown a weakness for smuggling little bits and pieces in there after nightfall, and Sissomak was quite shocked. So we put him in the bridal suite at the hotel. He was, in fact, its first guest.'

'And you mean you –?'

'Naturally. Who would miss such an opportunity? Eh b'en, I took him the stills afterwards, just as I have brought some to you today. He was very affable and hospitable. He gave me coffee, and he spent a long time looking at the pictures. Then, exactly like you, he asked: "How much?" '

Max paused and sipped his soda-water, eyeing Ivansong with a sly smile on his face.

'I told him that they were not for sale, but that if he were prepared to negotiate certain matters with representatives of my clients in a friendly and favourable manner, the photographs would never be seen again.

'But you know, he looked at me in complete astonishment. "What are you talking about?" he cried, as if I were some sort of an imbecile. "Never be seen again? Then I shall certainly not negotiate with your clients. I ask you once more, how much, how much? I don't want to suppress them, you fool. I want to buy them for myself. Some of them – look at that, for example" – and I assure you I could see the complacency stealing over his fat face – "some of them are truly excellent, even artistic. I am a generous man. You can name your price." '

'And did you?'

Max Alias threw up his hands. 'There you are again with your disgusting innuendoes. Of course not. I gave them to him as a present. He was very touched, and within a few weeks my clients were able, in consequence, to do business with him. There is nothing like creating goodwill.'

Max paused. 'Now, Larry, let's be reasonable. You know what your wife may do if she sees these pictures. Face up to it. You have no choice and you are going to cooperate. But,' he added, 'in the circumstances I think it would be best if I took Mini away with me now, inconvenient though that may be.'

Ivansong shook his head. 'Leave her,' he said simply. 'She will be perfectly safe with me, I can assure you.'

The ghost of a smile passed between them. Then they both laughed. The charade was over. They had short-circuited the odious Greeen, and each one now knew that the other knew he knew what he knew.

Except that Max Alias thought there really was a swinging chick called Miss Suzy Lee Flowerclass, and that illusion had to be preserved for posterity. So later that night Ivansong arranged to commit her to the safe custody of history. 'I'll fly out tomorrow,' agreed the fabulous Miss Flowerclass, 'and thank Heaven for that,' added Thinking Lotus, 'I so want to become the real Mrs. Ivansong again. It seems such a long time since I was. Have you noticed? Life is like money – what with one thing and another, I simply do not know where it all goes.'

17

I

Thinking Lotus flew back from Singapore two days later, but joy was not entirely unconfined, for Ivansong was constrained to rise at a cheerless hour next morning for certain religious observances. It was not yet seven when he left the house on the last day of the Feast of the Beasts, and he was still yawning and rubbing his eyes as he closed the front door behind him.

He therefore failed to see the seasonable gift that some stealthy friend must have placed beside it even earlier, and in the garden he passed the spirit house (which looked like a gaudy dovecote with upturned eaves) without remembering that he should be propitiating the guardian *phi* with food and flowers on this festive occasion if he wanted his home conscientiously protected.

Instead, he drove through reluctantly awakened streets to the Eglise des Deux Sisouphones, a small Catholic church on the southern outskirts of the city that had been almost deserted since Prince Kitay had frowned on all creeds but the state religion of Buddhism. The few local Catholic clergy and their small flock had fallen back on the main cathedral in the centre of Nava, as upon a beleaguered citadel.

Ivansong pushed open the door of the empty and silent church and crossing the central aisle quietly, knelt before a carved wooden confessional.

'When did you last confess?' asked a voice within.

'I can't remember, Father,' replied Ivansong through the gauze-covered pigeonhole, 'but isn't this a somewhat unusual hour for that sort of thing, anyway?'

'What hour can be unusual for hearing the sins of one in dire need of absolution?' came the prompt reprimand, 'and that is certainly what we have on our hands.'

'London came through?'

'London came through, my son. So now hear this. George McWimbledon Potterslee, born 1915 in the subdistrict of St. James and St. Anne, London – Carnaby Street to you – educated Romwood Grammar School, Essex, and employed by the Frugal Life Insurance Company, Finsbury Square. In 1935, he drew the rebate on an imaginary mortgage-reducing policy, banked the money in a new account under a false name, and left the company. He then used his small capital to finance a share-tipping operation, which consisted in writing to hundreds of subscribers weekly, telling each one that a different share or type of share would rise.

'By keeping careful records, he was soon able to draw up a short-list of pathetically trustful clients to whom he had correctly predicted market movements four or more times in a row, and these he took for a glorious ride one fine day by offering them fabulous returns for investing in a bogus palladium mine. He absconded with the funds, was caught and jailed. On release, he went into business with forged Irish Sweep tickets, until one of them most unhappily took first prize, the fraud was exposed, and he was jailed again.

'Let out during World War Two, he conned a flight to America out of a woman ferry-pilot and sold a ferociously anti-communist Chicago meat-pusher named Crutton the Anglo-Saxon Salvation Front, a purely imaginary ultra-right-wing political freemasonry in Britain for which he produced the printed manifesto, the statutes, and an imposing list of secret sponsors. The Front demanded the abandonment of the Soviet Union to Hitler, the subsequent defeat of the Axis powers, and the union between the United States of America and the British Empire. When the war ended and this gilded gull from the shores of Lake Michigan wanted to come to England personally to see what he had been pouring his lolly into, subject adroitly transferred himself to Manila with a faked passport and under another name.

'In the newly-independent Philippines he posed as a liaison officer from the Treasury and, after confirming earlier intelligence that the words "duty" and "corruption" were more or less synonymous in those delectable islands, sold a Filipino consortium interested in quick profits a half-interest in the British Customs and Excise Department, which they naturally assumed to be as venal as their own. He got away with two million pesos of the loot, but was caught, extradited, and sent up again.

'Prison reports show that while in jail he was, as he had always been in the past, an avid reader, but this time he concentrated on mysticism, clairvoyance and esoteric religions, devouring all that there was on the shelves from Old Mother Shipton to *The Third Eye.*'

It was very quiet and hot in the little church. Ivansong ached behind the knees, but his eyes were fixed on the gauze panel through which this tally of transgressions was coming out instead of going in.

'Now it starts to get fragmentary. But according to one old lag, our hero was urged to look up a Dutch occultist named Pekelvlees (see annexed telegram) who was said to have a unique collection of incunabula on oriental arcana – not getting too advanced for you, is it? – and then we lose sight of him.

'In 1969, however, the CID arrested an unfrocked plastic surgeon called Mulish whom they had been after for years for carving up criminals so that their own mothers wouldn't recognise them. Among his papers were "before" and "after" photographs of all his patients (they love to keep reproductions of their own masterpieces). These included mugshots of a man with exceptionally long ears who had paid him £250 for separrating them from the side of the face and creating fat hanging lobes out of them by pumping in silicone over a period of three months. The "before" picture, checked with police records, yielded our old fraud Potterslee. The "after" picture was our now slightly older fraud, the Paramahamsa Bonze.'

'That's it?'

'That's it. Except there were reports of a white thaumaturge who was being worshipped by the Balinese for his holy ears and his prophetic soul before the bonze turned up in Mekong. Thus primed, you may accompany me this afternoon to Nakhara Wat, where we shall have a few words with this fable which may or may not be taken down in evidence. London at last agrees that we know who has been betraying our resident agents to the Chinese, and that leaves me free to act. So same time, same place,. And now, my son,' Greeen's voice rose sanctimoniously, 'for your penance you will say one decade of the rosary, and by the powers conferred upon me, I absolve you from all your sins, past and present, in the name of. . .'

It was at that moment that the somnolent little church was gently shaken by the distant explosion.

Five minutes earlier Mango abandoned her game of stone-paper-scissors with Mini as she seemed to be losing, and besides she had suddenly remembered that this was the last morning of the Beast Feast and – who knew? – perhaps someone had brought her a present. Leaving the gibbon in the back garden, she ran through the living room and pulled open the front door. And there it was, standing on the threshold – a silly old horse on red wheels with a painted head and a stupid, friendly face, black hairbrush bristles for a mane and a tail, and a little cloth saddle on the round wooden body.

Mango jumped up and down twice, giggling with a mixture of excitement and ridicule. Then she dragged the absurd animal through the house and into the back garden before running indoors and stamping up the red stairs to shout 'Mummy, Mummy, look. Someone sent me a funny horse. Who was it, Mummy? Was it you?'

She found her mother on the landing, clad in a silk kimono and staring with a slight frown at a piece of pasteboard which she had just picked up from a small rosewood table. At the top of this was a thumbnail sketch of a toy horse, and underneath were typed two words:

PUNICA FIDE

Down by the pool Mini, one foot resting on top of her head, was also puzzled at first by the day's incomprehensible addition on wheels to the other works of nature in that part of the forest but, unlike the Latinless Lotus above, she was gradually absorbing its real and abominable significance. It had four legs. It had a tail. Then the thing at the other end must be a head, and, yes, in the head was an *eye*.

Mini whooped out her territorial challenge in the face of this act of naked aggression, and when the intruder did not budge, bit it ineffectually in the leg, seized it by the neck, pulled it rudely along the ground, and then leaped upon its back. But in her excitement she had forgotten the swimming pool. The horse bumped crazily down the steps towards the water she so hated, and her weight snapped the shear-pin that held back the tightly-sprung striker from the mercury fulminate cap concealed beneath the saddle.

Blasting gelatine has most commendable *brisance*. One pound of this material (nitroglycerine adulterated with eight per cent of nitrocellulose) when detonating at nearly 5,000 degrees centigrade will produce almost ten cubic feet of gas and a pressure of about 200,000 pounds per square inch. The blast swept through the ground floor of the house to the crash and tinkle of falling glass and crockery, a tidal wave rolled down the pool, splashing over clumsily on to the surrounding stone and grass, and bits of horse and gibbon were blown around indiscriminately over a radius of thirty feet. Ah King screamed in the kitchen, and Mango threw herself whimpering into her mother's arms on the floor above.

Ivansong arrived to find two policemen at his gate holding back a small crowd of Mekinese, and suddenly realised what they signified. It was Oliver Clarence who fielded him at the front door, staggering backwards under the weight of his big frame and his bigger fear, but hanging on hard to his two arms. 'It's all right, Larry,' cried the small, bald British first secretary with the unflappable eyes. 'It's all right, old chap. No one's hurt. The amah has a scratch on her arm, that's all. It was the monkey that got it. Otherwise no great harm done.'

Ivansong stood heaving before him, incongruously dressed in the sober suiting he had put on for Confession. He shut his eyes for a long moment as relief flowed through him. 'Well, God bless you, Oliver,' he stammered. 'For Heaven's sake don't go, but I must see Lotus and Mango, where are they?' They were already running down the stairs, Lotus leading, and for a moment Ivansong felt a little giddy.

'I'll see what the police are up to,' offered Clarence, 'they're all over the garden,' and tactfully left them to it.

'Ah King is suffering from shock a little,' Thinking Lotus murmured into Ivansong's lapel, 'but she is recovering quickly enough to start planning how she is going to boast about her own heroism. She is all tucked up with tea. Miss Ivansong appears relatively imperturbable, so we are playing a new game called business as usual which is, of course, only played when business is most unusual.'

'But *where* is Mini and Foxhunter?' asked Mango tearfully. 'Foxhunter?'

'The toy horse,' said Lotus, 'she'd already named it, so she's missing it,' and sitting down she began to explain what had happened.

'You said there was a card or something with this – this present,' Ivansong reminded her at the end of the story. 'You didn't give it to the police?' She took her head, took the card out of her sleeve and handed it to him. Ivansong glanced at it and pocketed it quickly.

Two timeless hours passed. The police questioned everyone in a desultory fashion (being careful, however, to satisfy themselves as to the maiden name of Ivansong's maternal grandmother), and then most of them left. Clarence returned to the embassy. Thinking Lotus was helping Mango make the beds, and Ivansong was alone in the living-room downstairs when Max Alias broke through the front door and demanded: 'What happened? Where is Mini?'

Ivansong stood up saying 'Look, I'm terribly sorry, Max,' and told him. As he spoke the head of the métis came slowly forward on its neck like that of some unbelieving but inquisitive animal, the eyes staring up in blind entreaty.

'No,' he whispered, 'No, no – ah, non, non, *non!*' Then the barrage burst, and he seized Ivansong violently by the lapels. 'Salaud! Lâche!' he spat into Ivansong's face. 'Mais c'est vous, c'est vous qui avez combiné toute cette cochonnerie, espèce de merde. Is this your Anglo-Saxon idea of vengeance or something? Killing a poor, bloody little beast without a sin or a lie to its silly name?' Max sobbed deeply, tremulously. 'Assassin, c'est vous qui avez fait toute cette saloperie, n'est-ce pas? Ah, que c'est monstrueux, ça, que c'est bien louche,' he shook his head almost sorrowfully. 'Very well, you son of a whore, you, it's finished. Bien, je m'enfous complètement de vous et de ce Greeen. *Chien!*' he added, suddenly violent again, beating his fist on Ivansong's chest. 'I will make you pay for murdering that little creature,' he shouted, biting his lip and raising a shaking finger, 'I swear to you. . .'

Ivansong shook him hard. 'Shut up, Max, for Heaven's sake,' he said roughly, 'I know you're upset and I'm sorry, but surely to God it's clear this had nothing to do with me? A wooden horse sent as a present to my daughter? Can't you see that it was intended for Mango, and it very nearly got her? It was only because she ran off to her mother, who was upstairs looking at the card –'

'What card?' asked Max Alias, his eyes still smouldering. 'What is this farrago of nonsense about cards? Ne me racontez pas de niaiseries parceque –'

'Will you shut up and listen?' cut in Ivansong, biting off the end of each word, and shaking Max again. Then he let him go and fumbled for the card. 'There you are. This was left with the wooden horse.'

Max looked down at it listlessly, and then with interest. 'Latin? What does it mean?'

' "With Punic faith".'

'Punic faith?'

'In plain language, "with treachery" – like saying "French leave" or "Dutch courage" in English. Sallust had a poor opinion of the Carthaginians, it seems.'

'Larry, show me where this happened, eh?' Max Alias was subdued, exhausted. They walked out to the pool. The water, discoloured by pale skeins of blood and littered with torn wedges of wood and fur-lined flesh, was draining out of it slowly. Like a scavenger in a public park, a skeletal Mekinese gardener with skin like smoked fish was stoically sweeping up the distasteful debris scattered over the surrounding lawn. The police had taken what they wanted and had promised to return later to inspect the bottom of the pool before it was cleaned and refilled. There was nothing else to see.

Max stood as if before a grave, his head bowed, his small hands clasped in front of him. 'A Trojan horse and a Latin tag about treachery,' he said quietly. 'All very classical. And you quarrelled with Pawkinson-Convoy at the American reception – oh, yes, don't think all that went unobserved.'

'Yes, well, all I can say to that is that, bright bastards that we are, we've both reached the same preposterous conclusion,' remarked Ivansong. 'I mean, you're not seriously suggesting that the British Ambassador would try to blow up the family of a journalist who had given him a piece of his mind unless he were raving mad, are you? Because it's absolutely ridiculous, Max.'

Max smiled briefly, almost imperceptibly, and pointed a finger at Ivansong. 'You said that. I didn't make any such suggestion. But I will tell you something, Larry. The pig who killed Mini is going to pay for it, and pay quickly. And I mean that, mon vieux,' he added, absolving Ivansong with the last two words. Ivansong looked into his face, and did not much care for what he saw.

'Larry?' Thinking Lotus called sharply out of an upstairs window, 'Larry, telephone.' He left Max at the pool, and ran indoors to pick up the extension downstairs. It was Miss Cholmoney.

'Oh, Mr. Ivansong, Mr. Clarence has been telling H.E. about the *unfortunate* affair at your house, and he would like to see you at one-thirty if you can manage it. It's a half-day but he will be in his office. He's on a diet, so he's skipping lunch. Are you all right there now? We were all terribly sorry and shocked to hear about it. Does your wife need any help?'

'No, thank you, Chummy, we're all right,' answered Ivansong, 'and please tell H.E. I'll be there, of course.' He returned to Max. 'It was the ambassador's secretary. He wants to see me at one-thirty.'

'Bon, je me sauve,' sighed Max, 'You will be hearing from me, Larry.'

'No doubt,' answered Ivansong a little woodenly, accompanying him to the front door. Just for a moment the joke seemed to be palling, he thought, as he stared unseeing at the little spirit-house on the front lawn.

2

By the time he and Thinking Lotus had warded off three local reporters, answered telephone calls from six foreign correspondents, and eaten a tin of skinless frankfurters with a purée of mashed yam, it was one-thirty, and Ivansong set off to see His Excellency.

British embassies are closed on Wednesday afternoons, but the chancery guard, heavily varicosed from nose to calf, told Ivansong he was expected and waved him upstairs. He knocked on the door of the ambassador's office, and it swung open at once. Pawkinson-Convoy gazed at him for a moment, his red lips pursed. Then he stretched out a hand like a tarantula and, grasping Ivansong's jacket, pulled him into the room.

'I want to know just what the devil you think you're up to, Ivansong,' he said, leaning back against his desk and staring at him belligerently over his arrogant nose. 'First you insult Her Majesty's accredited representative publicly on a diplomatic occasion, then you store explosives in your house as if you were involved in some sort of plot. Moreover, you store them so incompetently that you cause a dangerous explosion and create a major public scandal within a stone's throw of this mission.

'Well, speak up, man. Just what is your little game? I might as well tell you right away that my first agreeable task tomorrow morning will be to recommend to the Ministry of Foreign Affairs that your visa to Mekong be withdrawn and that your name be blacklisted.'

'Is that so?' cut in Ivansong sharply. 'And now you listen to me, because my child was nearly killed this morning and I am not in the mood for cross-talk. She was nearly killed by what was in effect a Trojan horse, as you well know, and this Trojan horse was surreptitiously delivered with a card reading "Punica Fide". Quite an academic performance, wouldn't you say? Except, of course, that there was nothing academic about it.'

Pawkinson-Convoy suddenly went as still as a jungle-fighter who has heard an ominous sound inaudible to others. Ivansong could see his discoloured teeth and tongue as he breathed silently through his wide-open mouth, and his instinct told him: he is not worrying about my asinine insinuation. It is something deeper.

The telephone rang. The ambassador picked up the instrument and twisted his head and shoulders away from Ivansong, as some men will when pulling money reluctantly from their wallets. 'Yes?' he said quietly, almost furtively.

'Is Ivansong there?' asked a muffled, neutral voice.

'Yes, but who. . . ?'

The telephone suddenly emitted the piercing metallic wail that malevolent callers can produce from the old-fashioned instrument still to be found in some public booths by touching the receiver to the mouthpiece. The startled ambassador hastily snatched the set from his ear, whereupon the voice shouted slowly and distinctly: 'Félicitations, Monsieur l'Ambassadeur.'

'What the devil? Felicitations for what?' Pawkinson-Convoy

bellowed back, keeping the thing well away from his head.

'Such a short memory, *comrade*?' The words could be heard all over the room. And then came the absurd, mournful reproach in a strong if erratic tenor: '*Monsieur, Monsieur, vous oubliez votre cheval. . .*'

'Sir, you are forgetting your *horse*,' said another voice behind Ivansong, and he turned to find that someone else had quietly come into the office.

The ambassador slammed down the receiver and glared up at Greeen, his hairy fists bunching. 'What the devil d'ye mean by barging in here like that?' he demanded irately. 'You fellows are beginning to think –'

'Sir, sir,' interrupted Greeen with horrible suavity, his sea-green eyes lengthening into a fraudulent smile, 'do please excuse me, but I heard the singing, and I see that you too are familiar with the tune. Alas, one does not hear it often nowadays, though one or two people in Nava perpetuate its memory.' He cocked his head at the ambassador, who was silent and pale again, his nostrils distended and his breathing heavy. 'I was in any case coming to see you, sir, to say that the explosion at Ivansong's place has apparently started all sorts of rumours of renewed violence, coups, or a communist attack. The city is disturbed, and as your security adviser I thought it best to let you know.' Greeen paused, and then went on in a voice like well-worn silk, 'In the circumstances, I trust that you will not attempt to leave the safety of the embassy compound.'

It was not a question, but Pawkinson-Convoy answered curtly: 'I had no plans to do so.'

'Splendid,' commented Greeen smoothly. 'I was certain you would see it my way. Then we can be sure that there will be no unpleasantness, can't we?' And beckoning to Ivansong, he left the room. Ivansong followed without a word.

Flodden was on the other side of the door, wearing a black synthetic alpaca suit and looking like a freelance mourner. 'He does not leave these grounds in any circumstance,' Greeen told him, straightening his tie for him. 'Be neat and tidy at all times. If you actually have to shoot him, I shall be very disappointed.'

167

'Very good, sir,' answered Flodden. 'Excuse me, sir, but was you expecting to come back later yourself, kindastyle?'

'In about three hours, at most,' replied Greeen, and turning to Ivansong, he added: 'You will meet me on the jetty of the Peninsula of Ten Thousand Years in forty minutes' time.'

'For God's sake,' protested Ivansong violently, 'you really don't expect me to go gallivanting around on the other side of the river after what happened in my own house this morning, do you?'

'No,' replied Greeen, 'never for God's sake. There are always more immediate reasons. Anyway, you've nothing to worry about. Trojan horses never come in pairs.'

3

The sky seemed to be enveloped in steam, and the sun continued to beat down mercilessly upon a Mekong already streaked with molten gold. From the little jetty over the shallows of the peninsula, Ivansong could see, if somewhat indistinctly through the haze, the summit of Mount Kham and the discoloured dentures of the Mayon. The Marines were still up there. A desperate attempt to break out in small parties had been stubbed almost on the perimeter wire. They had taken no serious casualties, but they had been forced to pull back precipitately to avoid being made prisoner. They were locked in a stone trap by an enemy who now outnumbered them to a sinfully extravagant degree, but who wanted them alive and never fired a shot at them as long as they stayed put and thought about. . .

'Come on in, the water's lovely,' shouted a voice behind him, chiming with his thoughts. Greeen had arrived in a smart little launch which had to anchor eight yards off shore, and was stumbling barefoot towards Ivansong over the pebbles, holding his shoes and socks above his head and grinning clownishly, his face half-obscured by an enormous pair of dark glasses.

'You look like a pre-war Margate tripper,' Ivansong told him sourly. 'What, no straw hat? No shrimping net? No piece of filthy pink rock to suck? Do you have to wear a linen suit and a tie for a caper like this? Don't you know it gives away your proletarian origins?'

'Ah, but they weren't, you see,' retorted Greeen, winding down his trousers and pulling his socks over his wet feet. 'In reality I am The Macdonald of the Minches, or some equally distinguished scion of Scottish nobility, and that entitles me to wear the tails of three male badgers over my private entrance, did you but know it. It's just that I'm not the showy type.' They began walking down the path between the tiers of Chinese graves that faced each other across it. Like Government and Loyal Opposition in the Mother of Parliaments, thought Ivansong. Had all those dead in Vietnam been saved for democracy, after all?

'Where's the card that came with the bomb?' asked Greeen.

Ivansong took it out of his pocket and showed it to him. Greeen glanced at it, raised his sandy eyebrows, and gave it back.

'Police find anything?'

Ivansong shook his head slowly. 'Only what you'd expect – bits of wood, flesh, bone, blood, smashed head and part of torso of both horse and ape, bits of striker mechanism –'

'Striker mechanism?'

Ivansong nodded. Greeen changed the subject.

'Max timed that phone call of his rather nicely, I thought,' he drawled after a short silence, stopping to peer at the framed photograph of an elderly Chinese in pince-nez fixed to one of the headstones.

'He knew I was going to see the ambassador. He was at my house when Chummy rang. And he said he was going to put paid to whoever had blown up the gibbon. But don't tell me you really fell for that ludicrous attempt of his to link Pawkinson-Convoy up with his communist chums in order to prove that Her Britannic Majesty's accredited envoy to Mekong was a Chinese agent? Or do you seriously suggest that H.E. would try to kill my daughter just because we had a stand-up row at the American Embassy?'

'If he were a Chinese agent he might have other reasons, mightn't he?' suggested Greeen.

'Like what?'

'Like the Te Wu didn't like you using your own wife for that display of amorous acrobatics in the bridal suite of the Asie, perhaps,' replied Greeen with gentle malice. 'Oh, what a tangled web we weave, when first we practise to deceive,' he sang to an imposing cenotaph commemorating the rise and fall of a Chinese duck-feather merchant.

'Christ, how did you find that out?' Ivansong was too puzzled to be abashed. 'Lotus was strange to Nava. No one knew her well here. And she's a born actress. She *became* Suzy Lee Flowerclass. So what went wrong?'

'Just the small mole on her right upper arm. It didn't go away.'

'Well I'm damned,' Ivansong grinned ruefully. 'I completely forgot about it. But I bet the Te Wu didn't even know it was there, and I still can't see Pawkinson-Convoy in their pay as an avenging saboteur.'

'Can't you? Are you forgetting that he had always cut Max dead in public, presumably as a security precaution since Max's dedicated career as a double agent is a well-known secret among all us girls. That made the comradely phone call we heard the kiss of Judas. And hasn't it ever occurred to you that for a British diplomat, P-C is too damned accident-prone? Wherever he is, we're in trouble, the embassy is mobbed if not wrecked and burned, and the name of Britain is mud – Kabul, Baghdad, Cairo, Djakarta, Peking, *and* Nava – you know, the riot over the funerary urns. In each case the *head* of mission was a different man – Gilchrist in Djakarta, Hopson in Peking, for example. But the common factor in all these charming little episodes in our stirring island story is always I-was-there Pawkinson-Convoy. Not even the most evil-minded member of your own repellent profession has a record as unblemished as his for being where the fun is. Isn't it all too much of a coincidence?'

'But the idea that the Trojan horse and the Latin tag prove H.E. rigged up that bomb is utter rubbish.'

'Now there I absolutely agree,' said Greeen soothingly, 'Pawkinson-Convoy didn't plant the thing. That was just my fun. The Chinese did it themselves. And that's what makes it so damning for him, doesn't it?'

'How on earth do you arrive at that?' asked the exasperated Ivansong.

'Dear me, I should have thought that was clear enough,' answered Greeen, appealing to the brassy heavens. 'It is, after all, very Chinese. They do not blatantly blow their agents to western capitalist intelligence services when they want to destroy them. It might give Peking a bad name in the trade. And killing accredited envoys is generally regarded as fiddling the rules, especially in these days of ping-pong diplomacy. Appearances must be preserved at all costs. So when they tire of H.E., they merely frame him with a couple of obviously farcical clues and then leave bloodhounds from the bourgeois reactionary governments like me to draw the inevitable conclusion.'

'The inevitable conclusion being?'

'That there would be no point in fabricating such fatuous evidence in support of so preposterous a proposition unless that proposition were true. A most subtle and polite betrayal, you see.'

'Oh, now I get it,' chimed in Ivansong with mock enthusiasm. 'They tip us the wink about a top-level spy planted right in the middle of our own Foreign Service so that we can knock him out of action, recall him to London, and grill the guts out of him. For subtlety that makes even the Emperor's new clothes look like rabbit fur.'

Greeen shrugged. 'All right. We don't yet know why they're shedding him, but agents are as perishable as pop-singers, remember, and the darling of yesterday can be the drag of today.' Greeen glanced at Ivansong obliquely through his absurd glasses, and then continued: 'Evidently they were satisfied that H.E. could tell us nothing of importance about their own organisation if questioned. They may even have fed him a lot of fallacious rubbish that they want him to repeat to us under pressure. And meanwhile don't forget that, being communists, they have a healthy respect for our democratic system, the Chinese. They know that the affair must come out into the open, that we shall be made to look fools again – Burgess, Maclean, Philby, and now this – that our security will be discredited, and the once touching, almost childlike trust shared between ourselves and the Yanks will curdle into even more vinegary mutual suspicion than before. Plenty of tax-free fringe benefits there, hm?

'On the other hand, our own profits seem to be dwindling.' Greeen stroked his lantern jaw lovingly. 'Your own uxorious activities have wrecked perhaps the biggest penetration of the Opposition that we have ever attempted in this region,' he continued unemotionally. 'And you've only saved your skin by uncovering this adipose bonze of yours. Was it too much to ask you to lose your virtue for a few searing minutes of illicit ecstasy? I really don't know what our younger men are coming to. Anyway, your little deception led to the horse business, and the horse business has led to Max going berserk about the killing of his gibbon. And once Max is mentally on the loose, it's like having the Mad Bomber around. None of us knows where he stands, or who will be blown to whom next.'

'But you can't complain,' protested Ivansong. 'It was the Trojan horse and the telephone call from Max that pinpointed H.E. today.'

'My dear Ivansong,' retorted Greeen, 'as I hinted to you at Confession, we already had him sewn up as the villain of the piece before breakfast.'

'Then how can you risk leaving him back at the embassy while you chase after the Paramahamsa Bonze?'

'The ambassador will keep in Flodden's rather nasty hands. What can he do? Fly to the Chinese, who have betrayed him? Skip the country and so admit all? As for your obese friend up in Nakhara Vat, on the other hand, I have my own reasons for wanting to see him rather quickly. But just do me a favour from here onward and keep quiet, will you? This is hallowed ground.'

They topped the last slight rise in silence and Stonecutter Village lay before them, peaceful in the afternoon sun but for the rhythmic tapping of the tomb-masons. Then small children erupted from the shophouses and surrounded the two men, eddying about them in a sly gurgling wake, and dancing along with them down the dusty street.

Greeen gave them his sharklike grin, stopped for a short game of tic-tic-toe, which he lost, forked out his ten cents like a man, and began talking again to the smiling Ivansong. 'Have you seen the Kuan Yin image here? Rather a nice little statue from Fukien.' They turned into a small temple and admired the garish figures of the plaster guardians at the entrance to the shrine, the coils of incense hanging from the ceilings, and the wooden carving of the gentle Goddess of Mercy with her pink enamel face and her long gown of gold leaf studded with glass.

'Charming,' said Greeen. 'Well, as I was saying, I shall see the ambassador at six, so we mustn't be too long, although I do enjoy these afternoons off over here among the ruins – you simply must come up and see my rubbings sometime.' He looked around. There was only a snaggle-toothed Chinese sage in pyjamas, sitting in a corner reading a folded-up newspaper through steel-rimmed spectacles. 'Anyway, you can be sure he will give us the full details – his brief, his controller, contacts, cut-outs, the works.'

Ivansong started to ask what he was talking about, but Greeen continued conversationally, 'No, don't interrupt. He's obviously completely disillusioned after that bomb explosion at your place. He knows his Chinese masters engineered it to frame him, of course, and that he's hopelessly blown. So we can really expect him to talk. But the main thing is to get him off to London as quickly as possible. The air attaché can fly him down to Singapore tomorrow morning first thing, and the RAF can handle it from there, I've no doubt. Shall we go on?'

He turned away from the goddess to preen himself in a looking-glass flanked by a shelf of small painted plastercast deities and a gaudy advertisement for a Japanese meat tenderiser. 'Mirror, mirror, on the wall,' he appealed to it plaintively, 'who is the unfairest of them all?'

18

Only desultory fire could be heard from the direction of the Mayon as Greene and Ivansong made their way towards the tall tower of the Paramahamsa Bonze, for there were no helicopters up now, and the thirsty Marines were painfully short of both ammunition and authorised targets. To Ivansong's lively imagination it seemed that the ruins themselves were rustling with Mekinese Reds, and they doubtless were, for more and more guerrillas were closing in for the kill on Mount Kham. But they saw no one in the courts of Nakhara Wat itself except a small party of Australian tourists and the three young monks who served the seer as doorkeepers. These let them pass up the steep stairway to his stone eyrie without begging for as much as a cigarette-butt from them. Evidently Ivansong was now on the approved shortlist of visitors.

The Bonze was meditating on his platform again, but when their perspiring foreheads topped the last step he rose and padded ahead of them into his large and well-appointed inner chamber, waving them to two chairs and dropping into a third himself with a sigh that set his ample flesh rolling gently.

'This is another seer of great knowledge,' explained Ivansong, waving towards Greeen, who took off his comic sunglasses and put them carefully into their case. 'I thought the Venerable Bonze would like to meet him.'

'Really, my son? asked the Bonze doubtfully, 'and what does he know?'

'He knows,' answered Greeen, 'that you are George Mc-

Wimbledon Potterslee alias Arthur Stimbridge alias Charles Maxwell Prattijohn alias Sir Henry Ardingly-Balcombe alias Howard E. Flatterletter alias the Paramahamsa Bonze. My dear fellow, what a name-dropper you are, to be sure. But then you're so popular. So many people want to see you, if you get what I mean. They have so many questions to ask you, because you know so much. The more egoistical among them even want to shut you up so that they have you all to themselves. Alas, the world is full of people like that.'

The Bonze observed Greeen through his heavy-lidded eyes, and clapped two small, fat hands. One of his young ladies, who had been sitting quietly in her niche, came to his elbow. 'Tell you what, my dear,' he said, turning briefly to look into the submissive little face and pat one diminutive haunch absent-mindedly. 'Open a little pot of the Beluga, make some nice buttered toast, and bring us a chilled bottle of Stolichnaya out of the icebox.

'Ah, peccadilloes, peccadilloes,' he remarked to Greeen with obese imperturbability. 'Our little weaknesses are our most endearing traits. How barbaric it is of Christianity to condemn them. I am sure you must be aware that in the great Hindu epics avatars who have, as it were, the standing of a Christ, are loved all the more for their small failings. And, indeed, where would we be without evil itself? For without evil there would be no good.'

'Nonetheless,' commented Greeen amiably, 'chickens have a way of coming home to roost.'

'I trust you are not throwing up what you would call my past in what I call my face, my son,' queried the Bonze, with a small smack of the lips, 'for as you must know the ego is an illusion. There is no enduring individual existence. The path of my self is like the path of a fish through water. When the fish is gone it is as if it had never been. And as its path does not exist, so my past does not exist. You are surely not trying to identify me with all those other people you just mentioned?'

'Personally,' confessed Greeen, spreading his hands self-deprecatingly, 'I am afraid I am not interested in those winning imperfections of yours that so attract the police except in so far as they give me what I must indelicately call a hold over you, Venerable Potterslee. I only care about one thing' – the sleepy verdigris eyes narrowed as he grinned disarmingly – 'and that is that you are a Chinese agent operating under the general directions of a disinformation bureau in Peking.'

The small mouth of the Paramahamsa Bonze opened and shut once or twice, rather in the manner of a fish passing through water and leaving no path. 'I am a holy man,' he said at last with quiet dignity. 'My person is sacrosanct. Any that touches me will be torn to pieces by the devout, and the most powerful in the land will revenge themselves cruelly upon him. So you can ruddy well stop bluffing, friend.'

'So can you,' rejoined Ivansong, stretching his long legs comfortably before him. 'We've got enough on you to break you. I can tell the whole world within three hours that you are a charlatan and a common cheat. Or we could overpower you, and drain the silicone from your famous ear-lobes simply by puncturing them. Then how would you dare face all those devout millions and their equally devout masters who were going to tear us to pieces?'

'Or would you like us simply to give you away to the Superiors of the Great Pagoda in Nava? suggested Greeen reasonably. 'You know they're so jealous of you that they'd like nothing better than to crucify you. Or shall we point out to Kitay that you're an old fraud from the wrong side of Carnaby Street? Or shall we just tip your Chinese friends off that you've blown the gaff to us?'

The Paramahamsa Bonze was breathing shallowly and shaking a little, the white flaccid skin of his underarm trembling in the golden afternoon sunlight.

'They wouldn't touch me,' he said, raising an unsteady finger and turning his head a little to one side to fix Ivansong with a single, admonitory eye. 'They'd be massacred by the Mekinese. When I moved in here and they gave me everything I asked for, they knew my value. "You deserve it all," they said, "you deserve it all". They need me, you see, but I swear –'

'And I swear they would cut you to rags and pin the crime on someone else,' Ivansong thrust in brutally. 'When they assured you "you deserve it all", that was simply their exquisitely polite Chinese way of saying "see that you bloody well earn it, or else". And you haven't earned it, have you? You still haven't told them that I detected those counterfeit ears of yours. That would have ruined your profitable little association with them, wouldn't it?'

There was silence, as if someone had forgotten his lines. The caviare, toast and vodka arrived. The Bonze ate greedily and threw his tot of vodka straight at the back of his throat. Ivansong and Greeen sipped and waited.

'How did you find out?' the Bonze asked hoarsely at last. Larry told him, and Greeen briefly reviewed his biography in and out of goal.

'I see nothing there,' said the Bonze in a soft, lilting voice, 'to justify the unwarrantable and foul accusation that I have worked for the cause of Chinese communism, a charge that I most categorically rej –'

'That,' interrupted Greeen, 'was confirmed when you made your latest little prophecy to my friend the other day. What was it? Something about pale men with smooth tongues deceitfully taking Mekong's jewel in the waters, and death and disaster following if it was allowed to happen? What does it mean, Bonzo?'

'I don't –'

'I said, what does it mean?' shouted Greeen, leaping across the intervening space like a tiger and seizing the great pudding of a monk in front of him by his cloth. 'Mekong only has one jewel in the waters, Potterslee, the island of Khammax. *What – does – it – mean?*' He shook the Bonze with each word, his eyes like narrow scuppers giving on to some malevolent northern sea.

'I swear I don't know,' gasped the Bonze. 'I was just told to say it.'

'To Ivansong, you infelicitous liar?' Greeen's knuckles were white against the yellow toga.

'Yes, and why not?' retorted the Bonze with that sudden

outburst of righteous indignation that afflicts rascals who abruptly find themselves telling the truth. 'This particular prophecy was to whom it may concern. U-certificate. Kitay, Americans, British, it didn't matter. It's rare, because normally I don't over-expose myself to the hoi-polloi. But it can happen.

'So I was half-inclined to give you and your American pal an audience anyway,' the Bonze twisted his head to look at Ivansong, 'though not in my inner sanctum, of course. And that's how I explained away my having talked to you both to my other chums. They seemed quite pleased I had. As a matter of fact –' he stopped in mid-indiscretion, but it was too late.

Greeen let him go, sat down, and stuffed some toast and caviare into his mouth. 'Well, bully for you, Bonzo,' he said equably, brushing crumbs from his hands and taking another sip at his vodka. 'Now, there's just one other little thing I want to get straight between us. You're in our hands. You're also in an extremely delicate and dangerous position. Your secret is no longer a secret. Only we can get you out of this, and not only will we do it, but we'll make the future easier for you if you cooperate with us in a proper manner. On the other hand if we have any nonsense from you, my man, we shall throw you to one of the many packs of wolves we have up our sleeves.' Greeen shot his cuffs and fingered his tie primly. The two young women had not moved.

Ten minutes later the Paramahamsa Bonze was warming to his own story, as men inevitably will.

'You see, I'd been caught out twice in the swami business (which is otherwise a very gentlemanly racket without being unprofitable) simply out of unforgivable ignorance,' he explained. 'That was why I boned up on it in jug. And when I got out I went to see this old Dutch boy, Pekelvlees, down at Carshalton. I spent days browsing around among the books in the back of his shop, and then he showed me this early nineteenth-century first edition of a work on Javanese mysticism. It had been written by an Irish colonel who had served under Sir Stamford Raffles when the British took over the administration of much of the Dutch East Indies during the Napoleonic Wars.

'Now,' said the Paramahamsa Bonze, taking a long, crooked cheroot out of a carved cedarwood box on the table beside him and lighting it from a small cloisonné opium-lamp, 'I'd already read a bit about the great twelfth-century Javanese seer, Djoyoboyo' – he blew smoke coolly at Greeen – 'you know all about him, of course, my son?'

'Like every schoolboy,' cut in Ivansong. 'King of Kediri from 1135 to 1157. He prophesied that a white buffalo would come to dominate Java, but it would be supplanted by a small yellow monkey, and the island would finally win back its freedom again under a man with supernatural powers. Right?'

'Right. And so was Djoyoboyo. The Dutch white buffalo colonised Java, to be succeeded for a short time during World War Two by the Japanese monkey, who in turn gave way to a native superman, President Sukarno. But, you see, this old book of Pekelvlees contained more about Djoyoboyo, in fact it had stuff about him not to be found anywhere else. It seems that when the king was getting on, some old ghoul who thought he was going to die asked him if he would return to his people in another incarnation. And you know what he said? "In thirty times thirty years will come one with the ears of the Buddha and with the *sakti* upon him. He will continue the story that I have begun, and he will be master of the world for one eternity."'

'Sakti?'

'Supernatural power. Well, thirty times thirty brought us, very roughly speaking, to the present era. And there were my ears. They had always attracted notice, being so long and fixed to the side of my face all the way down. That gave me like kind of a nudge,' (as he talked the round fruity tones of the Paramahamsa Bonze began to give way to more homely diphthongs, as when a butler retires to his pantry) 'and so I started to get the germ of an idea, a great idea – an idea, I might modestly say, gentlemen, of sheer genius.' The Bonze paused for agreement.

When this was not forthcoming, he continued with a small sigh: 'I bought the book for a horrible sum of money, but then I was going to make it worth millions, I reckoned. I went to see old Mulish, the plastic wonder – it was easy enough to pick him up on the grapevine – and in three months I was fixed up with my ears as they are now. My plan was quite simple. I would make the rest of good King Djoyoboyo's prophecy come true too.'

They finished the caviare and plunged further into the Stolichnaya as the Paramahamsa Bonze continued his unlikely tale. He made his way to Central Java, and with the help of his unique first edition was soon breaking even as a guru. In time Sukarno heard about him, and thereafter consulted him occasionally – at least once about his relations with the Indonesia communists and the Chinese.

Sukarno's own guru became jealous of Potterslee, but Potterslee was anxious to join him rather than lick him. 'You've got the flair, but I've got the ears,' he told the venerable soothsayer, who eventually came around to agreeing that it was his sacred duty to make Djoyoboyo's predictions prove correct.

'Now the Javanese don't believe in cut-throat competition. They have a tradition of mutual cooperation, you know, everyone in the village mucking in, agreeing what wants doing next, and then doing it together,' went on the Bonze. 'They call it *gotong rojong*. So the old boy brought a lot more gurus and medicine-men into the game, and in time we had a going club, so to speak. Mind you, most of them were pretty useless – getting on, too honest, and so on – you know. You remember I told you about the fellow who was eaten by the blokes in West New Guinea?' he reminded Ivansong. 'Well, he wasn't an Indonesian, but he was one of the club too.

'However, some were smart, and we worked together very nicely on occasion. For example, I would tell one of the Javanese princes that the stars said he should stop quarrelling with some general he didn't like, and another member of the club would tell the general that if he made a suitable contribution to our holy works, the prince would lay off him. So everyone would be satisfied. Oh, they were good days. We had some times, I can tell you.'

Then the Chinese, who had heard about him from Sukarno, approached the Bonze while he was preaching at the ruins of Borobodur, and a nameless man from their embassy in Djakarta began to see him regularly. He proposed that Potterslee be put on a proper footing as a sound money-making proposition. Peking would first take him in hand and see that he was given a better grounding in Hindu-Buddhist beliefs and philosophy. After that, he would expand his guru club to cover all South-east Asia, and perhaps in time an even wider area. The Chinese would feed him and his partners with advance information which they would then give out in the form of prophecies, and in this way they would rapidly acquire a reputation for being infallible. The Chinese would then tell them what advice as well as information they should pass on to men of consequence.

'It was an eminently plausible caper. You know how superstitious Asian leaders are. They consult astrologers and witchdoctors over all important dates and decisions. You've heard of Sukarno's guru, of the Blind Bonze of Laos, of the bomohs of Malaysia that the government even calls in to ensure fine weather on state occasions?

'But I must confess I could hardly believe my blessed ears just the same,' continued the Paramahamsa Bonze. 'The communists were going to use us, but I was going to use the communists to make Djoyoboyo's prophecy work, and once I was "master of the world for one eternity" I would ditch them. Can't you see it – a synchronised programme of rigged clairvoyance, stretching across a whole subcontinent? Who could refuse the biggest audience-assisted confidence trick in history? There was going to be billions in it.'

'But, my dear cretin,' interrupted Greeen, pulling out a small nail-file from his breast-pocket and setting to work with it languidly, 'you could not expect to startle the world with a string of prophecies which were in every single instance about the dubious intentions of Mao and Co. You would have to predict what anti-communist leaders were going to do as well. And how could you fiddle that?'

The Bonze shrugged resignedly. 'Of course it's difficult talking to people like you. My Chinese pal was just the same. You haven't got the head for this kind of thing. It's like me trying to discuss atomic fission with a nuclear physicist. Naive. Ignorant. Look, when I was a nipper no higher than this I had the answer to that question.' He pulled open a drawer in the table beside him and took out a well-thumbed deck of cards.

2

The Paramahamsa Bonze shuffled the cards expertly, riffled them from one practised hand to another held fully eighteen inches away, and explained: 'My Pa taught me the trick, God rest his gruesome little soul because we certainly don't want it around here. This is how it's done.' He swiftly laid out a row of nine cards on the table, face down. 'Now remember the cards I call carefully. Here we go: five of hearts' – he picked up the first card from the table and turned it so that he could see it but they could not, nodded, and kept it in his hand. 'Jack of spades' – he repeated the same process – 'four of diamonds' – and again – 'seven of diamonds, six of clubs, queen of diamonds, eight of spades. . .' When he had all nine cards back in his hand, he spread them out face upwards before them on the table. 'There you are, what did I say? Five of hearts, jack of spades, four of diamonds, seven of diamonds, six of clubs, queen of diamonds, eight of spades. . .' They were all there, as he had called them before he had seen them.

'Well, I'm damned,' exclaimed Ivansong reverently.

'My dear boy, don't be obtuse. If he knows the last one, he's got the lot.'

'Correct,' called the Bonze. 'Kewpie doll for the gent in the polkadot shoes. You see,' he explained carefully to Ivansong, 'before I lay out the nine cards, face down, I memorise the last one – easy enough to do, because I've palmed it from the bottom of the pack. It is the five of hearts. So when I touch the first card, I call five of hearts. I pick it up and see that in fact it's the jack of spades. So then I touch the second card and call "jack of spades". It turns out to be the four of diamonds, so I call "four of diamonds" when I name the next one, and I go on like this to the end where, of course, I get my real five of hearts, and all I've got to do is to slip that back to the top of the nine cards again and show them all to you face up. Can't go wrong. Silly, really.'

'What's this got to do with your latest swindle, though?'

'Everything. I've just demonstrated to you how you can make nine accurate prophecies together where you could not have made one singly, simply by linking them all up. Well, let me tell you. I travelled, studied – my God, how I studied – mugging up all that Sanskrit and Pali jargon. I brought in not only gurus but first-class professional con men. The Chinese suggested Mekong as an obvious headquarters for me, what with Nakhara and neutrality and so on, and I was all for that because there was obviously going to be a chance to wash a few brains in the gold and opium business. And then we got down to this peculiar form of knitting whose object was to pull the wool over the eyes of the beholder.

'Imagine it for yourselves,' the Bonze smacked his lips softly. 'The club by this time has its holy men or witchdoctors established in all the required countries, and we can now palm the one card we must know to begin the trick. This has to be a piece of Chinese communist information and, oh, what a bureaucratic lot they can be when it comes down to it, let me tell you.

'But anyway in 1964 we prophesy the first explosion of a Chinese atomic device to President Sukarno. In consequence, Sukarno pays heed thereafter when we strongly advise him to obey the stars over a series of crucial decisions which include intensifying his brushfire war against Malaysia, taking Indonesia out of the United Nations, and throwing in his lot with the communists in the coup of September 1965. We forecast Sukarno's actions accurately to the Filipinos in turn, and so they listen to us when we tell them they must without fail press home their own claim to a slice of Malaysian North Borneo, using military blackmail if necessary.

'Well, we now have Indonesia and Malaysia and the Philippines all embroiled with one another, and finally a bloodbath in Indonesia when the communist coup fails. But we have already been endearing ourselves to the Malaysians by carefully keeping them informed on what Sukarno is going to do next, so when the quarrel between Malaysia and Singapore comes to a head in 1965, we are in a position to make a prophecy that will be respected: if Tengku Abdul Rahman does not eject Singapore from the Malaysian Federation, there will be civil war and it will break up completely. Malaysia duly kicks Singapore out, which ensures that in fact the Federation is broken in two, and the five-power Commonwealth defence system of which it is the basis is thrown into confusion.

'In 1964 we also give advance news of a heavy communist offensive in Laos to General Khanh, who has become the new strongman in South Vietnam, and are thus later able to persuade him that he must bomb Cambodia on the pretext that it is swarming with Vietcong. We do not neglect to warn Prince Sihanouk of Cambodia what is going to happen, however, and when it does, he begins to consult us excitedly in his turn. Thereafter, it is child's play to convince him that he must sever diplomatic relations with the United States with a prophecy that he will be exiled within six months if he does not heed us, and then to advise the Mekinese and the Thais he is going to do so.

'Now, let me see, where are we? Yes, well, at the beginning of 1967 we forecast Chinese recognition of Cambodia's frontiers and Buddhist demonstrations in front of the presidential palace in Saigon, and we predict the communist offensive of February 1968 in South Vietnam, passing the information not only to President Thieu but to the Burmese and Malaysians.

'Subsequently this enables us to persuade Ne Win in Burma to push the former Premier U Nu into active rebellion against him, to convert certain Malays to the idea that the answer to the increasing political power of non-Malays is a bloody race riot, and to coax Thieu into launching costly operations across his frontiers into both Cambodia and Laos. Then we let the Mekong and Singapore governments know in advance –'

'Enough, no more,' interrupted Greeen, ' 'tis not so sweet now as it was before. But what did you tell the Americans?'

The Paramahamsa Bonze looked a little uncomfortable. 'We did get word to President Johnson early in 1965 that. . . but then later the Pope himself appealed to him to suspend the bombing of North Vietnam,' he ended with a fine, rapid flourish.

'You mean you influenced the Po –?'

'No, no, I mean, don't let's exaggerate, eh? We'd only been in the business three years by then, and you haven't heard half of it. We predicted the East Java uprising and the assassination of the communist insurgent boss in Burma in 1968, the increase in guerrilla activity in Malaysia in 1971 –'

'And thus put yourselves into a position where you could further encourage political leaders to make false moves, inflame hatreds, provoke insurrections, divide countries and break up alliances. Yes, I get the picture,' said Greeen, 'one of those massive masterpieces too big to be hung anywhere except in a public loo.

'And of course,' he continued slowly, 'it explains why Sissomak went to Peking, letting Yaksha mount his coup, why Kitay double-crossed Yaksha, and why we end up with a feudal lunatic as the country's leader and Mekinese Reds on our not very well scrubbed doorstep.'

The Bonze bowed modestly in acknowledgement. 'Mind you,' he said, 'I couldn't always direct things personally, and at one point I had trouble with the scars on my face. There was an inflammation of some kind and I had to hide out in a Chinese clinic, have them opened, and wait until they healed again. I used to powder them for months, but then all seemed well and I stopped it. My ruddy mistake, I now see.'

'Over-confidence,' sympathised Greeen, 'we can none of us

be too careful. However,' he went on, tilting his head to one side and smiling maliciously, 'I can see you're a man of discretion. You haven't told us that for the past year or two your Chinese friends themselves have been able to feed you forecasts which were not about future communist moves, but about future western or anti-communist moves, have you?

The eyes of the Bonze narrowed a little. 'It's news to me,' he said slowly, 'but come to think of it, you are right. I'd hardly noticed it, but it's true. Like this last one about white men tricking Mekong out of its jewel in the waters.'

There was a pause. 'Tell us,' asked Ivansong. 'Did Djoyo-boyo predict anything else?'

'Ye-es. But I can't figure that out. He said Borobodur would slowly crumble but Nakhara would die and be reborn many times like a man chained to the Wheel of Life.'

'Well-now,' said Greeen. 'Let's sum up. Here we have this mischievous monk in the heart of Nakhara Wat, protected – or imprisoned, if you look at it sideways – by several thousand Mekinese communist guerrillas, and victualled by one Flakey Garbageman, Provisioner by Appointment to the Paramahamsa Bonze. Problem, get the winkle out of the shell without using the pin.

'All right, friend, this is what is going to happen. You are coming away with us. You are going to make a final set of prophecies, and serve your illustrious private clients like Kitay with a final volume of information and advice, in order to undo what you have done. You and I are then going to wind up your Guru Club and sit down for a long, cosy chat about your nearest and dearest Chinese friends. And if you do all these things meekly and with a contrite heart, it may be that you will not have to spend the rest of your existence in a cell or a cemetery.'

'But I can't leave just like that, my son,' protested the Paramahamsa Bonze. 'If I walk out of here with you in broad daylight, my – er – my patrons are going to guess what the game is and we won't get two yards. And what do I say to my girls? And what about my young novices down at the foot of the steps? Look, give me time to make a few arrangements. I'll send them all away just before nightfall, then you come back when it's dark and bring me some ordinary clothes. That way we may manage it.'

'And what happens if your chums come along in the meanwhile to ask what you were doing talking to me?' demanded Greeen.

'Well, obviously, I'll just tell them you were another suitable customer for this yarn about the jewel-in-the-waters, my boy. And you bought it.'

'That's it,' assented Greeen, with an approving nod.

'But then what excuse can you make for sending everyone away from you?' asked Ivansong.

'That's easy too, my son,' answered the Paramahamsa Bonze. 'Why, it's staring you in the face. I just give them Djoyoboyo's prophecy – the hour has struck, Nakhara is to die in order to be reborn. They must go away at once, but I shall stay to contemplate, to watch, so to speak, over the body. I'll only tell them just before it gets dark, and if I am wrong and Nakahara is spared, I'll say, they may come back at dawn.'

The Bonze winked, Greeen laughed, and Ivansong felt like a gatecrasher. He was anyway aching to get to a telephone once more so that he could hear the voice of Thinking Lotus and make sure that all was well at home, and he now noticed with relief that despite his professional esteem for the old twister, Greeen, too, was getting impatient and beginning to fidget in his own secretive way.

'It would have been better if we could have split forces,' Greeen remarked pensively to Ivansong, 'but you'll have to come back with me to Nava to fetch a human disguise for His Unholiness here, I suppose. All right, first we take a look around, then we go.'

'I am bound to protest, my son, that I find your manner a trifle facetious, not to say uncivil,' said the Paramahamsa Bonze, bridling.

'Quite right too,' purred Greeen absently, beginning to open wooden chests and peer within. Then he turned to the

Bonze. 'But don't try to doublecross me, now, will you? Remember that clink is really just like the free world of illusion outside. The length of your stay is strictly a question of *karma*. There's always time off for good behaviour.'

19

'Not a scrap of the paper in place,' remarked Ivansong admiringly as they walked through the courts of Nakhara Wat towards the jetty, where Greeen's boat had already arrived from the Peninsula of Ten Thousand Years and was bobbing alongside next to a tourist ferry.

'Keeps it all in his head,' said Green, adjusting his dark glasses. 'You've got to have brains like that to be able to come a first-class cropper. Ordinary chaps can't do it. They stick to what is so amusingly known as the side of the angels and become cops or spooks or something.'

'Which is why they're always blowing their own operations sky high, I suppose,' rejoined Ivansong sarcastically. 'We've just paid a prolonged visit to the Bonze on a fine, sunny afternoon under the admiring gaze of everyone from his own ecclesiastical bodyguard to the self-effacing Mekinese Reds, and now we leave him alone for an hour or two so that the Chinese can get a fair chance to hear the glad news that he has been chatting to you, and thereafter remove him quietly to a place of safety. Tell me, does it hurt to be a high-grade moron?'

'Only when I cry,' answered Greeen, with a small frown of impatience. 'You know, you'll have to stop over-estimating the enemy, Ivansong. It cramps the style. Can't you see that the

Chinese would never tell a bunch of Mekinese guerrillas about the guru club? So even if they are briefed to protect the Bonze or even to contain him, they are certainly not briefed to spy on him. And although he's got three sacerdotal drop-outs in saffron robes at the foot of the steps to screen visitors, they're his end of the operation. Finally, he has a cast-iron excuse for seeing wicked whites like you and me – to spread word that his occult powers have unmasked the Khammax caper.' Greeen stopped and patted a stone apsara on her shapely haunch. '*Bas relief,*' he murmured equivocally. She had a crack in one eye which made her look as if she were winking.

'And just what is the Khammax caper?' asked Ivansong, thrusting his hands into the pockets of his faded blue trousers and leaning against a granite plinth.

Greeen stroked his chin. 'Well, all right, let me give you the birds and the bees on this one, though it's top secret, mind you. You see, sharing our old military bases and training grounds with their new native owners in this area was not working out too well, and since we were all pulling out of South-east Asia like decent, God-fearing Anglo-Saxons any-way, we got together with the Yanks and decided we might as well get a little place of our own. We British would make the running, so as not to create alarm and despondency, since we are the wrong size nowadays for imperialistic aggression or any of the more vexatious blood-sports. The Americans would stay discreetly in the background, cash in hand.

'Our choice of a site for this particular Asian development programme was Khammax. It belongs to Mekong but it is twenty miles off the coast. It has a deep fishing harbour that offers possibilities if you're looking for a cheap way to build a modest base for subs, destroyers and similar sardinery. It has two high peaks which please the radio-detection and listening-post hams. It has a fine shore-line for simulated assault land-ings, the beginnings of a respectable airfield, a big tangle of forest and swamp for jungle-warfare training infested with malarial mosquitoes, leeches and ticks, and altogether you can describe it as 100 square miles of military paradise.

'So we and Washington want to buy – buy outright. But if it was a delicate proposition to handle when Sissomak was in power, it becomes doubly delicate with Kitay. Everything would depend on the secrecy of the negotiations and the way it was presented to the public – preferably as a *fait accompli*. And now the Chinese have stolen the punch-line. If the Potterslee warning about white men stealing Mekong's jewel in the waters got out, we couldn't even open the bidding.

'Naturally, therefore, the Chinese didn't much mind who heard the prediction first. Once it was interpreted, our diplomats would be urging our governments to scrap the whole Khammax scheme, reports about it in the irresponsible western press would have every dove from Tacoma to Trafalgar Square up in arms, and Kitay would go through the roof of the Royal Palace. The point is that it would be a prophecy of the Paramahamsa Bonze, and it would be believed.'

'Even so, why did you come out in the open?' objected Ivansong. 'You've thrown away a chance to make the whole guru club operation backfire by using him as a double agent and feeding disinformation through him to the Chinese.'

Greeen shook his head. 'If we got him to make prophecies that suited our book, and not theirs, they'd very quickly smell a rat. Furthermore, we couldn't trust him, nor can we be sure that Max may not indulge in a little more destructive foolishness and denounce him to Kitay or the Bonze-Superior in Nava or some similar undesirable. No, dear boy, the guru club is counter-productive however you look at it. There's nothing to be done with it but unscrew it and bury the bits. The Khammax business is the clincher.'

They began to walk slowly towards the jetty again.

'Who knew about this on our side in Mekong?' Ivansong demanded.

'Pawkinson-Convoy, Clarence and me. No, you don't win a blood orange or a Burmese cheroot for guessing right first time. Ah, in Good King Charles's golden days,' Greeen burst out discordantly, 'When loyalty no harm meant, A furious H –'

'Shut up,' urged Ivansong, 'you're annoying the mynahs.

They think you're taking the mickey out of them. And how can you treat this so lightly? It sounds damned serious – the compromising of the Khammax plan, I mean.'

'Indeed, it would be,' agreed Greeen, nodding gravely, 'except that the plan doesn't exist.'

'Well, I do declare,' said Ivansong, after a short silence. 'Don't tell me it's yet another hothouse plant to add to the rest of the lush tropical greenery we already have around here?'

'What did you think? Of course it is. We fed the story through the FCO to Pawkinson-Convoy, and then just waited to see where it would come out. And now we've seen, haven't we? Because the Te Wu obviously assumed that the Khammax plan must have been given too wide a distribution for us ever to trace the leak – you know, Downing Street, Cabinet, Defence Ministry, White House, Pentagon, State Department and all the other compulsive gossips. They weren't to know, poor dears, that it was restricted to about ten people, all of whom knew it was a nonsense except H.E.'

'So the fuse ran from Pawkinson-Convoy to Max to the Chinese to the Paramahamsa Bonze?'

'Just so,' said Greeen, 'and that is why I am being a little peremptory today with our accredited envoy to Mekong.'

'But who was the Chinese link?'

'That pillar of Nava society, Mr. Lee Tian Kwang.'

'Hell, Greeen, you never warned me about him. He was at the Fourth of July reception, listening to an American air force general spewing confidential conjecture around the lawn.'

'Ah well, that sort of stuff is hard to keep down. Anyway, now you know. In the communist world he is known as Short March. He spends much of his time over in Stonecutter Village, ostensibly seeing how the marble is behaving under the knife. But approaching strangers are detected electronically and the whole place is wired to the rooftops for sound. Even the kids in the street and the Kuan Yin statue are bugged.'

Ivansong stopped dead. They were on the causeway leading to the waterfront. 'Just a minute,' he began slowly, the black flecks flashing in his eyes. 'Is that why we made the detour through the village this afternoon? You stood right in front of that statue and said that H.E. was going to tell you all tonight, and you would get him out to Singapore on his way to London first thing tomorrow morning. If that place is bugged, what you were doing was to warn your friend Short March that he only had a few hours in hand if he wanted to shut Pawkinson-Convoy's mouth for good.'

Ivansong examined Greeen more closely. 'But that would make no sense at all if in fact Short March had already framed him by planting the Trojan horse and Peking didn't care if we put him through the MI5 mangle in London, as you claimed. But you didn't really believe all that rubbish about the Chinese and the horse, did you, Greeen? That was just more of your fun. You were selling me a bill of goods, trying to scare me because I'd fooled you with my Miss Flowerclass, inimitable bastard that you are.'

'And whose fault is it if you believed me?' protested Greeen in a wounded tone. 'Really, I sometimes wonder what we pay you for. It was you who told me that the police had found bits of a striker mechanism at the scene of the crime. You're supposed to be familiar with the Chinese negative principle – the empty space on the canvas that suggests a lake, the technique of giving way yourself and using your opponent's own momentum to bring him down. Don't you realise the same applies to bombs?

'Normally the Chinese will never rig up a box of tricks with a firing-pin system that requires a positive act of percussion to explode it. They prefer to detonate their booby-traps electrically. Their victims don't have to hit something to make it go off. They just have to release it. You find a red flag stuck in the ground. You pull it out, and that's that. Why? Because the bottom of the post was in the grip of an ordinary clothes' peg, and when you jerked it away, the two ends of the peg snapped together. That closed a circuit fed by a standard nine-volt battery and up went the charge concealed underneath. Simple. Safe. Distinctly proletarian. Mao approves.'

'So in fact,' said Ivansong slowly, 'neither the Chinese nor

Pawkinson-Convoy tried to blow Mango or me up, which means that Pawkinson-Convoy was in the clear with the Chinese until you made damned sure in that one-sided chat you had with the wired-up Goddess of Mercy that Short March would think he was about to rat on Peking. And you did that because you calculated that the Chinese would then kidnap or kill him at once, if necessary, to stop him from talking. You came personally to Nava to see that Nigel Pawkinson-Convoy never got out of this place alive, Greeen, didn't you? But you then leave Flodden to guard him,' he concluded irritably. 'It simply doesn't add up.'

'No, it doesn't, does it?' exclaimed Greeen in mock astonishment. 'Well, we shall just see what we shall see, won't we?'

Flodden was not in the chancery building, but they found him standing motionless behind a big angsana tree and watching the door of one of the garages for official cars that adjoined it.

'He was in his office until sixteen hundred,' he murmured, his petal-lips pouting and fluting as he formed the words carefully. 'Then he come down to that garage' – he nodded towards it – 'and he's bin shut up inside ever since, kindastyle.'

Greeen walked up to it and the other two followed. He pulled open the right-hand leaf of the double doors, for they were not locked, and they stepped inside. There was no car, for the garage housed the broken platform machine which was normally used for weighing diplomatic bags. To replace this temporarily, a 75-kilogram spring-balance had been suspended by rope from a pulley fixed to a beam, and could be lowered or raised as required. This simple contrivance had very sensibly been hoisted about ten feet above the concrete so that the body of Nigel Pawkinson-Convoy could hang from it by a rope noose and there would still be a comfortable distance between his feet and the floor. A step-ladder left lying untidily on the ground indicated how he had been supported before he swung free. A trolley for moving the diplomatic bags stood in a corner.

Greeen stepped around the slack body in the dove-grey suit, looking up at it was if he were appraising a candelabra in a showroom. 'Right,' he said finally, 'lower away.' Flodden unwound the rope from a cleat on the wall, and the body came to rest untidily on the floor among them. Greeen pushed it on to its back and unhooked the noose from the spring-balance. Ivansong felt a hand. It was still warm, and when he touched the face he found no stiffening of the jaw. 'Too early for rigor mortis, eh?' nodded Greeen. 'But you notice those pinpoints of blood in the eyes? Petechiae haemorrhage, which means he strangled before he hanged, if you get me. Red face, slightly protruding tongue, that all fits. Nothing spectacular. Hanging would have taken about fifteen minutes, but he went much faster. The spring would have softened the fall, but not the contraction of the noose as it took his weight.'

'All right, spare us the Great Pathologist at work. Snoopy does that sort of thing better,' said Ivansong, looking at the dead, implacable eyes and half an octave of yellowing teeth, half-revealed. 'So how did this happen, Flodden? He was trying to bang his head on the ceiling and slipped?'

Flodden was silent. Greeen answered for him. 'My instructions to Flodden said nothing about preventing H.E. from letting someone in by the back gate and talking to them or whatever else it is you have in that suspicious mind of yours. He was simply told that Pawkinson-Convoy was not to leave the compound on any account. That was all. And he didn't. If your insatiable curiosity demands that you know more, you go through channels.'

'Very Chinese again, of course,' remarked Ivansong. 'There's nothing they like better than a neat little bit of poetic justice. Pawkinson-Convoy was always afraid his weight would kill him. And it did.'

'A suitable end for a man who only copulated with his wife in order to keep his figure, I'd say,' Greeen concurred unctuously.

'All right,' said Ivansong. 'One up for Short March. So what now, maestro?'

'You both stay here. Keep that door shut. I'll go and tell Dolly.'

Ivansong attempted no chit-chat with Flodden in the stuffy garage, but Greeen was back surprisingly quickly.

'How did she take it?'

'Like the little gallant lady she is, old boy,' answered Greeen in execrable taste, smoothing back an imaginary guardee moustache. 'She does not wish to see him. I persuaded her it would be better that way. The arrangements she leaves to me.'

'God bless us one and all. And what might they be?'

'All very straightforward really. We bring the Paramahamsa Bonze down here in H.E.'s clothes if he can manoeuvre the trousers over that belly of his, and get the air attaché to fly him down to Singapore with me early in the morning in the guise of our dear departed friend here. He can wear dark glasses, false moustache, that bushwhacker hat P-C loved, ear-muffs or something – even perhaps a scarf or bandage over the damned things – and keep his hat down and collar up and his hands over his face. With luck, it will rain. He goes by car to the airport, passes through the VIP lounge at, say, five a.m. No need for anyone to see him at all.

'Cover story: Pawkinson-Convoy has been recalled for immediate consultation to London and probable reposting. This means working all night so he doesn't go back to the Residence but naps on the couch in his office. Lady P-C can get his luggage packed and taken over to the chancery building this evening. She will follow him to England later when it is confirmed that he is not returning to Nava. Meanwhile London must get on to the FCO and din into them that we can have no murders or suicides in this embassy, and P-C must just quietly disappear. No one cares a damn about him anyway. The Bonze is the thing. Not going too fast for you, am I, duckie?'

'Sure you're not going too fast for yourself?' replied Ivansong ironically. 'Why all the knock-about farce? Couldn't Flodden have simply shot him in the back when no one was looking?'

'What will they send us next?' asked Greeen, appealing to the ceiling. 'Don't you know honesty is the best policy? You can't get caught out for something you didn't do. So the first rule for all men of integrity is to arrange that as far as possible all the dirty work is done by others. Now give us a hand with this.' He took the trolley from against the wall and, under his guidance, Flodden and Ivansong bundled the limp corpse on to it and covered it with some oily sacking that had been left in a corner.

'All right,' said Greeen when all was ready. 'Ivansong, you and I act as forward scouts. Flodden, you follow us up with the main body, so to speak. Destination: the small Buddhist shrine at the back of the compound. It's Wednesday, and it's everyone for tennis, so the coast should be clear if we keep well away from the courts.'

'Christ, you don't really think you're going to get away with this, do you?' protested Ivansong.

'Well,' replied Greeen with equanimity, 'I don't know. If we're lucky we'll be lucky.' And they were.

The shrine was small, dusty and deserted. Greeen switched on a single 40-watt bulb that hung from a rafter. A broken altar in faded gold and vermilion filled one wall, and the two big, broad-shouldered funerary urns stood side by side like sentinels against one another. Flodden tipped Pawkinson-Convoy on to the floor. Greeen kicked aside the sacking, went rapidly through the pockets of the corpse, bounced a bunch of keys in his hand for a moment, and then swung around to look at the urns with narrowed eyes.

'Dead right for size,' he said after a moment. 'Okay, inside with him. The one on the left.'

Ivansong looked at him in disbelief.

'Why, what's wrong with the left-hand one?' asked Greeen.

'You're going to put him in one of those? But where the hell do you think you're going to take it? And in what?'

'Time to think about that later. Where else were you thinking of putting him, anyway? No harm in being a bit sentimental occasionally. He loved these urns, remember?'

'But in this climate he'll be decomposing within three days.'

'That's right,' said Greeen approvingly. 'Now come on and stop trying to dodge the heavy work. Get him on Flodden's shoulder in a fireman's lift. That's it. Steady, now. Fine. I'll get the feet together. Don't damage the paintwork, there. Up a bit. Left a little. No, a bit more. Right-o, straight in, then.

Push it down a bit lower. Whoa! Good. A perfect fit.' Greeen dusted his hands against each other and straightened his tie.

'Flodden, we need cement. Half a carrier-bag will be enough, but we must have it quickly. We can make do with plaster if we have to, and you'll probably find that in the carpenter's store. You can also bring from there a tin of heavy gloss paint or lacquer – we don't need much – and a brush. Right. Move. Ivansong, you mind the urn. I shall be back shortly.'

Ivansong stood watch in the weak yellow light and pinched himself hard. But he was awake. Once there was a small noise from within the urn, and his hair rose. Rigor starting to set in, presumably. What happened if you were bald? He heard the crunch of tyres, and cautiously opened the door of the shrine an inch or so. But it was Greeen with one of the official cars, a sedate Rover saloon. 'The boot,' said Greeen, 'two jerricans and some rubber tubing.'

They fell to the mindless task of siphoning the petrol into the jerricans and emptying them on to the body in the urn until, fifteen gallons later, it was topped up. By this time Flodden had returned with a small bag of filler plaster, which he began mixing with water from the radiator of the car. Greeen pushed the earthenware bung of the urn over the neck and tamped it into place. Flodden then covered and sealed it with a generous layer of the cement, while his master stepped back to admire his handiwork.

'*Boeuf en daube*, so to speak,' he said, jingling Pawkinson-Convoy's keys. 'I've never seen him looking so good. When the plaster's dried, the excellent Flodden will give it a couple of coats of gloss, but you and I will now take a peek at the ambassadorial office, and afterwards, Ivansong, you will go about your business with the Bonze. For that we must get the good Dolly to give us some old cast-offs, which I am sure she will do, charitable soul that she is.'

'But damn it all, you revolting ghoul, you can't go and disturb her again after the shock she's already had. For God's sake have a little consideration for people. Some of them are actually human beings, though of course you have no means of knowing that.'

'Now don't fret, duckie,' soothed Greeen. 'Dolly can take it, I'm sure.'

'What did she actually say when you gave her the news?'

'She straightened up and her eyes met mine fearlessly, bless her,' answered Greeen, giving Ivansong one of his smaller smiles. 'And then she said, "Well, well, the people that die. But tell me, Mr. Greeen, what did the spring-balance actually *register*?" '

20

As soon as they reached the ambassador's office, Ivansong seized the telephone (which on a Wednesday afternoon was automatically switched to an outside line), dialled his home number, and held his breath while he waited for Thinking Lotus to answer.

'. . . courtesy of the Nava Telephone Board,' an impersonal voice said at last, 'at the third stroke it will be –'

'*Who?*' shouted Ivansong, angrily. 'What the –?'

'Oh, Mr. Ivansong,' said Thinking Lotus. 'How nice. I was only discouraging our worried well-wishers among the police, the press, and the shopkeepers with whom we have outstandingly outstanding accounts. They have been telephoning all afternoon. So touching. But you are different. You haven't been doing anything of the sort. Where are you, Larry? Are you coming home? Something awful has happened.'

Ivansong felt the blood leave his face and the sweat start in his hand. 'Lotus,' he begged, dry-mouthed, 'what is it?'

'There is a cable from your mother in London asking if anything is wrong because you forgot to send her a greetings telegram for her birthday on Monday.'

'Oh, my God, of course,' groaned Ivansong, faint with relief. 'Does she sound mad?'

'Middling hopping,' replied Lotus, 'but do not worry. I am cabling her back a soothing draft. There is also a faintly menacing note from the Singapore Comptroller of Income Tax. He says you owe him –'

'But hold on, for God's sake!' cried Ivansong. 'Hold on! What I want to know is, are you all right, and Mango, and the house, and what about Ah King, and –?'

'Us?' queried Lotus, surprised but brisk. 'But naturally. A detective came back to look at the pool when it was empty. The gardener has buried everything and is now washing it out. The police are still on the gate. Ah King has stopped boasting and has started cooking at last, and Mango is talking about becoming a spycatcher with a bowler hat and umbrella who performs brilliant brain surgery on the side. It will mean changing her name to Casey Steed, it seems, but she feels sure you will not. . . Larry, are you very busy just now?'

'Kind of,' answered Ivansong, tartly, all his loving anxiety ignominiously deflated. 'I'll be back sometime between seven and eight – probably with a guest for the night.' And with this Parthian shot he rang off.

Greeen had found nothing in the safe but a hand-written signed despatch with a note pinned to it saying, 'Clarence. Please deal with this. And kindly remember, *De mortuis*, etc. P-C.'

He detached the note, and Ivansong heard the pin drop. 'Suicide,' he muttered.

The despatch read:

Confidential.
The British Ambassador at Nava to the Secretary of State for Foreign and Commonwealth Affairs.

(There followed a short summary with numbered paragraphs, and then:)

To the Rt. Hon. Sir Dunstan Ronsmith

No. 15   H. M. Embassy, Nava.
Ref AM 314/5   Date:
Sir,

1. This despatch is designed to clarify and correct reports of questionable veracity that will doubtless be made available by other sources on the subject of my sudden demise.

2. My first contact with Chinese Communists occurred in 1943 when I was landed by submarine from Ceylon on the west coast of Japanese-occupied Malaya, and was guided to a group headquarters of the Malayan Communist Party (M.C.P.) in the jungles of the State of Pahang. The M.C.P. was the driving force within the Malayan People's Anti-Japanese Army which was harassing the invader with acts of sabotage and terrorism. Its members were almost entirely Chinese, and my duties were to instruct recruits in the use of the arms and explosives that South-east Asia Command was despatching to them, and to assure the liaison between the M.C.P. and our own men in Force 136 in my particular sector.

3. In consequence I lived and worked in a jungle camp with some fifty Chinese, ranging from party cadres to young girls who had offered to play their part against the Japanese enemy in this difficult and dangerous type of war. These people showed admirable fortitude and courage in all circumstances, and their discipline, their cleanliness, and their acceptance of the hazards and discomforts of a rain-forest in which they subsisted on a Spartan daily ration were just as impressive. After some months with these diligent and continent people, I was moved, and ultimately found myself for several weeks living almost cheek by jowl with their leader, and now Party Secretary-General, Chin Peng, for whom I formed a great regard.

4. I was able to meet Chin Peng again in Malaya just after the war ended in 1945, when I was on my way to take part in

a British military liaison mission to the Chinese Nationalist Government of Chiang Kai-shek in Chungking. Hearing of this, Chin Peng, who was fully aware of the high esteem in which I held himself and his movement, asked if I would permit him to put me into touch with friends of his who were negotiating with the Generalissimo on behalf of Mao Tsetung. I expressed myself agreeable, and it was therefore during that period that I was first approached by officials of what was to be the government of the People's Republic of China. In 1946 I was demobilised and joined the Foreign Service, and from then until 1954 was occasionally able to perform services which I deemed to be in the interests of better Anglo-Chinese understanding, even if at times they involved superficial sacrifices on the part of H.M.G.

5. However, I have the honour to inform you, Sir, that in 1954 my meetings with Chinese diplomats and officials multiplied, and a far closer working relationship was established. At that time First Secretary attached to the Delegation to the Geneva Conference, I was treated by the Chinese with unfailing consideration and deference, and my first informal interview with the Prime Minister, Chou En-lai, was an inspiring experience.

('Yes, but how was the *ping-pong*, Pawkinson-Convoy?' hissed Greeen.)

Thereafter a regular connection was established with representatives of the central Chinese department in Peking responsible for liaison with me ('Responsible for liaison? They were running you for all you were worth, you pompous ass') and as may have been observed from my career it was part of my duties to engineer for them little incidents that were calculated to inflame local feeling against H.M. embassies abroad. My recent attempt to set up funerary urns beside the statue of Queen Victoria at Nava was the last example of this aspect of my work.

('Just so, "superficial sacrifices on the part of H.M.G.",' Ivansong murmured.)

6. My fidelity to the Maoist theory of permanent revolution is absolute. As Chairman Mao says, there must always be

change and revolution, the constant solving of contradictions. The British system flouts this basic principle, seeking only to create an affluent welfare state in which all movement finally comes to rest at a point of inertia, and there is nothing left to do because all things are being done for all men irrespective of merit.

7. But I have to inform you further that there is no such thing as a free and equal society, for if there is to be total equality, it must depend on total control, since men are not born equal and therefore have to be made so. Conversely, total freedom means total competition, with the ruthless climbing to the top on the heads of the scrupulous. All western talk about equality and freedom is therefore so much cant. The Chinese, on the other hand, are building a new society whose members need demand neither equality nor freedom, for it is based on selflessness, diligence, thrift, discipline, self-reliance, courage, a strict morality, and an overriding sense of community. It will be a true classless society, and my experience in Malaya has convinced me that the Chinese communists are made of the stuff that can achieve it.

8. In the battery-chicken civilisation of the welfare state in the west, however, upstarts and ignoramuses with no values beyond the market quotation for the pound sterling are treated better than the dedicated, the self-sacrificing, the heroic, and the visionary, and through their materialistic opportunism are enabled to dominate worthier men. In the permissive society the clean and disciplined life of the young Chinese is mirrored by slovenliness and promiscuity, dirt and sloth, drug-addiction and the degenerate pseudo-philosophies of idlers and dropouts and long-haired ninnies. *Ubi solitudinem faciunt, pacem appellant.*

('Where they make a wilderness, they call it peace,' said Greeen. 'Not bad.')

9. Sir, I decline to be a second-class Englishman in this inverted and doomed society, much as the colonial Asians who joined the communists in post-war years declined to be second-class Frenchmen or Dutchmen. But today I learned that the communists themselves had rejected me, and had left

me to the mercies of my fellow-countrymen. Under the circumstances, therefore, only one course is open to me. I have to request, however, that my past actions be interpreted in their correct light – as a contribution towards a closer relationship between a sinking Britain and a rising China, and thus towards the regeneration and salvation of my own country.

10. As my last duty in this respect, I transmit to you the annexed report on the activities of my present temporary security adviser, Mr. Greeen, and his assistant, Mr. Flodden, in Athens in 1960 where I was myself *en poste* and therefore implicated. It may be decided that this should now be the subject of a formal enquiry and prosecution.

11. I am sending copies of this despatch to Her Majesty's representatives at Peking, Bangkok, Saigon, Phnom Penh, and Vientiane.

> I have the honour to be
> with the highest respect
> Sir,
> Your obedient servant
> Nigel Pawkinson-Convoy

Ivansong reached over to turn the last page and see the annexe, but Greeen gently detached it. 'I'll take that one, I think,' he said with a saurian smile. His eye seemed to lack its usual malicious gleam, however, and Ivansong suddenly realised that his own knowledge that the damning annexe on Athens existed at all – whatever it said – might now just possibly get him out of the pernicious clutches of this middle-aged monster. Athens might also explain why the diligent Greeen had painstakingly pursued his investigation of Pawkinson-Convoy, and then preferred him to be rubbed out in Nava rather than wrung out in New Scotland Yard, or wherever they kept their arc-lights these days.

But who had planted the wooden horse?

21

Young monks no longer guarded the foot of the stairway to the hermitage of the Paramahamsa Bonze, and when Ivansong climbed to the top of it in the gathering darkness, he found the holy man sitting by himself in the main chamber next to a battered expandable suitcase and a small plastic travel bag, twirling champagne in an ice-bucket.

'A farewell bottle of bubbly,' he said, lifting it so that the Veuve Clicquot label could be seen in the glow of the concealed fluorescent lights. He sighed, drew the cork with some difficulty, and poured out two glasses. 'Well, my son,' he said, looking around. 'This is a bit of a wrench, you know. I couldn't even say goodbye to the girls properly, as they're not in the act.'

'You haven't seen anyone else?'

The Paramahamsa Bonze shook his head.

'Cheer up,' said Ivansong. 'Everything has its compensations. At least you won't have to knock yourself out pretending to meditate for hours on end outside, where everyone could see you.'

The Bonze nodded without conviction. 'You know, I'll tell you something you wouldn't credit.' He paused, hesitating, and then he looked Ivansong in the eye a little furtively. 'I got hooked,' he admitted at last.

'Hooked?'

'Yes. I mean – and I've never dared tell anyone this before – I talked myself into it. I became a convert. There, now I've said it. Can you imagine? I've – well, not to put too fine a point on it, I've been seeking awakening, enlightenment, even Nirvana.

'Now, for Lord's sake don't go telling anyone else that, will you? It's more than my reputation is worth to let it out. But it's the truth. I sat out there meditating for hours on end, trying to open my mind to the realisation of the One. And you know what happened, what came into my head? Fiddles – I've dreamed up more and bigger fiddles out on that platform than I could ever possibly try to pull if I lived to a hundred-and-fifty. A gold mine in fiddles. When I was looking for God or whatever you want to call That. Marvellous, isn't it?' He smacked his small red lips, gave a ghost of a fat, mellifluous laugh, and poured out more champagne.

'Go on, you're just getting old,' retorted Ivansong. 'Youth is the booze-up, age is the morning after, and religion is simply the alcoholic remorse. Anyway, how could you ever hope to escape from the illusion, you of all people? You know the Hindu theory. Purusha, the One, is like a great actor, and we are all the different roles he has split himself into. If once we can get outside our individual part, this strutting paint-and-powder ego of ours, and step off the stage into reality, we shall see that we are in fact of Purusha himself.

'But you can't even get away from the string of imaginary individuals you've been posing as all your life in order to become George McWimbledon Potterslee again. So how can you hope to get yourself out of the bit-part of George McWimbledon Potterslee to discover that you are one with The Infinite? Here's how.'

'Cheers,' echoed the Bonze glumly. 'I know. Don't tell me. You must let go of your mind, forget the obscuring stars and absorb the void behind, the emptiness beyond thought. But you know how it is, my son. You can understand the principle that there is an underlying principle to the Cosmos, but the trouble is you can't get to see the underlying principle itself. Well, I thought before I got fuddled with years, you know, I'd like to have a bash at it. But nothing doing, it seems.'

'In that case I think we should squeeze you into your new

205

role, then,' suggested Ivansong. He opened the bag he had brought with him, and they set to work. The trousers were a dangerously tight fit, but the Paramahamsa Bonze managed to get the zip-fastener three-quarters of the way up. The bush shirt was adequate, the digger hat was a trifle too small but the chinstrap held it in place, and the shoes were much too large. 'Never mind,' said Ivansong facetiously, 'you'd pass all right in a crowd of Paramahamsa Bonzes dressed for the outback. Dark glasses – you needn't put them on yet – and that's it except for these.'

He pulled out a roll of Elastoplast and a pair of scissors, tucked the great Buddha-lobes up behind the ears, fixing them in place with the sticking plaster, and then taped the ears themselves close to the head. 'Well, it can't be helped, that's the best we can do for now,' he said. 'We'll fix you up better down in Nava. By tomorrow you'll have a moustache and you won't know yourself, as usual.'

'Moustache, what do I want that for, and where do I get it?'

'I think, as a matter of fact, it will have to be fashioned from a piece of my wife's favourite wig. But you'll be all right, you'll find,' Ivansong watched the Bonze for a moment, and walked past him to the entrance of the chamber. 'Oh, George!' he called abruptly.

'Yes?' answered the Bonze, turning casually.

'That's it,' said Ivansong, 'that's it, the perfect, natural, intuitive movement. There's your spontaneity. That is the way to escape from the illusion.' And as the heavy-lidded eyes widened in surprise, he snapped off the fluorescent lights.

Potterslee found himself plunged into sudden darkness relieved only by the odd bluish outlines, the images on his retina of the objects that had been before him until just a moment ago – the table, the champagne bucket, the suitcase, a chair, Ivansong. But they were figments now, fading rapidly, and beyond them was black, infinite, indivisible, unidentifiable nothing. After a long silence, the Paramahamsa Bonze muttered, 'Put the lights on, would you?' He looked at Ivansong intently when he reappeared and raised a trembling hand as if clutching at something. 'Just for a moment, there,' he said hoarsely, 'just for a —'

'Don't grasp!' yelled Ivansong, throwing a book that had been left on the table at him. 'Don't grasp!'

The Bonze shook his head and picked up the book — it was, Ivansong saw, a copy of the *Kama Sutra*. 'Gone now,' he said. 'But it was there all right, it was —'

'Don't try to describe it, you damned fool,' said Ivansong violently. 'Everyone knows it cannot be described.'

'*Satori*,' breathed the Bonze. 'Awakening or something very near it. I would never have believed it possible. What made you do what you did?'

'That Zen trick of calling someone's name and getting him to turn around spontaneously — just to show what spontaneity is — is an old con job as you would doubtless say. The other was a guess. You know, there was a Frenchman who achieved *satori* unexpectedly because he opened an umbrella against a bright night sky full of stars, and suddenly there was this great round black hole in the universe — the Void. That was his moment of enlightenment. I was thinking along those lines.'

The Paramahamsa Bonze nodded, but meanwhile his eyes, fixed on a far point that had no dimensions, were widening slowly with a curious mixture of perception and astonishment and disbelief. 'Tell you something, though,' he said suddenly yet faintly, struggling to his feet again. 'We've got to get out of here, yes, out of here, and fast. This place has had it, son.' And he spoke with the certainty of one who had been master of the world for the eternity of a single, isolated moment.

They left the lights burning in the big chamber to deceive any watcher, and slipped over the edge of the platform outside as quickly and quietly as they could. Once in the shadow of the steep, stone stairway, however, the Paramahamsa Bonze paused, his suitcase and travel-bag in his hand and his ridiculous clothes draped about him.

'So Djoyoboyo really foretold it all,' he whispered in awe, looking back at the dark silhouette of the tower.

'Except that he didn't,' retorted Ivansong. ''That book you

bought was a fake, and Pekelvlees is doing his third term right now for selling false first editions and souped-up treasure-maps to the gullible rich.'

The Bonze threw up his head and started to laugh softly, and he did not stop until he had somehow reached the bottom step without falling over Pawkinson-Convoy's size-eleven brogues. But in the shadowed courts of Nakhara Wat, inter-mittently illuminated by no more than a knife-edge of moon, he tripped heavily on the edge of a thick flagstone, and his plastic airbag flew out of his hands, striking the rough corner of a granite pedestal which ripped a three-inch tear in its side. He was on his feet with the speed of an athlete, but Ivansong reached the bag first. It was leaking trinkets, ingots, loose gems, diamonds, and small ornaments of beaten gold. He unzipped it and pulled out another handful.

The Bonze dusted himself down and shrugged. They both began picking up the fallen treasure without speaking. Ivan-song opened the empty case in which he had brought the ill-fitting mufti for Potterslee's latest illusory role, and dropped the broken travel-bag into it. After this, he took the other's hand and gently shook its glittering contents loose so that they fell on top of the bag. Then he closed the case.

'Look,' protested the Bonze, breathless but indignant, 'that's legitimately mine, you know. Treasure trove. When they built the temples and monuments of Nakhara, they buried these gewgaws under the foundations as offerings to the gods. Well, I found them. Come on, fair's fair. Anyway, how do I know what you're going to do with them? You'd probably keep them for yourself. Why not spare a struggling old man the little he has, and go and dig up your own fortune?'

'Well, well,' murmured Ivansong sadly, 'and I thought you were going to say something dramatic and touching like – "Now I have seen the light I want no baubles from this world of illusion. Take them, my son, take them." '

'Not likely,' riposted the Bonze. 'What do you think I was doing when I made you go away and leave me alone this afternoon? You don't imagine I kept them up in that chamber, do you? Hard work, it's been – finding them, then hiding them, and then digging them up again.

'And you forget something,' he went on, gaining momentum, 'I am the Paramahamsa Bonze, remember? These things cannot harm me because I am already beyond worldly greed. They are far safer with me than with those like yourself who might be tempted by them to cling to the Wheel of Life. Let me do you a favour and take them off your hands. You'll be all the nearer to Nirvana, I promise you.'

Ivansong held on to the case and started walking. The Bonze waddled along beside him. 'It's a terrible injustice you are doing me, you know,' he warned in his plummiest voice. 'Purusha plays all the parts in the cosmic comedy, the good as well as the bad, since he is a manifestation of the One. I mean it stands to reason, doesn't it? So I mean it follows that there should be no penalty for the transgressor, because he's as much part of God and God's extravaganza as the saint is.

'So I'll tell you what I'll do with you, my son, now we've got that settled,' concluded the Bonze in his well-rounded canonical tones, 'I'll split you in for twenty – yes, not eighteen, not nineteen, mind, but *twen – ty* percent of the take on this stuff. Now I can't say fairer than that, can I? How about it?'

'I think you had better stop burbling,' Ivansong admonished him, 'and be a little more self-effacing. We're almost at the jetty, and there's a man looking after the outboard I came in.'

'Thirty,' threw in the Bonze swiftly. 'That's my last word.'

But Ivansong said nothing, and the Bonze crossed the river, its waters gleaming faintly under the dying moon, in frustrated silence. However, as they walked towards The Bitch, which was parked opposite the bordellos along the Boulevard du Mekong, the seer renewed his attack.

'So your moment of awareness has changed nothing?' Ivansong asked at last.

'It's taught me I must be my natural, spontaneous, intuitive self,' came the quick rejoinder, 'and I'm grateful to you for that, really I am.' They reached the car, and Ivansong put the two suitcases into the boot.

'But you still talk as if I were the slave of greed and

ambition,' the Bonze added reproachfully. 'You forget that Hinduism and Buddhism teach a certain submission to destiny. "When the water level rises, the fish eat ants; when it falls, the ants eat fish," as the Laotians say.

'We are told to accept with indifference both pain and pleasure. I do not cry out against my change of fortune,' he went on piously as they got into the car and Ivansong turned the ignition key. 'Everything must be borne with fortitude, for what, after all, is pleasure but less pain?'

'I'm so glad you take things in that admirable way,' said Ivansong warmly, 'because then you won't mind if the fate of those movable assets of yours is decided by others. And you also won't mind pushing this *bloody* car, saving your cloth,' he added, 'because, you see, the battery's gone flat as a pancake again.'

22

I

'He is a little like a polythene bag stuffed with suet,' remarked Thinking Lotus, patting her dyed black hair carefully after she had installed the Paramahamsa Bonze in Ivansong's room, 'and Ah King has been a trifle discourteous in her forthright Cantonese way about his fine spread of barbarian posterior, but his relations with Mango are most cordial.'

They went upstairs together, an arm around each other's waist, to see who was winning. 'One for you,' Mango was saying, giving him a card, 'and one for me. Two for you,' she went on giving him a second card, 'and one, two for me,' she added giving herself two. 'Three for –'

'Now, have a heart, love,' pleaded the Paramahamsa Bonze. 'You can't pull that old dodge on me. That was in a Marx Brothers flick before even your mother was a twinkle in the otherwise inscrutable eye of your grandfather. No, you don't want to do it like that either. Always remember, there's a right way and a wrong way of going about every swindle in the book. Look, I'll show you. Take the pack in your left hand. That's it. . .'

The Bonze had cheered up a little, consoling himself with the thought that all was not yet lost. Moreover, he had delicately indicated that he had not reached the end of his resources by suddenly pulling a large and angry ruby from somewhere on his person and offering it to Thinking Lotus. 'Put a ring with that in it on your finger,' he had urged her, 'and every man will want to kiss your hand.'

Lotus had caught her breath characteristically but refused the stone with an elegant little gesture of rejection. 'I only want one man to kiss my hand,' she had told him, 'and he will do it without my wearing rubies.' And she had gone away to cut him a natty little moustache out of her black wig.

Greeen's preposterous operation had begun well. Evidently Short March, caught with very little time in hand between the two successive items of intelligence that Pawkinson-Convoy was blown and the Paramahamsa Bonze had sent away his acolytes, had failed to move fast enough in either direction. And thanks to the indiscretion of the pallid American air force general at the Fourth of July reception, the holy man's prediction that Nakhara was to be destroyed might not even have sounded suspicious to him. It looked as if they were in the clear. The Bonze had safely disappeared. The house was still guarded by police. Flodden was stretched out comfortably on a rattan chair in the downstairs living-room, listening with feet crossed and the faintest suggestion of a sneer on his face to a programme of Delius on the radio.

But Ivansong was in a less relaxed mood, for after a day

that seemed to have lasted three years Greeen had warned him that he must put in an appearance at a party thrown by Oliver Clarence. The party had been planned four weeks before as a dinner for ten, but had been blown up into a buffet at the last minute to take in as many people as were available, for the outside world must think that all was normal within the decapitated British embassy.

Clarence always entertained on the flat roof of his house, which was lit by coloured lanterns and decorated with potted orchids. Ivansong inevitably arrived late. White-coated boys were already pushing trolleys bearing not only drinks but platters of food among the guests, and the chatter was rising skyward with that mounting volume and urgency which always gives the impression that an entire diplomatic reception may suddenly take off at any moment and migrate elsewhere, like a flock of wild geese.

'No, the old man won't be coming,' the air attaché was saying loudly to anyone who would listen. 'He's burning the midnight oil in his office. I'm flying him down to Singers tomorrow for a pow-wow. Got to give 'em the gen on what's happening up here, what with everything getting so flaming dicey.' And indeed guests could see from the parapet that a lamp was burning on the first floor of the chancery building.

Ivansong was quickly surrounded by compassionate friends who were themselves dying to hear the shocking details of Mini's sudden translation into sound and light that morning. Only Charlie Polak seemed genuinely sorry. A dazed Max stood apart, blood-and-thunder* in hand, arguing sulkily with Felicity Slipstream and swaying slightly from side to side. The death of Mini had evidently pitched him off the water-wagon as brutally as the death of Cigar had pitched him on to it. Ivansong slipped through the circle of ghoulish sympathy around him and joined them.

'Max,' Miss Clipstream was saying, unwise with worry, 'I hope you realise that's your fifth.'

'You see?' the métis countered unhappily, spilling some of it down his heliotrope Hawaii shirt. 'She is already counting

*Four parts cognac and one party cherry brandy, served on the rocks.

my drinks. Yet a gibbon does not even count his years.'

'He still grows old,' remarked Ivansong mildly.

'If he is allowed to by his so-called betters,' Max returned at once, and Ivansong saw the wild light in his eye and caught a quick warning grin from Felicity.

'Bah,' Max continued disgustedly, taking a long swallow. 'You are all savages. Vous n'y comprenez rigoureusement rien. Why the hell do I still have to live among you?'

This could become dangerous, thought Ivansong, and took a chance.

'And I,' he echoed, looking Max in the eye. 'Why the hell do I still have to live with you and your dubious friends?'

Max frowned, hesitating. Ivansong sensed the ghostly presence of a moment of truth and held his breath. Then the métis shook his head. 'No,' he declared finally, in a flat voice, as if suddenly drained of emotion, 'you do not have to live with me and my – my dubious friends any more, Monsieur Ivansong. Parceque je te dirai franchement, j'en ai marre de tout ça, tu sais? Enough is already too much. A few scores to settle, and after that –'

'What are you planning to do, then, Max?' Ivansong asked anxiously, drawing him aside and helping himself to a spring roll from a trolley of hot Chinese delicacies a few feet away.

Max chewed glumly on a deep-fried prawn. 'There is nothing left for me here. Nothing! So, a partnership in wild life survey work' – he shrugged and stuck out his lower lip sceptically – 'well, but it has attractions. Miss Clipstream is, of course, already working for the International Foundation, and it seems possible that I also could –'

'I wouldn't worry too much if that did not work out, anyway,' Greeen interrupted smoothly, stretching between them from behind to seize a curry puff. 'If all else fails I am sure some big American organisation could be persuaded to fork up for you as a small token of appreciation, don't you think? And then of course the Soviet Academy of Sciences. . .'

Oh, God, not the CIA and the KGB too, prayed Ivansong. Max was like that small pagoda in North Vietnam, built on a single wooden pillar, which was supposed to concentrate upon itself all the geomantic forces of the land. The death of Mini and life with Miss Clipstream had between them invalidated the entire established pattern of security and intelligence work in the area, he was thinking. The wiring and insulation on the diagram could no longer be trusted, for everywhere that Max had touched it there might at any moment be a short-circuit.

'If you "settle old scores" as you say, Max,' he warned, 'you are going to throw out everyone's charts and calculations here – British, Chinese, American, Russian – for the balance of security that depended on your discretion will have gone. So why not just drop out silently?' Ivansong poured himself a whisky and soda. 'I shall be the first to congratulate you.'

'What was that?' asked Miss Clipstream, coming upon them suddenly. 'Congratulate him on what?' She extended a long simian arm towards Max and, taking off her glasses, looked at him with the vague cupidity of the myopic female. 'Does this mean you are planning to cast me off, or take me on?'

Max swayed back on his heels and looked down his nose at her with the fine disdain of the slightly boiled. 'Take you on?' he repeated. 'Are you suggesting I should risk making an honest woman of you, as you hypocritical Anglo-Saxons say?' He swallowed more of his drink, but Ivansong sensed that while his body was tipsy, his mind was sober, nagged by its own indecision.

'What's so hypocritical about it?' he asked sharply. 'I thought you believed that the only honourable way to do things was for money? Well, in our income bracket, wives get paid, lovers don't. You have to go up in the scale before men keep mistresses and wives keep husbands.'

'Eh bien,' muttered Max, glancing at Miss Clipstream and looking a little lost. 'I suppose there is more than one way to cook one's goose.'

'Don't be so sure of her, either.' Ivansong pressed his advantage. 'If you procrastinate, she may go off with some fine young blue-eyed British intellectual from the faculty of one of our more zoologically-minded universities.'

'Not effing likely,' retorted Miss Clipstream, chastely up-

214

dating Pygmalion in a loud voice. 'I'm sick of men who only want to press me sentimentally between the pages of a book. My first word of advice to my daughters will be "don't take any wooden academics".'

'You see?' Max regarded her morosely. 'Elle est folle, mais elle est adorable, that's the trouble.' There was capitulation in his voice. 'You have no idea what those arms can do.' He sighed. 'And then again I must confess that life has really become *obscenely* complicated.'

'Then uncomplicate it, for Heaven's sake,' said Ivansong, and turned away tactfully in search of shrimp dumplings.

'Look,' he urged a few minutes later when Miss Clipstream had retired to cure a sudden fit of hiccoughs. 'Go while the going is good, Max. Someone may want to eliminate you and all the compromising cross-indexed information that still remains inside your head. You have been playing it a bit too close to God, you know.'

'Peuh! And why not?' rejoined Max sardonically. 'Let me tell you something about this God of yours. Perhaps I acknowledge him, but I do not have to like his attitude. Enfin, je trouve qu'il n'est pas très sérieux, tu sais, même pas très *correct*. Nevertheless, perhaps his penchant for playing one side off against another is his secret of success, because please note one thing about him above all else' – and Max tapped Ivansong on the chest to emphasize each word – 'despite all his enemies, he *survives*, mon vieux, he *survives*.'

'That does not prove that you will,' retorted Ivansong promptly. 'It's always dangerous to generalise from the particular, you know.'

'Clichés again!' sneered Max. But Ivansong saw he had won.

2

Ten minutes later Charlie Polak button holed Ivansong and swung him around. 'Get a load of that chick over there,' he breathed. 'Wouldn't you just love to teach her the fictions

15

of life?' Ivansong turned to see that the etiolated American air force general had brought the igneous Miss Cannabière to the party with them, undressed to kill.

'No problem,' he told Polak. 'If you have the lolly, she has the love.'

'No kidding? The Mosaic type? A roll for your roll? A screw for your screw? You mean she doesn't just do it for secrets? Jees, I took it she was some kind of Mata Hari working for the French. After all, this place is stiff with spooks tonight. Or hadn't you noticed, Larry?' asked Polak with a you-son-of-a-gun glint in his eye.

'Max at work again, I suppose,' answered Ivansong, after a pause, smiling wryly at the large New Yorker. 'But it's quits, Charlie,' he added, staring steadily back at him. 'Yes, I had noticed the place was stiff with spooks.'

'How come?' But the question was not to be answered.

'Hello, Charles,' said Greeen affably, coming up before Ivansong could reply. 'Your friend Inqvist been planting any more Trojan horses lately?'

A kind of numbness crept over Ivansong, not dissimilar to the dizzy detachment that isolated him from his body when he was in deep relaxation. 'Inqvist?' he heard himself say at last.

'Larry,' interpolated Polak quickly, 'I swear I didn't know anything about this until we heard the explosion and he thought the operation had succeeded and was so happy he gave the game away. That was when I found I was fresh out of tranquillizers.'

But Ivansong hardly heard him. Feeling, a sudden sense of the urgent present, was flooding back into his body. 'By Christ, I'll kill that bastard,' he whispered harshly, 'where the hell is he?'

'Over there.' Greeen pointed to where the flat cropped field of Inqvist's grey bristle shone in the lamplight next to Straw-bury's hay and the lacquered black of General Keo's coif. 'But leave him alone, Ivansong. He wasn't going for you or yours. Believe it or not,' Greeen's eyes lengthened slowly with amusement, 'he was trying for Kitay and his.'

'*Kitay?* Well then how the devil could –?' Ivansong stopped short, the memory of all those misdirected letters coming back to him. 'Well, for God's sake, our house and Kitay's,' he muttered in a slow, deliberate voice, 'the two one-hundred-and-seventy-ones of rue du Bassac. The geomancers love giving that number because it's reversible, which is lucky for a start, it adds up to nine and is therefore three times three, it's got Oneness on each side and blessed seven in the middle, and it's more than your life's worth to try to change it. But you'd think he'd have made sure that the man who delivered the horse could tell our two places apart.'

'Does your postman even know the difference?' asked Greeen. 'After all, they're both large and ornate wooden houses in traditional Mekinese style. Inqvist's Santa Claus was probably some half-literate Vietnamese legman for the CIA who wouldn't know Buck House from the Shwe Dragon Pagoda – especially in the evil hour before dawn. And another thing. You never entertain Inqvist. Perhaps he isn't aware that there are two houses numbered 171 in rue du Bassac and didn't even warn his man.'

They both looked at Polak, who waved his hands in front of his face, warding them off. 'I don't know how the sonofa-bitch arranged it,' he protested, 'though I guess that's just about the way the balls-up bounced. Don't ask me. The initials of my organisation are N-A-B-S-. Got it? NABS – North American Broadcasting System. Don't confuse me with any other acronym from now on, gentlemen.'

'But what was the idea?' asked Ivansong. 'Liquidate the uncooperative Kitay? Throw a scare into him and persuade him to resign and go into exile? Break his heart over the death of his youngest kid? – sanctimonious little brat, mind you, but still.'

'Well.' Greeen nodded his head towards the silver fuzz and the dead-pan face of the CIA man. 'He has his successor standing by, hasn't he?' They could just hear the voice of General Keo grinding out the word 'democracy' as if he were mincing it for a gettysburger. It was followed by a buoyant, mellow lilt that ran: 'Yup, the population explosion em-

217

phasizes the dichotomy between establishment and people and so traumatically obfuscates any meaningful qualitative evaluation of future democratic institutionalisation, I guess. But with due respect, General, our findings are that compulsory sterilization or surgical emasculation and even induced effemination and virginity are only superficial solutions. On the other hand, I have a team working on something really fundamental and groovy.'

'Groovy, Monsieur Strawbury?' asked the bewildered police chief.

'Yessir, General.'

'And what is that? Human rites, perhaps?'

'Smaller people.'

'Ah!'

'How in Heaven's name did you know it was Inqvist all the time,' Ivansong asked Greeen fiercely when Polak had wandered away in search of Miss Cannabière and consolation, 'and why didn't you tell me, you bastard?'

'Be your age, Ivansong. I've been guessing up to now myself, and Polak has only just confirmed a fairly wild hunch. Anyway, I'm sure all that fatherly fury of yours has been good for the adrenalin, so what are you complaining about, duckie?'

Greeen glanced around sleepily to make sure that they were alone. 'Look, half-baked though your education may have been,' he began amiably enough, 'only a damned fool would send a fine upstanding product of our nightmarish Graeco-Roman-Christian civilization a simple Latin tag which even you could probably translate, and which would therefore put you on your guard at once. And only a congenital idiot would have made quite sure that you had plenty of warning by taking the appalling risk of telling his sidekick to break in and leave his card upstairs on a table almost outside your bedroom door.

'Can you see the Chinese, who are maniacs for quotations, making a mistake like that? Can you see the fastidious Pawkinson-Convoy being so academically impure as to use a phrase about Carthaginian treachery to describe an outstanding example of *Greek* horseplay?

'No, my good fellow, the tag was a dirty joke, possibly intended to teach a haughty Asian prince who thought himself a cut above the Caucasians and all their cultural works that he had lost a child because he couldn't read two words of Latin, the goddamned monkey.'

'But that's just it,' broke in Ivansong. 'Where do you get this goddamned monkey business? Why should it have been Inqvist or any other American?'

'Look, Inqvist has taken up western culture in a big way through a series of rich, handsome volumes offered at derisory prices by certain philanthropic American publishers who let you have the books because they are only interested in the money. He is just the man to start throwing around tags like "Punica Fide" that he's memorised from some list in one of them – you know: "Casual classical quotations for smart cosmopolitan occasions. Baffle your friends. Surprise your enemies." That sort of thing. And it had to be an American, of course.'

'Why of course?'

'Well, you don't really think anyone was mad enough to insist that his agent leave the card on the landing, do you? He probably wanted to make sure it wasn't blown to bits with the horse, and simply told him to ease open a shutter and slip it inside somewhere on the ground floor. There wouldn't be much risk. After all, he had an excuse for sneaking up as far as the front door. He was just delivering a Feast-of-the-Beast gift. Are you with me?'

'For my sins,' sighed Ivansong, but he was listening carefully, and suddenly it was there. 'British ground floor equals American first floor.'

'There are moments when you quite surprise me,' murmured Greeen. 'We shall be on to fetching sticks and bringing in the morning paper in no time. Just so. When Americans say "first floor", they mean street-level. When the rest of us *hear* "first floor", we think of the floor up the first flight of stairs. And this applies throughout most of Europe and Asia. A CIA officer tells a Vietnamese agent to put something on the first floor, and he automatically takes it up to what the

American fondly thinks of as the second floor. So between them they not only get the wrong house, they get the wrong floor, too.'

'Amazing,' exclaimed Ivansong with spurious awe. 'Wonderful. But how you do run on, don't you? Shouldn't all this deductive reasoning by our voluble amateur crimebuster be saved for the last chapter?'

'There is no last chapter,' countered Greeen with dignity. 'So now we had better not be seen talking too intimately for too long, despite the way everyone is letting down their hair around here. Nasty minds might misinterpret our innocent relationship.'

'Oh, I wouldn't worry, I don't think,' said Ivansong. 'I have a feeling that after that little bit of business of yours with Flodden in Athens, you and I are going to be imperfect strangers to each other once the Bonze is off our hands.'

Greeen flashed him a long smile, and then said the one thing best calculated to worry him: 'Do you want to bet on it?'

'Well, *au revoir*,' he concluded, accentuating the last two words. 'I see Short March over there, or rather, our esteemed friend Lee Tian Kwang. It is a rather distressing time for him and I feel I should pay him what you might roughly describe as my respects. We share a common love of Siamese cats, you know, but while I call mine "Bolshie", he regards his as bourgeois-reactionary. Which only goes to show something or other, doesn't it?'

Ivansong found that Keo had left, but Charlie Polak was standing with Chuck Strawbury beside one of the wagons and pouring scotch-on-the-rocks for both of them while ignoring Inqvist completely. Ivansong joined them and gave himself a drink. 'I was just telling Chuck about the Paramahamsa Bonze,' said Polak, 'and I want to get together with you over a possible story on him. Okay?'

'Of course,' agreed Ivansong. 'Any time.'

'You seen him since?'

'Yes, I went back to try to find out what that prophecy he made to us meant, but he didn't seem to know himself.'

'Did he make any more?'

Ivansong sipped scotch. 'As a matter of fact, he did make one,' he replied doubtfully.

'What was it?'

'He said Nakhara was going to be destroyed tonight.'

'How did he know?' almost shouted Inqvist and Strawbury in unison, the face of one a hard mask of suspicion, the eyes of the other a flurry of fish startled within their plastic-rimmed aquaria.

Ivansong stared back at them, expressionless and unwinking.

Polak was the first to move, but Inqvist seized him fiercely by the arm. 'You don't take one single step towards that cable office,' he said in the voice of a slot-machine robot, his lips almost motionless. 'That story is a lot of crap.' He turned accusingly to Ivansong. 'It's just that, who knows, sometime we may have to get the commies out of there to save our own boys, even if it does mean blowing up a few lousy ruins.'

But across the pale piscine eyes of the polysyllabic ecological warfare expert there stole a small, fanatical gleam. Strawbury had his own answer to non-populated socio-psychological pseudo-military targets.

23

Paradoxically, the overtired man is often a good lover. At two a.m. Ivansong left Thinking Lotus wrapped in a warm luxurious cocoon of fulfilment and, softly closing the door on her sleeping figure, walked on bare feet across the upstairs lounge clad only in a sarong. He could not sleep, and he would have to be up a little after four to take the Parama- hamsa Bonze to the airfield ('better get the old crate off the tarmac as soon as it's light, old boy,' the air attaché had said)

He mixed himself a weak whisky-and-soda and wandered over to the balcony. Flodden glanced up at him for a moment from the shadow of the jacaranda. Ivansong ignored him.

The honed-down moon was riding high, cutting its way through white locks of uncombed cirrus, and the river was striated by thin strands of silver light. The fractured silhouette of Nakhara Wat and, beyond it, the dark breast of Mount Kham with the Mayon at its summit, were wreathed in a gossamer mist. A man could stand here for ever, thought Ivansong, filled with the euphoria of his own melancholy.

But tomorrow was another day. Thinking Lotus had given him a list of shopping chores – draw housekeeping money, pay the Chinese 'Green Grocer', buy some quarto carbon paper and get some cable forms from the post office. Mango had gone to bed with a slight temperature and tummy trouble. Lotus would stay at home to watch it, warning the British Council school she attended and calling the embassy doctor in if necessary. The national lottery results would be out this morning. He must not forget to check their tickets. Anything else? Hell, he still had to go to police headquarters to make a formal statement about the bomb. And he would have to file a story to Worldover, of course – but what? That was the agent's eternal problem after a caper like this, sorting out what he could write from what he knew.

What did he know? The Paramahamsa Bonze business was clear enough, but the rest had been a ridiculous comedy of negatives. The ambassador had not sent him the wooden horse. And the Chinese had not sent him the wooden horse either. The Chinese did not know that Miss Suzy Lee Flower-class had been Thinking Lotus, and presumably believed, therefore, that they still had him on a hook as a double agent. Nor had the Chinese killed the ambassador, for they had obviously regarded Greeen's report to the Goddess of Mercy in Stonecutter Village as an attempt to trick them into doing so. The obscurity of their motives in deliberately betraying Pawkinson-Convoy and trying to harm the Ivansongs was explained. They had done neither.

Most of the time, in fact, the Chinese had been noteworthy

for their masterly inactivity – what the Taoists called 'wu-wei' or 'non-action', the principle that they even extended to the detonation of booby-traps. But they had quite unnecessarily blown P-C and the Paramahamsa Bonze in order to unmask the non-existent Khammax plot, Max had quite mistakenly betrayed the British Ambassador, and the ambassador had committed suicide for quite the wrong reason. The Chinese had lost two key agents in Pawkinson-Convoy and Max, and with any luck they were going to find that because Max had defected they had also lost a third – Ivansong. Up the imperialists.

Up the imperialists? Inqvist had sent his bomb to the wrong house, but it was only a matter of time before he would have Keo in Kitay's shoes, and Mekong would move into a new circle of hell. It had been left to the Paramahamsa Bonze to point out the best bit of the joke, however. When Greeen had spuriously promised that the case against George Mc-Wimbledon Potterslee might be treated with greater leniency if the Bonze would undo some of the damage he had done by making a judicious public prophecy that would restore sanity to the situation, the Bonze had promptly agreed. 'I am ready to say anything you like,' he had said in his fruitiest manner. 'But what *do* you want me to say?

'Do you want me to tell the millions of Mekong that their salvation lies with Kitay, and he should be kept in power at all costs? That may finesse Keo, but I would venture to suggest that Kitay has already discredited such a prophecy in advance with his feudalistic policies, and in the long run you would only be making it easier for Sissomak and the communists to rouse the people against their rulers and then take over the country.

'Or do you want me to urge everyone to fight for the return of Sissomak and the overthrow of Kitay? That again will only open the door to communist and Chinese domination, and even if Sissomak could stop the Reds from crowding him, once they had helped him to win back his capital, it would still be no good. Before he was chucked out, he was distrusted by all the neighbours, and Mekong was looked upon as a dagger pointed at the heart of the South-east Asia Treaty Organisation. The situation is changing, but you would still be undermining regional resistance to communist subversion in this area at a time when the Americans are pulling out of it, Is that how you arrange for Asians to settle Asian problems?

'I tell you, if you'd had as much experience of double-headed coins as I have, you'd know you can't win this one, my son. In my humble opinion there's nothing for it but to leave all these unfortunate wretches to their own charades. Still, it's up to you.'

In the end it had been decided that the Paramahamsa Bonze would make no more prophecies.

George McWimbledon Potterslee was packaged and ready for delivery to Singapore and London, it looked as if Max Alias would be able to duck out with the long-armed Miss Clipstream, and even the Ivansongs might just scrape clear of their entanglements with Greeen and the Chinese. But the rest of it was too much like life – loose ends, question-marks, black patches of ignorance, unfinished business, an untidy, throwaway situation opening on to a future that looked about as neat and hygienic as a well-filled garbage can.

If only it could be a tasteful piece of fiction with no odds-and-ends left lying around, instead of having this slovenly lived-unhappily-ever-after look about it, thought Ivansong regretfully. How was the power game really working out in Peking? What was in the ambassador's annexe about Greeen and Flodden in Athens? And what would Greeen do with his body? What about Strawbury and Inqvist, and Kitay and Keo and, Christ, what about those poor bloody Marines up there on Mount Kham?

Ivansong pitched the dregs of his drink over the balcony, and returned to the bedroom. 'Absolutely scrumptious, *dawling*,' murmured the quondam Miss Flowerclass without waking, as he lay down beside Thinking Lotus. And then, in no time at all, he had drifted into sleep and was dreaming that he had woken up.

He did not, therefore, hear the first faint drone of the bombers, prophetic as the smell of burning phoenix. Nor did he hear the soft, flat explosions as the casings burst over Nakhara Wat and the stone ring of ruins that encircled Mount Kham, spreading the seeds and the fertiliser in the B.I.R.C. (Beanstalk Instant Refoliant Canisters) like pollen on the wind.

'What the hell they got in those bombs, sawdust?' Smearer asked disgustedly, peering out of a shallow trench down near the wire. 'Sawdust?' scoffed Chomsky. 'What kind of sawdust is that ferchrissakes? Ain't you got ears?' And they listened in wondering silence to the curious crepitation that rose towards them from all sides, insidious as the thin, vanishing mist.

It was only at first light that Chomsky gave his verdict, unaware that he was about to prove the Buddhist claim that pleasure and pain are all one. For within thirty-six hours he would be sitting safely aboard the USS *Spiro Agnew* in the Gulf of Khammax – but refusing an illicit shot of scotch and calling compulsively for yet more water.

'Well, if that ain't the goddamnedest air support I ever saw in all my years of fighting the gooks, the charlies, the army and the U.S.A.A.F.' he said, shaking his head in disbelief.

'The bastards haven't blown up the stonework or burned out the goons. No, that'd be too easy and kinda old-fashioned. Just get a load of that stuff, will you? It's not even killing the lousy jungle, lookit. It's bringing it alive!'

*　　　*　　　*

It was one month later, and everything had gone according to plan. The Marines had been rescued by helicopter from the Mayon without difficulty, for as Burghausen records,[*] the muscular shoots of the miracle refoliant had grown so fast that in the first two days the other architectural wonders of Nakhara had been submerged in an impenetrable tangle of jungle to a height of twelve feet. The creeper had then set about tearing them apart, stone by stone, until the entire complex had disappeared beneath a sea of synthetic vegetation.

The two men – one tall, one short – were leaning over a broken wall side by side to contemplate other, more recent

* Ibid., Vol. III, pp. 239–243.

havoc, however. A small temple in the grounds of the British compound in Nava had been razed by a mysterious explosion and a raging fire during a freak storm that the superstitious attributed to the wrath of the *phis* over the desecration of Nakhara. But a blackened corpse and the shards of a sacred funerary urn had been salvaged by the firemen, and word spread quickly that the holy remains of the Paramahamsa Bonze, who had marvellously foretold the fate of Nakhara and then vanished without trace, had now been found. These were ceremonially cremated on a massive pyre erected in front of the Royal Palace amid much public lamentation, and the outraged mob of Mekinese mourners around it then seized burning brands from the catafalque and converged on the British Embassy to take their revenge. Within an hour the residence had been ransacked and the chancery building was ablaze. Pawkinson-Convoy had done it again.

But now it was almost unnaturally quiet.

'How is that nameless cat of yours, my dear fellow?' the taller of the two men asked, glancing down at his companion with a thin feral grin.

'Physically fit, ideologically unregenerate,' sighed the other. 'But at least she is company.'

'Just so. It is becoming a little lonely here with so many friends going away, isn't it? Mr. Alias, Mr. Ivansong, the Paramahamsa Bonze in his own inimitable way, and, of course, Sir Nigel Pawkinson-Convoy.'

'It will not be so for long. I expect to be surrounded very soon by an increasing number of – technical? – colleagues from Peking. But I fear you will not meet them. I hear you are also leaving us soon, Mr. Greeen?'

'Ah, yes, alas. My heart bleeds, but my work here is done.'

'So I see, Mr. Greeen,' Short March sighed again and nodded moodily towards the wrecked British compound. 'So I see.'

'An act of God, my dear Short March. An act of God, I assure you.'

'Act of God?'

'Our pious Christian term for any sudden, merciless blow

226

which we consider completely undeserved and grossly unfair. Why the sudden influx of Chinese?'

'You are forgetting, Mr. Greeen, that just as the United States imperialist aggressors have earned the stern condemnation of all peace-loving peoples by destroying Nakhara, China has earned international acclaim by offering to put it together again. But that will require the presence of hundreds, perhaps thousands of Chinese specialists and technical workers, personnel administrators, security guards, interpreters, teachers and cultural groups, welfare workers, cooks, transport drivers, and so on, for Peking has promised that the contingent will be completely self-sufficient.'

'I presume that they will all be concentrated in this area?'

'Most of them will be here, but there will be quarrying teams in the Coriandra mountains, and detachments studying the structure of other ancient temples throughout Mekong, including, of course, on the island of Khammax. It seems that Prince Kitay is so angry with the Americans about Nakhara that he is ready to accept the Chinese offer despite strong opposition from the other feudalistic gangsters around him.' Short March glanced at his watch suddenly. 'But we should know in a few seconds,' he exclaimed, pulling a small transistor radio out of the pocket of his cotton jacket. 'Confirmation of his decision is expected to be on the news today, and it is almost noon now.'

'Ah, noon,' murmured Greeen. 'The peaceful hour of the siesta. You know, I rather doubt if we shall hear from Prince Kitay today, after all, as a matter of fact.'

'What makes you say that?'

'Just something I overheard Mr. Inqvist discussing earnestly with General Keo a few evenings ago. You know how incorrigibly *nosy* I am.'

They turned to look incuriously into each other's eyes, unfathomable black and unfathomable green, and it was just then that the first machine-gun opened up so startlingly close that both men instinctively dropped to the ground, where they lay side by side on their stomachs in the dirt, and began to laugh gently, even, you might say, companionably.

WALK DON'T WALK
Gordon Williams

By the bestselling author of *The Straw Dogs, The Man Who Had Power Over Women* and *The Camp*.

'Hugely successful . . . this is a swiftly placed, finely written novel, and it's a great deal of fun' – *The Times*

'Extremely funny . . . It is a pleasure to recommend a book that flies higher than its blurb' – *New Statesman*

Fiction 40p

AT FEVER PITCH
David Caute

Winner of the John Llewelyn Rhys Memorial Prize and Authors' Club First Novel Award

'This is that rare and beautiful thing, a novel too short for its contents . . . a most impressive piece of work. It is funny, accurate, exciting' – *The Observer*

By the bestselling author of THE DECLINE OF THE WEST, THE OCCUPATION, THE FELLOW TRAVELLERS.

Fiction 40p

MURGATREUD'S EMPIRE
Bamber Gascoigne

'It is hard to convey the sheer delight of Mr Gascoigne's humour ... it is a treat, and I read it with intense pleasure from beginning to end' – Auberon Waugh, *Spectator*

'A splendid comic verve ... rises to a brilliant climax' – *Evening Standard*

'An absolute gem, dazzlingly funny and bitingly satirical' – *Hibernia*

Fiction 40p

THE LUCK OF GINGER COFFEY
Brian Moore

The Luck Of Ginger Coffey is a brilliant example of Brian Moore's shrewd observation. Ginger Coffey is a thoroughly likeable failure; his new life in a new land (from Ireland to Canada) is hardly off the ground before it starts to crumble around him. At his lowest ebb, Ginger suddenly decides to fight back against his fate, and armed only with the luck of the Irish and a lot of bravado, he starts running uphill in hope, into a hilarious series of misadventures, disasters – and victories. *The Luck of Ginger Coffey* is a superbly entertaining novel.

Fiction 35p